EART
REMA

Donna Leon was named by *The Times* as one of the 50 Greatest Crime Writers. She is an award-winning crime novelist, celebrated for the bestselling Brunetti series. Donna has lived in Venice for thirty years and previously lived in Switzerland, Saudi Arabia, Iran and China, where she worked as a teacher. Donna's books have been translated into thirty-five languages and have been published around the world.

Her previous novels featuring Commissario Brunetti have all been highly acclaimed; including *Friends in High Places*, which won the CWA Macallan Silver Dagger for Fiction, *Fatal Remedies*, *Doctored Evidence*, *A Sea of Troubles* and *Beastly Things*.

Praise for *Earthly Remains*

'Donna Leon's recreation of Venice and her depiction of the series' core characters . . . is, as always in this long-running series, a triumph.'

Literary Review

'Leon is a wonderful writer, the sentences as beautifully crafted as the *puparìn* Casati's father had long ago built.'

The Arts Desk

Donna Leon

EARTHLY REMAINS

arrow books

1 3 5 7 9 10 8 6 4 2

Arrow Books
20 Vauxhall Bridge Road
London SW1V 2SA

Arrow Books is part of the Penguin Random House group of companies
whose addresses can be found at global.penguinrandomhouse.com.

Penguin
Random House
UK

First published by William Heinemann in 2017
First published in paperback by Arrow Books in 2017

www.penguin.co.uk

A CIP catalogue record for this book is available from the British Library.

ISBN 9781784758141
ISBN 9781784758158 (Export edition)

Map © ML Design, London

Typeset in 10.93/13.84 pt Palatino by Jouve (UK), Milton Keynes
Printed and bound in Great Britain by Clays Ltd, St Ives Plc

MIX
Paper from
responsible sources
FSC® C018179

Penguin Random House is committed to a
sustainable future for our business, our readers
and our planet. This book is made from Forest
Stewardship Council® certified paper.

For Justice Ruth Bader Ginsburg

E scenderem col fiume, e in seno accolti
il mar ci avrà pria che risorga il giorno.

We'll go down with the stream, and the sea
Will have us before the day dawns.

Handel, *Ottone*, Act 2, Scene 9

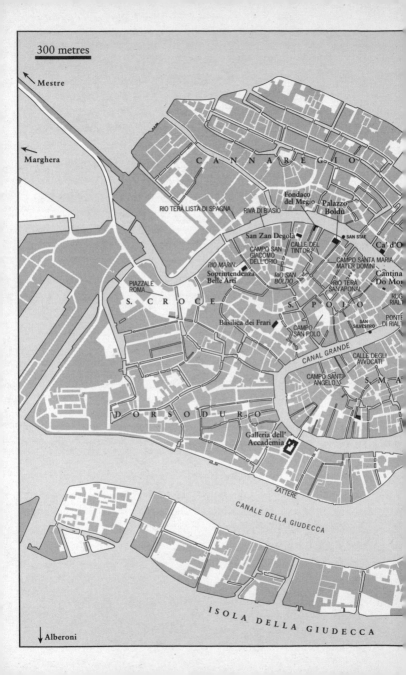

Treviso &
Preganziol

MURANO

Torcello

N

Cimitero

ISOLA DI
S. MICHELE

Sant'Erasmo

L A G U N A

Multisala Giorgione

Ospedale Civile

CAMPO
SS GIOVANNI
E PAOLO

Basilica
SS Giovanni
e Paolo

The Church
of the Miracoli

Ballarin

CAMPO
S. MARINA

CAMPO
SAN BARTOLOMEO

San Lorenzo

Questura

Rosa Salva

PONTE
DEI GRECI

C O

PIAZZA SAN
MARCO

C A S T E L L O

SAN
ZACCARIA

Basilica di
San Marco

CAMPO SAN FILIPPO
E GIACOMO

BACINO DI SAN MARCO

ISOLA DI
S. GIORGIO
MAGGIORE

Lido

1

After an exchange of courtesies, the session had gone on for another half-hour, and Brunetti was beginning to feel the strain of it. The man across from him, a 42-year-old lawyer whose father was one of the most successful – and thus most powerful – notaries in the city, had been asked to come in to the Questura that morning after having been named by two people as the man who had offered some pills to a girl at a party in a private home two nights before.

The girl had washed them down with a glass of orange juice reported also to have been given to her by the man now sitting opposite Brunetti. She had collapsed some time later and had been taken to the emergency room of the Ospedale Civile, where her condition had been listed as 'Riservata'.

Antonio Ruggieri had arrived punctually at ten and, as apparent evidence of his faith in the competence and probity of the police, had not bothered to bring another lawyer with him. Nor had he complained about the heat in the one-windowed room, though his eyes had paused for a moment on the fan standing in the corner, doing its best – and failing – to counteract the muggy oppression of the hottest July on record.

Brunetti had apologized for the heat in the room, explaining that the ongoing heatwave had forced the Questura to choose between using its reduced supply of energy for the computers or for air conditioning and had chosen the former. Ruggieri had been gracious and had said only that he'd remove his jacket if he might.

Brunetti, who kept his jacket on, had begun by making it amply clear that this was only an informal conversation to provide the police with more background information about just what had happened at the party.

Registering this bumbling commissario's badly disguised admiration for the stature of Ruggieri's family, the famous people in the city who were their clients and friends, and the circle of wealth and ease in which Ruggieri travelled by right, it had taken the lawyer little time to lapse into easy condescension towards the older man.

Because the officer sitting next to Commissario Brunetti was wearing a uniform, Ruggieri ignored him, though he kept his sensors active to ensure that the younger man responded in a manner proper to the speech of his elders and betters. When the young man failed to react adequately to his self-effacing superiority, the lawyer ceased to use the plural when addressing the two men.

'As I was saying, Commissario,' Ruggieri went on, 'it was a friend's birthday party: we've known one another since we were at school.'

'Did you know many people there?' Brunetti asked.

'Practically all of them: most of us have been friends since we were children.'

'And the girl?' Brunetti asked with faint confusion.

'She must have come with one of the invited guests. There's no other way she could have got in.' Then, to show Brunetti how he and his friends safeguarded their privacy, he added, 'One of us always keeps an eye on the door to see who comes, just in case.'

'Indeed,' Brunetti said with a nod of agreement, and in response to Ruggieri's glance, added, 'That's always best.' He reached forward to push the upright microphone a bit closer to Ruggieri.

'Do you have any idea whom she might have come with, if I might ask?'

It took Ruggieri a moment to answer. 'No. I didn't see her talking to anyone I know.'

'How was it that you started to talk to her?' Brunetti asked.

'Oh, you know how it is,' Ruggieri said. 'Lots of people dancing or standing around. One minute I was alone, watching the dancers, and the next thing I knew, she was standing beside me and asking me my name.'

'Did you know her?' Brunetti asked, in his best old-fashioned, slightly puzzled voice.

'No,' Ruggieri said emphatically. Then he added, 'And she used "*tu*" when she spoke to me.'

Brunetti shook his head in apparent disapproval, then asked, 'What did you talk about?'

'She said she didn't know many people and didn't know how to get a drink.' Ruggieri said. When Brunetti made no comment, he went on, 'So I had to ask her if I could bring her one. After all, what else is a gentleman to do?' Brunetti remained silent, and Ruggieri said hurriedly, 'It

3

didn't seem polite to ask her how it was she didn't know people there. But it did cross my mind.'

'Of course,' Brunetti agreed, quite as though it were a situation in which he often found himself. He put an attentive look on his face and waited.

'She wanted a vodka and orange juice, and I asked her if she were old enough to have one.'

Brunetti conjured a smile. 'And she said?' he asked.

'That she was eighteen, and if I didn't believe her, she'd find someone else who would.'

Imitating a look he had often seen on the face of his mother's aunt Anna, Brunetti brought his lips together in a tiny moue of disapproval. Beside him, Pucetti shifted in his seat.

'Not a very polite answer,' Brunetti said primly.

Ruggieri ran a hand through his dark hair and gave a weary shrug. 'It's what we get from them today, I'm afraid. Just because they're old enough to vote and drink doesn't mean they know how to behave.'

Brunetti found it interesting that Ruggieri again remarked on her age.

'Avvocato,' Brunetti began with every sign of reluctance, 'the reason I asked you to come in and talk with us is that you've been said to have given her some pills.'

'I beg your pardon?' Ruggieri said, sounding puzzled. Then he gave an easy smile meant to include Brunetti and added, 'I've been said to have done many things.'

Smiling nervously in return, Brunetti went on, 'The girl – I'm sure you've read – was taken to the hospital. The Carabinieri questioned a number of people and were told you'd been speaking to a girl wearing a green dress.'

'Who were they?' Ruggieri's voice was sharp.

Brunetti held up both hands in a gesture bespeaking weakness. 'I'm afraid I'm not at liberty to tell you, Avvocato.'

'So people are free to lie about me and I can't even defend myself against them?'

'I'm sure there will be a time for that, Signore,' Brunetti said, leaving it to the lawyer to work out when that might be.

Ignoring Brunetti's answer, Ruggieri asked, 'What else did they say?'

Brunetti shifted in his chair and crossed his legs. 'I'm not at liberty to say that, either, Signore.'

Ruggieri looked away and studied the wall, as though there might be some other person hiding behind it. 'I hope they said something about the girl.'

'What about her?'

'The way she was all over me,' Ruggieri said angrily, the first strong emotion he'd shown since they entered the room.

'Well, someone did say that her behaviour was, er, forward,' Brunetti answered, letting the word stumble out.

'That's putting it mildly,' Ruggieri said and sat up straighter in his chair. 'She was leaning against me. That was after I brought her the drink. Then she started to move to the music, against my leg. She put the glass – it was chilled from the ice – between her breasts. They were almost hanging out of her dress.' Ruggieri sounded indignant at the shamelessness of youth.

'I see, I see,' Brunetti said. He was conscious of the tension mounting in Pucetti beside him. The junior officer had recently questioned a young man accused of violence against his girlfriend and had produced a report that was professionally neutral.

'Did she say anything to you, Signore?'

Ruggieri considered this, started to speak, stopped, then went on. 'She told me she was hot because of me.' He paused to let the other men understand fully. 'Then she asked if there was some place we could go, just the two of us.'

'Good heavens,' said an astonished Brunetti. 'What did you tell her?'

'I wasn't interested. That's what I told her. I don't like it when it's that easy to get.' Seeing Brunetti's nod of agreement, the lawyer went on, 'And no matter what these people told you, I don't know anything about any pills.'

'Was the girl you talked to wearing a green dress?' Brunetti asked.

Eventually, the lawyer gave a boyish smile and answered, 'She might have been. I was looking at her tits, not the dress.'

Brunetti felt Pucetti's reaction. To cover the young man's slow intake of breath, he slapped his hand to his mouth and failed to stifle his appreciative chuckle.

Ruggieri smiled broadly and, perhaps encouraged by it, said, 'I suppose I could have taken her somewhere and done her, but it was hardly worth the effort. Nice tits, but she was a stupid cow.'

Brunetti and Pucetti had learned an hour before the interview that the girl had died in the hospital earlier that morning. The immediate cause of death was an asthma attack; the presence in her blood of Ecstasy provided another. Beside him, Brunetti heard the rough grind of the feet of Pucetti's chair against the cement floor of the interrogation room. From the corner of his left eye, he saw Pucetti's legs pull back as the young man got ready to stand.

Fear of what would happen gripped Brunetti's heart, and his left arm shot up as a low grunt escaped him. This changed to a sharp whining sound that rose up the scale as if forced out by pain. Brunetti lunged crookedly to his feet, gasping for breath while pumping out the tortured whine.

6

The two other men froze in shock and stared at him. Brunetti pivoted to his left, propelled by a force that shifted his entire body. Arm still raised above his head, he collapsed towards Pucetti, his arm crashing down on Pucetti's shoulder as the young officer rose from his chair.

Self-protection, perhaps, forced Brunetti's hand to grab at Pucetti's collar and yank the younger man towards him. Pucetti automatically braced his left palm flat on the table, arm straight, elbow locked, and took Brunetti's weight as it fell across him. He turned and wrapped his right arm around the Commissario's chest, steadied him, and started to lower him to the floor, fighting down his panic.

Pucetti shouted to Ruggieri, 'Go and get help!' From his place above Brunetti, feeling for his heartbeat, Pucetti saw the other man's legs and feet under the table: they did not move.

'But there's nothing—' Ruggieri started to say, but Pucetti cut him off and screamed again, 'Get help!' The legs moved; the door opened and closed.

Pucetti leaned down over his superior, who lay on his back, eyes closed, breathing normally. 'Commissario, Commissario, can you hear me? What's wrong? What happened?'

Brunetti's eyes snapped open and he looked into Pucetti's.

'Are you all right, Commissario?' Pucetti asked, struggling for calm.

In an entirely normal voice, as if making a point about proper procedure, Brunetti asked, 'Do you know what would have happened to your career if you'd attacked him?'

2

Pucetti pulled himself back from the supine man. 'What do you mean?' he asked.

'You were about to grab him, weren't you?' Brunetti demanded, making no attempt to temper his reproach.

Pucetti was silent, his eyes still on the perfectly relaxed Brunetti. He struggled for speech, but it took him some time to achieve it. 'The girl's dead, and he's talking like that,' he finally sputtered. 'He can't do that. It's not decent. Someone should slap his mouth shut.'

'Not you, Pucetti,' Brunetti said sharply, propping himself up on his elbow. 'It's not your job to teach him manners. It's to treat him with respect because he's a citizen and he hasn't been formally accused of any crime.' Brunetti thought for a moment and corrected himself. 'Or even if he'd been accused of a crime.' Pucetti's face was rigid. Brunetti didn't know if it was from resentment or embarrassment and didn't care. 'Do you understand that, Pucetti?'

'Sì, Signore,' the younger man said and pushed himself to his feet.

'Not so fast,' Brunetti stopped him; he'd heard the sound of approaching voices. Seeing Pucetti's confusion, he added, 'You heard what he said when he was leaving, didn't you, that there was nothing wrong with me.'

'No, sir,' Pucetti answered.

'It's what he started to say before you shouted at him again.' The voices grew nearer. 'Get back down here and put your palms on my chest and give me CPR, for God's sake.'

Blank-faced and looking lost, Pucetti did what he was ordered and knelt beside Brunetti, who lay back down and closed his eyes. Pucetti put one palm on Brunetti's chest, his other palm on top of it, and started to press, counting out the seconds in a low voice.

'He's in there,' Ruggieri said from the corridor.

Brunetti opened his eyes to slits and saw two pairs of uniformed legs come through the door, followed closely by the dark grey slacks of Ruggieri's suit. 'What's going on?' came the voice of Lieutenant Scarpa.

Pucetti suspended his counting, but not the rhythmic pressure, and answered, 'I think it's his heart, Lieutenant,' then went back to counting out the seconds.

'An ambulance is coming,' Scarpa said. Brunetti saw the other uniformed legs turn to the side, and Scarpa said, 'Go down and wait for it. Bring them up here.' The legs turned and left the room.

'What happened?' Scarpa asked.

'I thought he was going to attack me,' Ruggieri began, 'but then he stood up and fell against him.' Brunetti realized this confusion of pronouns was unlikely to make any sense to the Lieutenant, so he closed his eyes and started to pant softly in rhythm with the pressure of Pucetti's hands.

Brunetti heard footsteps move to the end of the table and then approach. 'Has he had heart trouble before?' the Lieutenant asked.

'I don't know, Lieutenant. Vianello might.'

After a long silence, Scarpa said, 'You want me to take over?' Brunetti was glad his eyes were closed. He kept on panting.

'No, sir. I've got the rhythm going.'

'All right.'

The approaching two-beat of the ambulance's siren slipped into Brunetti's consciousness. Good Lord, what had he done? He'd hoped to create a momentary distraction to stop Pucetti from attacking the man, but things had got out of control entirely, and now he was on the floor with Pucetti feigning CPR and Lieutenant Scarpa offering to help.

Would they try to find Vianello? Or call Paola? She'd been asleep when he left that morning, so they hadn't spoken.

He hadn't considered the consequences of his behaviour, had done the first thing he thought would save Pucetti. He could have blamed it on not having slept last night, or having slept too much, because of what he'd eaten or not eaten. Too much coffee, no coffee. But he'd gone too far by falling against Pucetti. And here they were, and here was the ambulance crew.

Footsteps, noise, Pucetti gone, different hands, mask over his nose and mouth, hands under his ankles and shoulders, stretcher, ambulance, siren, the calming up and down of motion on the water, slow slide into the dock, bumbling about, transfer to a harder surface, the sound of wheels on marble floors as he was rolled through the hospital. He peeked through slitted eyes and saw the automatic doors and huge red cross of Pronto Soccorso.

Inside, he was wheeled quickly past Reception and parked alongside the wall of a corridor. After some time, he heard footsteps approach. Someone slipped a pillow under his head while another person put something around his wrist, a blanket was placed over him and pulled to his waist, and then the footsteps moved away.

Brunetti lay still for minutes, eyes tightly closed until he remembered he had to think of a way to put an end to this. He couldn't jump up and pretend to be Lazarus, nor could he push the blanket aside and step down from the bed, saying he had to get back to work. He lay still and waited. He lapsed into something approaching sleep and was awakened by movement. He opened his eyes and saw that he was in a small examination room, a white-uniformed nurse lowering the sides of his rolling bed. Before he could ask her anything, she left the room.

Very shortly after this, a woman wearing a white jacket entered the room and approached his bedside without speaking. Their eyes met and she nodded. He noticed that she carried a plastic folder. She reached out her hand and touched his, turned it over, and felt for his pulse. She looked at her watch, made a note in the file, then peeled down his lower eyelid, still saying nothing. He stared ahead.

'Can you hear me?' she asked.

Brunetti thought it wiser to nod than to speak.

'Do you feel any pain?'

He looked up at the woman, saw her nametag, but the angle prevented him from reading it.

'A little,' he whispered.

She was about his age, dark-haired. Her skin was dry, her eyes weary and wary.

'Where?'

'My arm,' he said, having a vague memory that one sign of a heart attack was pain in one of the arms; the left, he thought.

The woman made a note. After a moment, she turned away from him and slipped the file into a clear plastic holder attached to the top rail of his bed.

'Can you tell me what's happened, Dottoressa?' he asked, thinking that was the sort of thing a person would ask if he'd been taken to the hospital in an ambulance.

She turned back to him, and he saw her name: Dottoressa Sanmartini. Her expression was so neutral that Brunetti wondered if she knew she was speaking to a human being. 'Your vital signs,' she began, pointing to his file suspended from the bed, 'offer a wide range of interpretation.' She closed her eyes for a moment and took a deep breath.

Then she looked across at him, this time appearing to notice him. 'What work do you do?'

'I'm a commissario of police,' he answered.

'Ah,' escaped her lips. She pulled out the file, opened it, and wrote something on the top sheet.

'I'm feeling better, I think,' Brunetti said nervously, thinking it was time to stop all this and get out of there.

'We still have to do some tests,' she cut him short by saying. Then, perhaps in response to his expression, she added, 'Don't worry, Signor . . .' she looked at his chart, '. . . Brunetti. We'll check a few things, just to be sure what's going on.'

'I don't think anything is,' he said calmly, hoping that the certainty in his voice would persuade her.

'Perhaps it would be better if you left this to us to decide,

Signore,' she said quite amiably, convincing Brunetti that he was going to have to pay for his rashness.

Brunetti closed his eyes in resignation. He had set this in motion; now he could do nothing but play it out until the end.

Voice suddenly brisk and professional, she went on, 'We'll take blood and do further tests. I'd like to exclude some possibilities.'

It occurred to him to ask what it was she wanted to eliminate, but he realized that wisdom lay in raising no opposition. 'Good,' he forced himself to say.

Another set of footsteps approached. A male voice said, 'Elena told me to come, Dottoressa.'

Brunetti looked towards the voice then and saw a white-bearded mountain of a man carrying a small metal tray. The man set it on a cabinet next to the bed, rolled up Brunetti's left sleeve, and wrapped a piece of rubber tubing tight around his upper arm. He removed a syringe from the tray and tore off the plastic covering. His immense hand rendered the syringe minute and because of that somehow more threatening. Straight-faced, he said, 'I hope this won't hurt, Signore.'

Brunetti closed his eyes. He felt the man's hand on his wrist, then the faint touch of the cold needle on his inner arm, then nothing at all while he waited for something to happen. He was conscious of pressure, heard some clinking noises, but he kept his eyes closed, waiting.

A sudden brush on his arm caused him to open his eyes, and he saw the man untying the rubber tubing. Three glass vials of blood stood upright in a plastic rack on the tray.

The doctor placed a sheet of paper on it, saying, 'All of these, Teo. And I'd like them to do the enzymes immediately.'

'Of course, Dottoressa.' He took the tray and turned away. Brunetti listened to his footsteps disappear down the corridor. What have I done? What have I done?

'I'd like to call my wife,' he said.

'I'm sorry, but *telefonini* don't work in the examining rooms. There's no reception,' Dottoressa Sanmartini explained.

Brunetti reached his newly freed hand to the edge of the sheet and began to push it back. 'Not so fast, Signore,' the Dottoressa said. 'We still need an electrocardiogram. You can call her after that. A nurse will take you to where you'll be able to call.' As if conjured up by the doctor's words, a female nurse arrived and placed herself at the foot of the bed.

The doctor stood back while the nurse pushed him from the room. She wheeled Brunetti across the large atrium in front of Pronto Soccorso and then directly into the cardiology emergency room. But once he was inside, things slowed down. Some sort of mix-up in scheduling meant that he had to wait while three people were examined.

Having once thought of her, Brunetti now became agitated at the idea that Paola knew nothing of what was going on. He looked at his watch and saw it was just after noon: there was still an hour before she'd begin to worry.

Finally a different doctor did the electrocardiogram, after which Brunetti was wheeled to another room where the same man slathered cold gel on his chest to prepare him for an ultrasound. The doctor told Brunetti he could watch the monitor with him, but Brunetti declined the chance to do so.

The doctor squeegeed the gel around on Brunetti's chest for what seemed a long time, then began to rub a blunt wand across his chest. Occasionally he tapped at a computer screen, taking pictures from various angles, never saying a word. At last he ripped a long strip of paper towel from an enormous roll and passed it to Brunetti. When Brunetti had finished wiping his chest clean he dropped the towels into a large plastic bin beside the bed, still no wiser than he had been at the beginning of the exams.

'Humm,' was the doctor's only comment when Brunetti asked if there was anything wrong.

Realizing it was the only answer he was going to get, Brunetti asked, 'Can I go home now?'

The doctor could not contain his surprise. 'Go home?'

'Yes.'

'That's not a decision I can make, Signore. I'm not in charge of your case.' Then, glancing at the screen, he added, 'I think it would be wiser if you were to stay here a bit longer.'

Before Brunetti could say a word, they heard a commotion outside the small room. A female voice was raised loud in protest, and then another one, even louder. Suddenly the door opened and Paola appeared.

Brunetti pushed himself up on one elbow and held out his other arm towards her. 'Paola, don't worry. There's nothing wrong,' he said, hoping to quell her fears and assure her he was all right.

She came quickly to the side of the bed, and he glanced at the doctor, hoping to enlist his support.

Paola leaned down, and when she was sure she had his attention, said, voice tight with badly contained anger, 'What have you done now?'

3

The doctor, evidently shocked by the woman's words, to say nothing of the tone in which she said them, asked, 'Who are you, Signora?'

'I'm this man's wife, Dottore,' Paola said in a voice she managed to make sound calm. 'I'd be very grateful if I could have a few minutes alone with my husband.'

Brunetti watched the other man's reaction. The doctor moved his head backwards, as though the distance would afford him a better view of these two people, then tilted his chin to one side and then the other, then upwards, much in the manner of a curious bird. He turned off the machine, and the light in the room grew dimmer. He left silently, closing the door very quietly after him.

'I've never seen that happen,' Brunetti observed.

'What?' asked his distracted wife.

'That someone bounced a doctor from his own examining room.'

Brunetti heard Paola take a few deep breaths. He wondered what form her anger was going to take. He should have insisted on phoning, should have got up and found a phone that worked, borrowed one, used his warrant card to commandeer one at the nurses' desk. But he had not, had completely given himself over to the passivity that hospitals want to instil in their patients.

She said nothing for so long that Brunetti began to fear her silence was a presage of the consequences of his thoughtlessness.

'Who told you?' he finally asked.

Suddenly her right hand was over her eyes, the left tucked under the other elbow. Brunetti said her name, but she turned away from him. 'Paola. Tell me,' he said, struggling to keep his voice calm.

He pushed the blanket back, swung his legs over the edge of the bed, and sat up, suddenly light-headed and woozy. He clung to the edge of the mattress with both hands. He took two deep breaths and lowered his feet to the floor; then he stood.

Paola must have heard him, for she uncovered her eyes and looked at him. 'Pucetti came to the university. He appeared at the back of the classroom where I was teaching. In his uniform. With a terrible look on his face.'

Ah, faithful, dutiful Pucetti, trying to amend things by bringing the real news, the good news, to his commander's wife. Brunetti could imagine the scene: the pale-faced officer at the door, distress written plain across his face.

'I'm sorry,' he said.

'I thought you were dead, Guido,' Paola said in a ravaged voice. 'I thought that was why he'd come, to tell me that you'd been killed. By someone who was trying to rob a bank or some crazy person who had a hostage. I saw him, and I knew for an instant that you were dead.' Her voice was hoarse, and the words came out with rough edges, as though she had been screaming for hours.

Paola had not cried, he saw; there were no traces of that around her eyes. She was a woman who lived in her imagination, who immediately turned what she saw into stories, who caught a person's expression and made up what had happened to them, and she believed in tragedy. She lived a happy life, but her vision of life was tragic.

'And then what happened?' he asked, still on his guard.

'And then he smiled and held up his thumb to show me things were all right. I still didn't know what had happened, but he was telling me not to worry.' Paola stopped and breathed deeply a few times.

Brunetti waited.

'I looked back at the students. Some of them were turned around, watching Pucetti; the others started to talk.' She raised her right hand in a gesture that could have signified anything. 'So I told them class was over.'

Brunetti nodded. That made sense, letting them go, not pretending that she'd be able to concentrate any longer.

'You'd think they'd never seen a policeman before,' she said in something that approached her normal voice.

Brunetti looked down and saw that his feet were naked. Where had his shoes gone? He urgently wanted to be wearing them, to be able to joke with his wife, to sit in his office and be bored.

'When they were gone, Pucetti came across to my desk and told me that it was all an act, done to protect him. I had no idea what he was talking about, and I don't think I really understand it now, either.'

Brunetti walked to the chair standing against the wall and brought it back for her. He touched her then, holding her shoulders and guiding her to the chair as though she were an old woman and needed help.

'Tell me what you've done, please,' she asked, the same request that had accompanied her dramatic entrance into the room, but, oh, so different now.

'I was questioning a suspect together with Pucetti. All of a sudden, Pucetti lost control of himself. I thought he was going to grab the guy's throat. So I jumped up to block him and cause confusion – I really didn't think about it – and a few minutes later, I was lying on the floor with Pucetti giving me CPR and Scarpa looking down at me.'

'You think Scarpa understood what had happened?' she asked.

'God knows,' Brunetti answered. 'I was on the floor with Pucetti pumping away at my heart, so I didn't have a clear vision of what was going on.' Brunetti cast his mind back over the Lieutenant's behaviour and said, 'He was worried, but I'm not sure about what.' How difficult, to think the Lieutenant could have felt concern for him. Perhaps Pucetti would know: after all, he had seen Scarpa's face and had spoken to him.

'Next thing, Patta will be sending you flowers.'

'I think I'm going to let him,' Brunetti said.

'What?' she asked.

'I think I'm going to keep this.'

'Keep what?' she asked, clearly not understanding.

'This thing. Collapse. Sickness. Attack. Whatever it was.'

'Or wasn't,' Paola corrected him.

Brunetti smiled. Life was good again: his wife could joke with him.

'I can't stand it any longer, doing what I do,' Brunetti surprised himself by saying. 'I had to fake all this and end up here in the hospital, with doctors prodding and poking at me, just because I have to protect the people I work with from reacting to the work they do.' He had never spoken this aloud, never thought it out in this fashion before.

He leaned against the mattress, glad to have its solidity behind him. Brunetti wanted, even though he was speaking to the one person he trusted without reserve, not to have to explain anything more. He was tired of the whole thing.

'It sounds like you want to run away,' she said, trying to make it sound like a joke.

Brunetti nodded.

She looked at him the same way the doctor had, even tilting her head at the same angle to study him. He watched his response mirrored in her face: her eyes widened and she glanced away. Her lips grew tight as they sometimes did when she was reading a difficult text. Experience had taught him that he had no option save to give her time to study the text, wait and see what she would decide.

The door to the room opened, but neither of them bothered to look to see who it was. Silence. The person retreated and the door closed.

She studied his face for a long time before she asked, 'Are you sure?' Then, as though she wanted to be sure they were talking about the same thing, she added, 'Run away from home?'

His soul knew that she was his home. 'In a way,' he admitted, shocked at how it must sound to her. 'Not from you. Not from the kids. But from all of the rest.' To make the distinction clear, he waved at the room in which they found themselves, as though asking her to see it as evidence of everything he was talking about.

'I've been thinking about it for a long time,' Brunetti continued, discovering truth as he spoke it. 'I need not to have to do this work for a while. Not think about it and not do it, and not end up in a hospital because a suspect said something offensive about a girl.'

'What girl?' Paola asked.

'A girl who was given pills at a party and who died here last night,' he said, remembering where the girl must be.

Paola let some time pass, the way people do when they hear of an unknown person's death. Finally she said, 'If you shot Patta for every offensive thing he's said, he'd look like Swiss cheese.' She smiled; Brunetti's life straightened out and returned to its normal course.

'Pucetti's young,' he explained.

'It's a while since he was the bright young recruit, Guido. He's in his thirties now.' Brunetti wondered if she would draw her conclusion, and she did. 'He should be able to control himself, Guido. He carries a gun, for God's sake.'

Brunetti wanted to explain that Pucetti had not been wearing his gun that morning, but he realized it made no difference. He had lost control of himself, or would have, which merited an official reprimand, but Brunetti's grand-standing had eliminated that possibility. Wasn't what he had done to save Pucetti a distortion of the truth? Was it any different from kicking a weapon closer to the fallen body of an attacker who might have been about to use it? Or saying that the suspect had resisted arrest and had to be restrained?

'You're right,' Brunetti said. 'I didn't think. All I wanted to do was stop him before he did anything violent.'

'You're his boss, Guido, not his father.'

'Would you do the same thing to stop one of your students from ruining his career?' he asked, knowing it was not at all the same thing, not really.

'I probably would,' she said and got to her feet.

Her answer didn't change much, he realized. He had done it and would do it again. Where could he find another Pucetti?

'And so?' he asked.

She let a moment pass and then said, 'We were talking about your running away.'

'You make me sound like a child,' he said petulantly.

'Not at all, Guido. I've watched you during the last few months, and I agree with you that you need to get away from waiting for the next horrible case you'll have to work on.'

In all these years, she had never criticized the work he did: she had always been the interested, supportive wife, who listened to him as he described the mayhem he had observed and the consequences of the violence that lay so close to the surface of human behaviour. She had listened to his accounts of murder, rape, arson, violence, and she'd had the grace to ask him questions and had often suggested new ways to view people and events.

And in return, he asked himself, how much interest had he paid to the work that was equally part of her life? He had turned her passion for the prose of Henry James into a running gag and had refused to read more than a few of his books. Murder was for real men, and books were for girls. And now he couldn't bear it any more, and she was encouraging him to run away from it.

'I've just had a vacation,' he reminded her.

'That was two months ago, and you didn't like it.'

'It rained all the time,' he said, remembering how he'd sulked his way through London, Dublin, and Edinburgh, complaining about the rain and the lousy coffee, not caring that his mood dampened his family's spirits as much as did the weather.

'We can talk about this when you come home,' she said. 'Did they tell you when that will be?'

'No. Only that they have to do more tests,' he said, sounding casual.

'Does that mean they've found something?' Paola asked, sounding anything but casual.

The door opened, and Dottoressa Sanmartini came in. 'Good afternoon, Signora,' she said coolly. 'Might I ask you to leave me alone with my patient?'

Ordinarily, Paola would have reacted to any sarcasm lurking among the words, but there was none, only the request of one polite person to another. She said, 'Of course, Dottoressa,' and left the room.

'Would you like to sit on the bed, Signor Brunetti?' the doctor asked.

Brunetti sat and waited for her to continue, curious about what a civilian would think of the costs of their work.

When she realized that he was not going to prompt or question her, she went on, 'You must sometimes have to deal with dreadful people who have done terrible things and are incapable of seeing them as that.' Had someone played her the tape of the conversation with Ruggieri? he wondered wildly.

'You've certainly seen the results of what people can do to one another,' she added.

'You've see the same things, Dottoressa, I'd imagine,' he said.

'Yes, but my responsibility ends when I cure the victim of her wounds.' Interesting, Brunetti thought, that she automatically said 'her'. 'I don't have to listen to the person who did it deny what he did or say that he had the right to do it.'

'And you think this could lead to what's wrong with me?' Brunetti asked.

She set the papers down and turned the full attention of her eyes towards him. 'Signor Brunetti, may I speak frankly?'

'If you're my doctor, don't you have that obligation?' he asked.

She made a noise, something between a snort and a laugh. 'Hardly.'

'Then yes, please speak frankly.'

She indicated the file. 'I think the results in there have very little to do with what's wrong with you.'

Brunetti shrugged and waited for her to continue. When she did not, he asked, 'Then what does?'

'Your work. The need to do something when you can do nothing.'

She looked down, studying either her answer or her feet. Eyes still lowered, she said, 'Because of the limits put on your powers, you can only arrest and question people you believe guilty of a crime. You can't *do* anything to them, and you have little chance of making them see what it is they've done.'

She raised her eyes and looked at him. 'That's why I said "*need*", Signore. I'm talking about a sense of ethical obligation. Because you consider yourself powerless, you ended up here.'

'You make it sound like a very simple conclusion, Dottoressa,' Brunetti said quite amiably.

'When I look at the results of your tests, it *is* simple,' she answered. 'Would you like to know why?'

'Yes.'

She picked up the file and opened it, then said, 'I spent some time looking at these results, and I find no sign that you had a heart attack, nor demonstrable problems with your heart. The electrocardiogram and ultrasound are normal, and there's no sign of problems with your blood enzymes.'

Brunetti flashed a relieved smile and closed his eyes for a moment. 'That's a great relief,' he said, feeling uncomfortable at continuing with his performance as a worried patient.

'But your blood pressure is very high: 180 over 110.'

Brunetti made no attempt to disguise his nervousness.

'In your case, since there's no sign of damage – of any sort – to the tissue of the heart, what's left is stress.'

Brunetti interrupted here to ask, 'Is that better or worse, Dottoressa?'

'Neither better nor worse, Signore.' She left him time to digest that, then said, 'I've made copies of our results. You can show them to your own doctor. My diagnosis is that you are at risk because of stress, and you should do something to reduce it.'

'I'm too old to find a new job, Dottoressa,' he said.

Finally, she smiled. 'And too young to retire, I'd venture.'

'I'm afraid so.'

'Nonetheless, and regardless of your age, I think what you need, Signor Brunetti, is time away from the circumstances that cause your stress. I've indicated that in my report, which says that you are suffering from exhaustion brought on by your work that might have adverse consequences for your heart.'

'Does that mean what I think it does?' he asked.

'I've written a letter recommending two weeks – renewable to three – away from your place of work. You should not be contacted for anything to do with your normal duties. Only for emergencies.' Here she looked at him directly, and he noticed that her nose was bent just minimally to the left, as though from an old injury that had not been attended to properly. 'Whatever those emergencies might be. And you should not be bothered for normal bureaucratic problems.'

He risked saying, 'You sound like a person who has worked within a bureaucracy, Dottoressa.'

'For my sins,' she said. And then smiled again.

'And when may I go home?'

'If your wife will go with you, you can leave now.'

'That's very kind of you, Dottoressa,' he said, trying to mask his relief.

She nodded but said, 'It's also very pragmatic of me.'

'Excuse me.'

'We need the bed.'

4

Outside the room, Brunetti found Paola, and in the corridor where he had lain while waiting to be seen by a doctor, he found his shoes. Some time later, they emerged, arm in arm, into the pounding light and worse heat of a late afternoon in mid-July. Stepping from the coolness of the enormous entrance hall of the Ospedale, Brunetti felt as though someone had wrapped him in an electric blanket after first throwing a bucket of hot water over his head. The interrogation room in which he had staged his collapse had been hot, but nothing like this.

Turning to Paola, he said, 'I should have booked a return ticket with the ambulance.'

'And gone back to the Questura?' she asked, opening her bag to search for her sunglasses. Not finding them at once, she retreated into the shade until she did, then emerged with them in place.

'Let's go home,' Brunetti said. 'This is unbearable.'

They walked slowly, taking the shortest way, deliberately cutting through Campo della Fava to avoid the crowds in Calle della Bissa. When they arrived at the foot of the Rialto bridge, they looked up at it, horrified. Anthill, termites, wasps. Ignoring these thoughts, they locked arms and started up, eyes on their feet and the area immediately in front of them. Up, up, up as feet descended towards them, but they ignored them and didn't stop. Up, up, up and across the top, shoving their way through the motionless people, deaf to their cries of admiration. Then down, down, down, the momentum of their descent making them more formidable. They saw the feet of the people coming up towards them dance to the side at their approach, hardened their hearts to their protests, and plunged ahead. Then left and into the underpass, where they stopped. Brunetti's pulse raced and Paola leaned helpless on his arm.

'I can't stand it any more,' Paola said and pressed her forehead against his shoulder. 'I want Il Gazzettino to have a headline saying there's cholera in the city. Plague.'

Brunetti kissed the top of her head. 'Shall I pray for a tsunami?' he asked.

He felt the motion of her giggle. She pulled away from him and said in her calmest voice, 'No, I don't want anything that would hurt the buildings.'

By the time they got to the front door, Brunetti had perspired through his shirt and jacket, and Paola had strings of damp hair falling across her forehead. They climbed the steps, saying nothing, wanting only to get to the top and let themselves into the current of air that flowed from one end of their apartment to the other.

Inside, Brunetti peeled off his jacket, convinced that he heard it suck free from his shirt. He moved into the living room and into the stream of merely warm air that flowed from north to south. He unbuttoned his shirt and flapped its open sides in the breeze. When he turned to Paola, she was running her fingers through her hair to hold it up in the same breeze.

Without thinking, he said,
'la pastorella alpestra et cruda
posta a bagnar un leggiadretto velo,
ch'a Laura il vago et biondo capel chiuda.'
Paola let her hair fall to her shoulders and smiled at him. 'If you can watch the shepherdess wash the veil that binds her hair from the wind, then I hope the burning heat of the day will fill you with the chill of love,' she said, completing the poem.

'Don't I ever get to quote something you don't recognize?' Brunetti whined.

'You'll have to try someone more obscure than Petrarch,' she answered amiably, and then added, 'Why don't you take a shower first? You're the one who was in the hospital all morning.'

'My own stupid fault,' he said and went back to their room to find fresh clothing.

A new man emerged from the shower, one who had stood briefly under a stream of water as hot as he could endure and then switched to cold and stood stoically, though for a far shorter time. It was this man who found his wife sprawled across the sofa, sipping at a glass of pale liquid that, because of the moisture condensing on the outside of the glass, had to be cold. Silently praising his powers of observation, he noted a second glass on the tray in front of the sofa.

'Mine?' he asked.

Too tired, or too hot, to make a joking response, Paola contented herself with a nod. He sat beside her and picked up the glass. He set it down after the first sip. 'Is this lemonade?' he asked, doing his best not to sound like a policeman.

'Don't you like it?' she asked. 'I can't bear the thought of drinking anything else.'

Brunetti took another sip. 'You're probably right. I asked only because I'm surprised.'

'That it's not wine?' Paola asked.

The question made him uncomfortable, as if she'd suggested he would not drink anything that did not contain alcohol. 'It's fine,' Brunetti said and took another sip. But it wasn't a *spritz*, was it?

When Paola finished her lemonade, she set the glass down and asked, 'Well?'

Brunetti gave the question some thought. 'I've been authorized two or three weeks of complete rest,' he finally said.

'And you're going to take them?'

'Yes,' he answered without hesitation. 'Yes.'

'Good,' she affirmed. 'It's what you need.'

'If only to stop me from doing stupid things?' he inquired.

'What you did wasn't stupid, Guido, not at all,' Paola said. 'Rash, perhaps, or impulsive, but by no means stupid.'

Brunetti wondered if the children reacted the same way to her approval, if they, too, felt uncertainty or guilt fall away the instant she said what they'd done was right. 'I'm glad you think that,' he said, unable to stop it from coming out awkwardly.

Ignoring his remark, she asked, 'What will you do with your two or three weeks?'

Brunetti realized he hadn't given it any thought, other, that is, than knowing that he would take the time for himself. He kicked off his shoes and put his feet on the table in front of them. How nice a *spritz* would be, he thought again, and shifted himself down in the sofa. 'I'd like to go somewhere and look at the water,' he said.

'Here in Venice, or somewhere else?' she asked, as if his remark had been the most natural thing he could possibly have said.

'Here,' he said, and then surprised himself by adding, 'I'd like to go rowing,' an idea that had just come to him – as much the result of impulse as had been his original response to Pucetti's action.

'In this heat?' she asked.

'It's different out in the *laguna*,' Brunetti said, recalling his younger self: harder-muscled, harder-headed, and, he had to admit – though only to himself – probably harder-hearted. 'You don't feel the heat because there's always a breeze.'

'And currents and mosquitoes, and crazy young men in speedboats.'

'With happy dogs on their prows,' he countered. 'And the light on the water, the feel of the boat under your feet, and no sound when you get to the smaller canals,' he said, but then, seeing that she still failed to swoon at the magic and mystery of the *laguna*, added, 'and young girls in bikinis.'

'And you in your T-shirt, showing all your muscles.'

Brunetti leaned towards her, bent his elbow in an arm-wrestler's L and made a fist. 'Go ahead, feel it,' he said. And when she raised a hand towards him, added, 'Be careful you don't hurt your hand.'

Instead of feeling his muscle, she poked him in the ribs, saying, 'Oh, stop it, Guido. Be serious: where do you want to go?' But she said it, Brunetti thought, like someone who had an answer in mind.

'I don't know. I haven't got that far. But I could go out and stay on Burano, I guess, or even out to Torcello. There are fewer people there.'

'In a hotel?' she asked in her prosecuting magistrate mode, thus enforcing his belief that she already had an answer. 'And the boat about which you are so rhapsodic? Where do you have that hidden?'

Brunetti shoved himself to his feet and went into the kitchen. He pulled some ice cubes from the freezer and dropped them into two glasses, thought of the heat and poured in a lot of mineral water, added a shot of Campari to both, and opened one of the bottles of prosecco in the door of the refrigerator. He filled the glasses almost to the rims and took them back into the living room.

Handing one to Paola, he sat back down beside her and took a long swallow. 'I'm ready now,' he said.

'For what?' Paola asked and took a ladylike sip.

'For whatever it is you have in mind. Where I can go. And probably where I can have a boat to use, as well.'

She set her drink, barely touched, on the table and leaned back next to him. 'Zia Costanza's house,' she said, as though it were the most obvious thing in the world. 'Well, I suppose it's really a villa.'

Brunetti paused to try to remember Aunt Costanza, and finally he did: a much-married, much-widowed cousin of his father-in-law's who had one son and a great deal of property both on the mainland and in Venice as well as on the islands around it.

He had heard talk, over the years, of apartments, the odd *palazzo*, a few shops, but he failed to recall any mention of a villa. 'Where?'

'Out at the tip end of Sant'Erasmo. She has a villa and some land.'

Long familiarity with the Falier family had alerted Brunetti to the need to seek clarity about expressions such as 'some land' or, as had happened in the past, 'a few apartments'.

'Is it empty?'

'Sort of,' Paola answered. 'The custodian and his family live in another house on the property and keep the main house ready for anyone she might send out to stay there.'

'You make it sound like the perfect place for a rest cure,' Brunetti said, smiling as he spoke.

He took a few small sips of his *spritz*, placed the half-empty glass beside hers and nodded. 'How big is this place?' he asked.

Paola pressed her head against the back of the sofa and closed her eyes. 'I was sent out there for a few weeks most summers when I was in school. It seemed very big to me then. The land around it was covered with artichokes.'

'Why were you *sent out*?' Brunetti asked.

'My father thought it would be a good thing for me to see what life on a farm was really like.'

'Marie Antoinette?' he asked.

Paola had the grace to laugh. She opened her eyes and looked at him. 'I suppose so. He wanted me to see how ordinary people lived and worked.'

'And did you see that?'

'Well,' Paola hesitated, 'the artichokes pretty much took care of themselves and grew on their own.'

'So what did you do?'

'Oh, I went swimming and lay on the sofa and read.'

'And then?'

'And then it was time to go back to school.' She put her hand to her forehead as if she had just remembered something. 'That was more than thirty years ago.' She shook her head as though to clear it. 'Good grief, it sounds so long ago.'

'Have you been there since then?'

'Once. I went out for a week the summer after my third year at university.'

'To do what?' he asked.

She turned her head and looked at him. 'Something like what you want to do: look at the water and not have any noise around me.'

'Did it help?'

She looked at him for a long time before she answered. 'Not as much as meeting you in the library at the university a few months later did.'

'Ah,' was all Brunetti allowed himself to say.

After they both, no doubt for different reasons, allowed Brunetti's 'Ah' to fade to nothingness, they returned to the question of Zia Costanza's place. The villa, Paola explained, was one of the oldest on the island, built in the eighteenth century by Zia Costanza's branch of the Falier family as a refuge from the dreadful heat and pestilent air of summertime Venice. The flood of 1966, however, showed there was no refuge from the water, which rose to the second floor, destroying everything but the walls and roof. Zia Costanza, proving that she could master the art of losing, jettisoned what was ruined, cleaned what had survived, and waited until springtime to begin to dry the place out. The restoration took two years, left the exterior intact, and turned the interior into the comfortable house where the young Paola was meant to learn about life in the country. Since then, it had been offered to members of the extended family for use during the summer.

'Is anyone staying there now?' Brunetti asked.

'No, only the custodian. He's been there for years, although he wasn't there when I went out as a kid, but I met him only once. He seemed formidable, but I've been told he's absolutely reliable. He lives in the gardener's house at the back of the property with his daughter and her family.'

'Your Zia Costanza must be in her nineties by now,' Brunetti recalled.

Paola laughed. 'That branch of the family is indestructible. She's ninety-six and lives in Treviso with her son, Emilio, who's in his seventies. He tells me she goes out for a walk every day, alone. She carries a cane, but she says it's only to hit away any dogs that come too close to her.'

'They take care of the villa, even though no one lives there?'

'That's what Emilio told me. Davide's been there for twenty years or so.' Then, before he could speak, she said, 'Emilio calls me every summer to ask if I'd like to use it. He says he hates it to sit empty all the time.'

'You think he's serious?' Brunetti asked, always uncomfortable about being indebted to her family in any way.

'I read books, not minds, Guido. I can't say he's begged me to go, but he's asked if I'd like to go out with you and the kids more times than I can remember. And each time I say we're busy, he says he's going to ask me again. And he does.'

'It sounds like he wants us all to go.'

Paola closed her eyes and returned her head to the back of the sofa for long enough to take a deep sigh, then leaned forward and said, 'I suppose it wouldn't help if I recited the words of the wedding ceremony to you?'

'About being united as one heart and one spirit?' Brunetti asked.

'Yes.'

'If I remember correctly, there was nothing in the ceremony about the husband's being able to go and spend time in a house that's offered to his wife,' Brunetti said. The subject had always so troubled him that he could speak of it only in jest.

'Guido,' she began in the voice he identified as the one she used to address his social insecurities. 'We also have a legal contract – even if we forget for a moment the poetic words in the ceremony – to joint property. To joint everything. So please stop fretting about accepting Emilio's offer.' She looked at her watch and, changing the subject, asked, 'I think we'd have a better chance of survival if we ate on the terrace, don't you?'

The children were eating with their grandparents, making it easier for Paola to decide it was too hot to cook, so their meal was an *insalata caprese* with olive oil they'd brought home from Tuscany in the autumn. Brunetti grumbled that it was impossible to find decent bread in the city any more, while Paola poked aimlessly at the leaves of *basilico* she'd picked from the pot on the terrace. Finally she set down her fork, saying, 'I've never known this to happen, but it's too hot to eat.' She looked across at his plate, where the slices of *mozzarella di bufala* lay sweating in shallow pools of oil.

Then, more decisively, she asked, 'Do you want me to call Emilio?' When he failed to answer, she said, 'You don't have to listen.' She pushed her chair back and went inside the apartment, leaving Brunetti to his grumbling and his unwanted lunch.

After a few moments, Brunetti heard her voice from the open window of her study. He stacked the plates and took them to the kitchen, left them on the counter and went back to their bedroom to retrieve his copy of Pliny's *Natural History*, a book he had been wanting to read for ages.

He was just coming to the end of the fawning dedication to the Emperor Vespasian, embarrassed that a writer he so admired could be such a lickspittle, when Paola came back into the living room and sat opposite him. 'Everything's arranged,' she said. 'Emilio will call Davide and tell him you'll be there either tomorrow or Thursday and will stay for a few weeks. He said everything you'll need is in the house. Davide's daughter will put fresh sheets on the bed and see that there's enough food in the kitchen.' Brunetti, who thought that what he would most need in the kitchen was Paola, refrained from saying it for fear that she would howl at hearing such a thing.

'What are you going to do?'

'Stay here in my home, with our children, and go about the business of my life.'

'And that is?'

'Reading the books I put off all year for the summer, preparing my classes for next term, listening to my children and talking to them, feeding them, visiting my parents, reading.' She smiled, as if at the simplicity of the list.

'Couldn't you do all that on Sant'Erasmo?'

'Most of it, I suppose, though that would require that we persuade the kids to come.'

'You think they wouldn't want to?' Brunetti asked. Considering what he knew about Sant'Erasmo, he realized the kids would be isolated at the end of an island where they knew no one, with two choices for entertainment: swimming or rowing. And stuck in a house with only the company of their parents. Before Paola could reply, therefore, he said, 'Maybe it's better I go there alone.'

Without waiting for her answer, he returned his

attention to Pliny, held up the book and read aloud to her what Pliny had written to the Emperor:

'I am well aware, that, placed as you are in the highest station, and gifted with the most splendid eloquence and the most accomplished mind, even those who come to pay their respects to you, do it with a kind of veneration.'

He looked up from the page to see her response and saw her, standing at the door, mouth agape, and so he moved to a previous paragraph.

'Nor has the extent of your prosperity produced any change in you, except that it has given you the power of doing good to the utmost of your wishes. And whilst all these circumstances increase the veneration which other persons feel for you, with respect to myself, they have made me so bold, as to wish to become more familiar.'

This time, he looked at her and raised his eyebrows in inquiry, having decided to spare her the cringing servility of Pliny's next line: 'What a fertility of genius do you possess.'

When she had recovered from her surprise, Paola asked, 'Is this the preface to your letter to Patta, asking for time off?'

5

The next morning, Brunetti was careful to arrive at the Questura at nine. When he entered her office, Signorina Elettra stared at him in astonishment. Before he could try to explain, she said, 'Pucetti said you were in the hospital. That you'd had problems with your heart.' She raised a hand towards him, and he wondered if she was going to ask if she could put it into the wound in his side to be sure he was still alive. Instead, she pulled it back and waved at the telephone, saying, 'I've called them at least four times, but each time I get a different answer: that you're in Cardiologia, Gerontologia, or that there's no record of you, or that you were there but you'd been sent home.'

'The last one is right,' he said evenly, hoping to calm her with his tone.

'Pucetti said you were taken there in an ambulance,' she insisted, as if his being sent home could weigh nothing in the face of this.

'Yes, I was,' Brunetti conceded. 'But it was all a mistake.' Slowly, then, with some repetitions and going-backs, Brunetti told her the story, minimizing Pucetti's contribution and making it sound as though it had been his fault to misinterpret the young man's behaviour and thus exaggerate his own response, with the unhappy result that he had landed in the hospital and caused the staff unnecessary concern about the consequences to his heart.

'We work in a profession that has consequences for the heart,' was Signorina Elettra's deadpan reply; then she asked, 'What happens now?'

'I'm going to take the weeks of medical leave the doctor gave me,' Brunetti said, aware that each time he said it he was more fully persuaded that it was the right – even the necessary – thing to do.

'And do what?' she inquired.

'Nothing. Read. Go to bed early. Get some exercise.' He'd added this last when he remembered that Paola had said there might be a boat at the house on Sant'Erasmo. Two weeks of rowing was nothing, he knew, but perhaps it would begin to get him back into shape. Even as he thought this, Brunetti knew he would not persist in any routine of rowing once he left the island, but it made him feel better to tell himself that he wanted to.

'Is there anything really wrong with you?' Signorina Elettra asked.

'I hope not,' was Brunetti's cheerful reply. Before he could explain the details of the doctor's findings, he heard footsteps approaching the door, and when he turned he saw their superior, Vice-Questore Giuseppe Patta.

If rude good health and masculine vitality could be combined and somehow transformed into a sellable product, the Vice-Questore's photo would be on the packet. The whites of his eyes made the irises shine a deeper brown; his hair was boyishly thick and just turning white at the temples, apparently having decided to eschew the telltale ageing displayed by grey. His teeth were obviously his own and glowingly white; his walk was a combination of easy glide and irrepressible bounce. Brunetti knew from Signorina Elettra that Patta was only three years from retirement; no one, seeing him, would believe it.

In the time it took Patta to cross the room and reach Signorina Elettra's desk, Brunetti had managed to hunch himself over and sink his head lower on his neck in the very likeness of ill health. Patta, in his ineffable way, displaying the tact and discretion that had for years endeared him to his colleagues, seeing Brunetti, stopped dead and demanded, 'What's wrong with you now?'

'My doctor thinks it's my heart, Signore,' came the response from a newly timid Brunetti.

'You look terrible. He's probably right. What are you going to do?'

Brunetti sighed, as though the thought of having to respond to any of this was too taxing for him. 'He's told me to rest completely for two weeks, Vice-Questore,' he said, agreeing to Patta's change of the doctor's sex to one that would not lead Patta instantly to suspect a plot of some sort, or at least professional incompetence. Brunetti permitted himself to take out his handkerchief and wipe at his brow, then stuffed it back in his pocket. 'He thinks I should get out of the city.'

'And go where?' Patta demanded.

'Sant'Erasmo, Signore.'

'Where's that?' Patta asked, although he had been working in Venice for decades. The severity of his voice suggested he thought this was all a hoax and that Brunetti was going off to Cortina for fresh air and lounging around a hotel pool.

'Out there, sir,' Brunetti said, waving a hand in the general direction of the east.

'How long did you say?'

'Two weeks, Signore.'

'Good. That's enough to set anyone straight,' Patta declared and turned towards his office, leaving Signorina Elettra to see to Brunetti, now no doubt reclassified in Patta's mind from troublemaker to malingering troublemaker.

When their superior was gone, Brunetti returned to his normal height and stature, and Signorina Elettra asked, 'Sant'Erasmo?'

'Yes. There's a place where I can stay.'

'You're going alone?' she asked. 'What about your family?'

'They'll stay here,' he said, nothing more.

His voice must have warned her, for she asked no more personal questions, only when he was going and how it would be possible to get in touch with him. Just in case. He didn't have a phone number for Davide, nor, for that fact, a surname. 'I'm taking my phone with me.' Should it happen that she could not reach him, he added, she could always call Paola: she'd know where he was.

She started to ask something, stopped, then asked, 'You're as well as ever?'

Brunetti resisted the impulse to pat her arm, fearing that the gesture would seem condescending. 'I'm fine, Signorina. It was all a confused mess, but I'm going to take advantage of it and try to . . .' words fled him for a moment, then he retrieved the right one . . . 'decompress.' He smiled as he said this, and she smiled in return, no doubt relieved that her concern had not passed over some border of deportment or rank.

He quickly turned to business and explained that, for the moment, any documents concerning the investigation into what Avvocato Ruggieri had or had not given to the girl at the party should be handed over to Commissario Griffoni.

Seeing the change in Signorina Elettra's expression, he inquired, 'Yes, Signorina?'

Her smile was modest, almost self-effacing. 'Pucetti spoke to me yesterday about the interview with Avvocato Ruggieri. I took the liberty of having a look at him.'

'And learned?'

'That he lives with the daughter of Sandro Bettinardi,' she said, naming a powerful member of Parliament. She gave him a few moments to consider the wisdom of pursuing a case against the companion of this man's daughter and then added, 'She's seven months pregnant.'

After leaving her office, Brunetti wondered if he should go up to his own to take a look around for anything he might need in the next weeks: reports from an ongoing investigation, his pistol, a light raincoat he'd left in the closet sometime in the spring? But no, he'd leave all thought of work behind. What did a man of determination and muscle need with police reports, with a pistol, with a raincoat, for heaven's sake? If he got wet, then he'd be wet; if imperilled by some unknown terror from the sea, he'd beat it back with his single oar and then return to his bachelor home and cook the fish he'd caught that morning, eat it with a glass of local wine, then sit in the dimming light with a small glass of grappa while he listened to the chatter of marsh birds as they prepared themselves for sleep, and then go and do the same himself, the dreamless sleep that comes of sunlight, simplicity, and long hours rowing under the sun.

That night he packed, determined to make everything fit into a small wheeled suitcase, the one he used when they went away for a weekend or he travelled on police business for a few days. He packed a pair of tennis shoes that had soles good for rowing, a pair of leather sandals, and decided he'd wear an old pair of brown leather loafers he'd had re-soled and heeled more times than he could remember. Four T-shirts; uncertain whether there would be a washing machine in the house and embarrassed to ask Paola, he threw in two more. Underwear, two white cotton shirts and then a third, a button-down Brooks Brothers Oxford cloth he'd bought in New York and that had now matured to the perfect softness. An old beige cotton jacket he could no longer remember buying, a worn cashmere sweater he'd refused for years to part with, bathing trunks, a pair of light blue jeans, and a pair of navy blue Bermudas he'd bought but never worn. He paused as he picked up his razor, uncertain about putting it into the leather case Paola had given him for his fortieth birthday. Did rustic men shave every day? he asked himself. Paola's voice somehow channelled itself into the room, saying, 'Yes, they do,' and he put in the razor. Toothbrush, comb, toothpaste, and that was that.

Now the hard part. Presumably, he'd have no guests; not unless Paola decided to come out and visit, with or without the kids. He would be by himself for two weeks, in a house that might or might not possess books. It would be light until after nine, when he'd eat, then go to bed. But the mornings: he'd be free to make coffee and go back to bed to read, what bliss. And if it rained? Faced with this prospect, Brunetti's sense of heroism diminished, allowing him to admit he'd probably prefer days alone, undisturbed, with a book, to days spent rowing a boat aimlessly around the *laguna* in the rain.

He went into the bedroom, where his books were kept, exiled here a decade ago by the encroachment of Paola's books on the shelves of her study, where space had once been promised to his. He stood and stared at their spines for five minutes, running his eyes across them, counting the days he'd be on the island. How long since he'd read the *Odyssey*? His hand reached towards it but came back empty: his memory was too clear; besides, his days would provide enough travel on the wine-dark sea. He went and took the Pliny from the sofa, came back, and placed it on the foot of the bed. Then Herodotus, a new translation which he'd had for three years and not once opened. He returned to studying the books, and when his eyes fell upon Suetonius, whom he had not read for ages, he took him and tossed him on the pile: what would be better than gossip for a rainy day?

He hesitated then, anticipating the panic that came when there was nothing left to read. Real men busied themselves, he had always been told: hunting, chopping firewood, defending their territory and women from marauding hordes, buying low and selling high. Faced with two weeks on the outer edges of a city that had always needed brave men to defend it, Brunetti stood and looked at his books, pulled down a copy of Euripides, to have as many Greeks as Romans, put the four books into his suitcase and closed it.

6

After a consciously non-dramatic farewell from Paola, Brunetti took the Number One from San Silvestro to Ca' d'Oro and walked back towards Fondamente Nove, arriving on time for the 10.25. Because it was midweek, there were not many people on the enormous Number 13, and, even though it was July, he identified few people as tourists. He wore a pair of faded cotton trousers and one of the white cotton shirts, which was clinging damply to him by the time he got to Fondamente Nove. He had called the number Paola gave him for Davide, whose surname was Casati, and told him he'd be arriving at the Capannone stop on Sant'Erasmo at 10.53. He assumed that the grunt of acknowledgement he'd received had included the promise that Davide would meet him there. The idea of walking any distance on the island, pulling his suitcase behind him, in no way appealed.

The first stop was Murano Faro, where he watched idly

as people got off and on. One woman caught his attention: tall, white-haired, more than robust, wheeling an enormous shopping cart while at the same time holding the hands of two little blonde girls, perhaps three and five. The taller one broke loose and started towards the door at the back of the vaporetto that led to the outside seats. 'Regina!' the woman called, and Brunetti heard the fear in her voice. The swinging doors led to seats, but they also led to a railing and then the drop into the water.

Just as the child passed him, Brunetti leaned closer and swept her up, saying, '*Ciao*, Reginetta. You don't want to run away from your *nonna*, do you?' Speaking automatically in Veneziano, Brunetti said it loud enough for the woman to hear and was careful to hold the child under the arms and at a good distance from himself, familiar as he was with the fears – groundless or not – of parents and grandparents.

He set Regina back on her feet and released her, hunched down in his seat to bring his eyes on a line with hers. She looked at him, startled, and Brunetti crossed his eyes and moved his ears up and down, a trick that used to drive his daughter Chiara to a delirium of giggles. Regina laughed aloud and clapped her hands in delight. Turning to the woman, she cried out in that piercing voice of child-joy, 'Nonna, Nonna, come and look at the funny man.' She, too, spoke in dialect rather than in Italian.

He stood and turned to the woman, who called out, 'Guido Brunetti, is that you?'

His surprise left him without words, but he used the time it took him to recover to darken her hair, let it grow longer, take away fifteen kilos, and smooth the lines from her forehead and around her eyes. And yes, it was Lucia Zanotto, who had sat in the seat in front of him for four years of elementary school.

'Lucia,' he said, delighted. He had seen her only once – no, twice – in more than thirty years, and yet he knew her in an instant. Sweet-tempered, funny, generous Lucia, who had married her Giuliano Sandi while still in her teens and had three children, and here she was, on the boat to Sant'Erasmo.

They hugged one another, stepped back to have a better look, then hugged again. Then two kisses on the cheek and unconditional delight at having found an old friend. 'I'd know you anywhere. You look just the same,' they said simultaneously. It was the truth for them, although the years had changed them.

Lucia called the girls – the daughters of her son Luca – to her and introduced them both – Regina and Cinzia – to 'Zio Guido'. They put out their tiny hands and shook Brunetti's. Regina asked him to move his ears again so that Cinzia could see, and when he did, both of them clapped their hands at the sight.

There was little time to talk, but Lucia managed to say she was going home from grocery shopping on Murano, and he managed to tell her where he was going and who he hoped would pick him up at the landing, asking if she knew him.

'Everyone on Sant'Erasmo knows everyone else on Sant'Erasmo,' was her answer.

'And what they had for dinner?' Brunetti asked.

'And where they caught it, too,' she said and laughed out loud. Then, more seriously, she added, 'If Davide said he'd be there, then he will be.'

'Well, all he did was grunt when I said I'd arrive at 10.53.'

Lucia laughed again, the same loud noise he remembered from those years of school. 'With Davide, a grunt's as good as a yes, and a yes is something you could put in the bank.'

'Real chatterbox, eh?' Brunetti prompted.

'Really good man,' she corrected him. 'You couldn't be in better hands out here. He and his daughter keep that house as if it were their own. The Faliers are lucky to have them.'

Brunetti acknowledged this but went back to the subject of Davide. 'How old is he?'

'At least seventy,' Lucia said, 'but you'd never know it. Not to look at him or to see him work. Like a man half his age.' She looked through the window of the boat, searching for the man they were talking about. Then, in that voice people use for passing on sad news, she said, 'His wife Franca died four years ago, and he hasn't been the same since then. She took his heart with her.' Her voice deepened to that used for tragedy as she added, 'She was a long time dying. It was one of the bad ones.'

He heard the engines slowing and reached down for his suitcase. Beside him, Lucia pushed herself to her feet. 'We get off here, too,' she said. The girls rose; Cinzia took her hand; Regina took Brunetti's.

Hand in hand with the child, Brunetti disembarked. He looked upon the land and found it rich and pleasing. Trees and fields made a green assault upon him, reminding him that not only stone and the world of man could be beautiful. To his left stood rigorously straight files of grapevines, their pendulous triangles pink in the morning light. The fields to the right were a mess: unruly grass beaten down in paths that led to overladen apricot trees, so heavily burdened that even the thieves couldn't carry away all the fruit. He and his friends had come out here during their school holidays, Brunetti remembered, and made tracks of their own to the ancestors of these trees.

'Signor Brunetti?' a man's voice asked. Brunetti turned and saw a solid trunk of a man dressed in a shirt that had faded and a pair of brown corduroy trousers worn smooth just below the knees. Pale blue eyes stood out in his sun-worn face. Just to the left of his mouth was a Euro-sized patch of smooth, shiny skin. Seeing how cleanly shaved Casati was, Brunetti wondered if the smooth patch gave him trouble.

Still holding Regina's hand, Brunetti approached the man, set down his suitcase, and extended his right hand. Seeing the telltale rower's calluses on the tips of the other man's fingers, Brunetti gave only a mild grasp and quickly released Casati's hand.

'Davide Casati,' he said in the grumbling voice Brunetti had heard on the phone. Turning from Brunetti, Casati went down on one knee and kissed Regina on both cheeks and then did the same when Cinzia ran over to greet him. 'Zio Davide,' the elder one implored, 'when can we go out on the boat again?'

Casati got lightly to his feet. 'Your grandmother's the one who decides that, *ragazze*, not me.' He, too, spoke in Veneziano, Brunetti was pleased to hear. Casati turned to look at the girls' grandmother, who had joined them. She nodded in assent.

'But you're a man,' Regina said, pulling the last word out to twice its natural length.

'I'm not sure that counts much,' Casati answered. 'Women are a lot smarter than we are, so I always try to do what they tell me.'

The girls looked at their grandmother, but she said nothing, leaving it to the other man to solve this mystery. Like two tiny owls, they swivelled their heads towards Brunetti, who nodded and said, 'Your Zio Davide's right. We're really not very smart. You're much better off listening to your *nonna*.'

Hearing this, Lucia smiled at Brunetti and said, 'I can't wait until they ask Giuliano about this at lunch today.'

'What's he likely to say?' Brunetti asked.

'If he knows what's good for him, he'll agree with both of you,' she answered, then laughed at what she'd said. She looked at her watch, told Brunetti hurriedly that their number was in the phone book, under Sandi, and he should call and come to dinner one night. Then, calling to the girls to come along, she tilted her cart back on to its wheels and started walking directly away from the water, towards the other side of the narrow island.

At no time during their brief conversation had she asked why he had come to the island alone. Perhaps married people didn't dare to ask that question of other married people.

When Brunetti turned his attention back to Casati, he saw the man walking away from him on the *riva*, Brunetti's suitcase in one hand. Brunetti called goodbye to the little girls and Lucia. The girls turned and waved; Lucia raised a hand but did not turn to look.

Brunetti hurried after Casati, who was walking towards a rope tied to one of the bollards. As he reached him, Brunetti looked into the water and saw floating a metre below them a *puparìn*, the wood glowing in the sun. Closest kin to the gondola, though a bit shorter, the *puparìn* was Brunetti's favourite rowing boat, responsive and light in the water; he had never seen a lovelier one than this. Even the thwart glowed in the light, almost as though Casati had given it a quick polish before he left the boat.

Casati set the suitcase on the *riva* and crouched down at the edge. For a moment, Brunetti thought he was going to jump down into the boat, as if a young man's stunt would show Brunetti who was the real boatman. Instead, Casati sat on the *riva*, put one hand, palm flat, on the pavement and hopped down into the boat. He steadied himself before reaching up for the suitcase. Brunetti moved fast and handed it to him, sat on the *riva*, judged the distance, and stepped down on to the thwart.

Involuntarily, it escaped Brunetti: 'My God, she's beautiful.' He couldn't stop his right hand from running along the top board of the side, delighting in its cool smoothness. Looking back at Casati, he asked, 'Who built her?'

'I did,' he answered. 'But that was a long time ago.'

Brunetti said nothing in reply; he was busy studying the lines where the boards were invisibly caulked together, the hull's gentle curves, the floor planking that showed no sign of moisture or dirt.

'*Complimenti*,' Brunetti said, turning away to face forward. He heard noises from behind, then Casati asked him to haul in the *parabordo* that served as a fender between the side of the boat and the stone wall. When Brunetti turned again, he saw Casati pull in a second *parabordo* and set it in the bottom of the boat, next to a piece of iron grating standing upright against the side. Brunetti faced forward again and heard the slap of the mooring rope tossed into the bottom of the boat, and then the smooth noise of the oar slipping into the *fórcola*. A sudden motion pushed them away from the wall, and then he thought he heard Casati's oar slide into the water, and they were off.

All he heard after that was the soft rubbing of the oar in the curve of the *fórcola*, the hiss of water along the sides of the boat, and the occasional squeak of one of Casati's shoes as his weight shifted forwards or backwards. Brunetti gave himself to motion, glad of the passing breeze that tempered the savagery of the heat. He hadn't thought to bring a hat, and he had scoffed at Paola's insistence that he bring sunscreen. Real men?

Brunetti had rowed since he was a boy, but he knew he had little to contribute to the smoothness of this passage. There was not the slightest suggestion of stop and go, of a point where the thrust of the oar changed force: it was a single forward motion, like a bird soaring on rising draughts of air, or a pair of skis descending a slope. It was a whish or a shuuh, as hard to describe as to hear, even in the midst of the silence of the *laguna*.

Brunetti turned his head to one side, then to the other, but there was only the soft, low hiss. He wanted to turn and look at Casati, as though by watching him row, he might store the motions away and copy them later, but he didn't want to shift his weight and thus change the balance of the boat, however minimally.

A fisherman stood on the *riva*, looking both bored and impatient. When he saw the *puparìn*, he raised his pole in salutation to Casati, but the heat rendered him silent as a fish.

They reached the end of the island and turned eastward, following the shoreline past houses and abandoned fields. Even the turning had been effortless. Brunetti watched houses and trees glide past and only then did he realize how fast they were moving. He turned, then, to watch Casati row.

Seeing the perfect balance of his motion, back and forth, back and forth, hands effortlessly in control of the oar, Brunetti thought that no man his own age or younger would be able to row like this because he would spoil it by showing off. The drops from the blade hit the water almost invisibly before the oar dipped in and moved towards the back. His father had rowed like this.

It was perfection, Brunetti realized, as beautiful as any painting he had ever seen or voice he had ever heard. He turned himself forward and looked to the right as they entered what seemed to be a wider canal.

'It's just up there,' Casati said from behind him. Brunetti saw a tangled mass of vines that had managed to crawl over and repossess a brick sea wall, and behind it sick, desiccated trees, their lower parts moss-spattered and apparently fruitless. Like bones tossed to dogs under the table, dull orange fragments of the wall lay scattered among the tin cans and plastic bottles on the tidal beach that had washed up against it.

'No, farther ahead,' Casati said. Brunetti saw that the colour of the bricks lightened as the wall grew straight and more solidly made. Behind it he saw the tops of trees, each a vernal Lazarus, sickness cast aside, peaches and apricots rich on the branches, leaves as brightly polished as the boat they rode in. And amidst them the multi-chimneyed tiled roof of a countryside villa. From so low, he could see only the top floor and roof, but he noticed that the white paint on the plastered walls was fresh, as were the copper gutters and drainpipes.

Casati steered them towards an opening in the wall in front of the house, where three moss-covered steps led down to the water. He passed the steps and pulled close to the sea wall. As the boat slowed, Brunetti, without being asked, tossed the *parabordo* over the side and put out his hand to slow them by grabbing a metal ring in the wall. When they came to a full stop, he moved forward and tied the rope lying at the front of the boat to the ring.

Brunetti turned towards the back of the boat, and saw another rope already tied to a second metal ring, the second *parabordo* already over the side to protect the boat. Casati clambered up the three steps, suitcase in hand. In ordinary circumstances, with a friend, Brunetti would have made a joke about hoping the other man did not expect a tip, but he didn't want to risk offending Casati.

When he climbed up, Brunetti saw the villa standing fifty metres back from the brick wall. It looked like a square box covered with a four-segment tiled roof that peaked in the centre. A thick wooden door stood in the middle of the façade, three large windows on either side of it. A wide stone pavement led to the private mooring.

Casati had already started towards the villa, and Brunetti followed him. The man opened the door, prompting Brunetti to ask, 'You don't lock it?'

Casati looked at him as if he'd spoken in some language other than Veneziano, then answered, 'No. Not out here.'

'Just like when I was a boy,' Brunetti answered, hoping it was the right thing to say.

Apparently it was, for Casati smiled. 'Come in, Signore.'

It took about fifteen minutes for him to show Brunetti around the house. He started with the ground floor with a central staircase leading to the upper floor. In a large sitting room stood a random selection of easy chairs that had in common with the single sofa only the look of being comfortable and well worn; the library – Brunetti sighed with relief at the sight – had four walls of books. The dining room held a long walnut table scarred by centuries of use, and another, smaller sitting room had walls filled with fragments of ancient Venetian pottery that must have been rescued from the underwater dumps of the old pottery workshops on Murano. An enormous kitchen spanned the back part of the building and had what appeared to be the original brick floor and six French windows giving out to a walled-in garden.

The centre of the garden was a sea of flowers, only flowers, growing in reckless abandon and with no apparent order, not of variety, colour, height, nor size. Brunetti recognized roses, marigolds, zinnias, and saw others that looked familiar but remained nameless to him. The back wall was covered with climbing plants: cucumber and what looked like squash as well as some trellised fruit trees. The trees he had seen from the water stood near the right wall, in front of them a long row of coloured boxes on waist-high stands. An equally long row of rosemary and lavender was planted to the left. Colour rioted, shapes stood where they pleased, yet the whole was strangely harmonious.

Casati called to him from the front of the house, and Brunetti went towards his voice. 'I'll show you your room,' Casati said and started up the stairs, still carrying Brunetti's suitcase. At the top, Casati turned left and, passing a closed door, said, 'That's the bathroom.' He passed the next door and continued to the last on the right side and opened it.

'This is your room,' Casati said and set the suitcase on a wooden rack next to a tall old wooden *armadio* that showed signs of having once been painted green. 'I'm sorry you're not closer to the bathroom, but this room has a view of the garden.'

'It's perfect,' Brunetti said, glancing around. Brunetti loved square rooms, which answered some sort of impulse towards harmony in him. The double bed was of dark mahogany with a high headboard, like the bed his grandparents had slept in. There was a long walnut desk against one wall, east-facing windows to either side of it, another window in the wall to his right, this one facing south. Curious to see what was visible from the first windows,

Brunetti went to take a look. As he approached, light flooded across his feet, warming his sockless ankles. There was the water, and, he thought, Treporti just on the other side of the canal.

He turned back to Casati, repeating, 'It's perfect. Thank you.'

Casati smiled as he said, 'I'm not the one to thank, Signore. It's Signor Emilio, who called me.'

'Then I thank you for coming to get me and for carrying my suitcase.' Before Casati could speak, Brunetti added, 'And for rowing so beautifully.'

7

The compliment must have pleased Casati, who lowered his head in an attempt to hide his smile. To fill the silence, Brunetti went on. 'I've rowed – though only off and on – since I was a kid, and recently I went out again with an old friend. But I've seldom seen anyone so completely in command. I could have been in an armchair.' He decided he'd said enough and feared embarrassing the other man.

'Thank you,' Casati said. 'I value your opinion.'

It was now Brunetti's turn to be embarrassed. 'I don't know why you should, Signor Casati.'

'You rowed with one of the best, so you know the difference,' Casati said, a remark that confused Brunetti utterly.

'I'm sorry,' he said, 'but I don't understand.'

'Your father,' Casati said. 'You rowed with him, didn't you?'

Brunetti's mouth fell open in surprise he could not hide. 'How did you . . . ?' he began. 'Did you know him?'

'We won the regatta in 1967,' Casati said.

Brunetti stared at the other man. 'Davide?' he asked. 'You're *that* Davide?' Without thinking, Brunetti crossed the room and wrapped his arms around the older man. 'No, it can't be.' He stepped back from Casati and looked at him as though seeing him for the first time.

'My father talked about you all the time, about that regatta and how you told him to take the oar at the back, and how you almost had a fight about it.' Memories buzzed into Brunetti's mind, and for an instant he could hear his father's happy voice, telling about his day of glory.

'He was the better rower,' Casati said, then seemed to drift off to that same race, half a century ago. 'We had a good boat, and that helped.' He smiled again. 'Old man's chatter, I'm afraid.'

'It was one of his happiest memories,' Brunetti said. 'Maybe the happiest.'

'He didn't have many happy ones after he came back from the war, I know,' Casati said, then added, 'I didn't go to his funeral. My father was . . . and the doctor told me I should be with him because . . .' He stopped and said, 'Doctors.' Then added, 'I saw your mother once and tried to explain, and she told me I'd done the right thing. But I don't know. My father had another week, but I didn't know that at . . .' His voice died away, and neither spoke for a time.

Brunetti turned away from the other man, and walked over to the window and looked down at the garden.

Unconsciously, Casati had slipped into the familiar *'tu'*.

The window was open, the air perfumed by the flowers below. Brunetti, urban to his marrow, was incapable of distinguishing the scent of one flower from another, but the scent pleased him. He looked down at the garden and at second sight made out the pattern more clearly: variegated colours in the middle; then the straight lines of fruit and herbs down the two sides. He could see shapes that from here looked like stacked boxes; packing cases, perhaps. 'What are those?' he asked, pointing at them.

Casati cleared his throat and came over to the window. 'Flowers,' he said.

Brunetti laughed and said, 'No, the boxes. What are they?'

'Beehives,' Casati answered and gave Brunetti a puzzled look. 'Haven't you ever seen them?' he asked, continuing to address Brunetti as *'tu'*, and thus establishing that he was speaking not to the son-in-law of Conte Falier come out for two weeks, but to the son of an old friend.

After some thought, Brunetti answered, 'I don't think so, but I probably wouldn't have known what they were, anyway.' He glanced down at the garden again and added, 'They look like plastic.' Brunetti knew, or thought he did, that beehives were of wood or straw.

'These are,' Casati said, sounding as if he'd been caught out in a lie. 'I've got others that are made of wood.'

'Down there?' Brunetti said, waving down at the garden.

'No, out in the *laguna.*'

This made no sense to Brunetti. The *laguna* was salt water. Bees needed, he thought, land and flowers to find pollen. Come to think of it, though he'd read about them, he really didn't know much about bees. But he did know that he loved honey.

Curiosity got the better of him, and he asked, 'Where in the *laguna*?'

'Oh, on some of the *barene,*' Casati said, suddenly sounding evasive.

'But they're just marshland in the middle of the water. Nothing can grow on them, can it? What happens when the tide comes in? To the hives, I mean.'

'I've got the hives up on stands on the man-made *barene* because some of them are lower than the natural ones. So even when a high tide comes, the water doesn't reach the hives,' Casati said, moving away from the window and towards the door. 'Is there anything else I can do for you?'

'I'd like you to find me something to do.'

Casati's eyes narrowed. 'I don't understand.'

'I'm going to be out here for a while,' Brunetti said, suddenly conscious of how long two weeks might be. 'And I'd like to do something physical.'

'Such as?' Casati asked, honestly puzzled, then suggested, 'Ride a bicycle? Go jogging?'

Did he look so irredeemably urban? Brunetti wondered. 'No, more like work. I don't know, chop firewood or work in the fields or help you if you have to transport goods.'

Casati surprised him by asking, 'You're a policeman, aren't you?'

Usually, when asked this, Brunetti tried to make a joke of it, but Casati was very much in earnest, and so Brunetti answered, 'Yes, I am.'

'Does that mean you don't talk about what you do?'

'Usually.'

'And if I ask you not to?'

Immediately worried that he was going to be caught up in semi-legal activity of some sort, Brunetti answered, 'Then I don't tell anyone,' but thought it more honest to be frank with him and added, 'so long as it isn't against the law.'

Casati shook the idea away with his head. 'No, it's perfectly legal. I just don't want people to know about it.' That, Brunetti thought, could cover a wide range of actions.

Casati looked at his watch and must have calculated something, for he said, 'It's almost twelve-thirty. There's some lunch for you in the kitchen. If you eat now, we could leave in an hour, and we'd be back before five. You want to come?'

'Yes,' Brunetti said, and went down to the kitchen to look for his lunch.

At one-thirty promptly, Brunetti, now wearing his tennis shoes, left the house, telling himself not to worry about leaving the door unlocked, and walked down to the mooring place where Casati had tied up the boat. He heard the older man before he saw him, shifting something around in the bottom of the boat.

He noticed that the water was higher than when they had arrived. He stepped easily into the boat, saw a second oar lying on the gunwale, the second *fórcola* in place on the left side of the boat. 'Rub some of this on you,' Casati said, handing him a metal tin. The label said it was dark brown shoe polish, and he wondered if this was some sort of miracle suncream known only to sailors: Paola would be amazed. He prised up the lid and saw that the label had got the colour wrong: the goo inside was beige.

'It's for the mosquitoes. Rub it on, and they won't bother you.' When Brunetti hesitated, Casati said. 'My daughter made it: it works.'

Brunetti did as told and rubbed it on his hands, arms, ankles, and neck: he could smell camphor, lemon, and something sharp and acid. He handed the tin back to Casati, who put it in a wooden box under the platform at the back of the boat and pulled out a pair of leather gloves.

'Put these on,' Casati said, tossing them to Brunetti. When Brunetti hesitated, Casati added, 'I shook your hand. You'll need gloves the first few days.'

'First few days. First few days.' Brunetti repeated the

words to himself like an incantation while Casati cast off and pushed the boat away from the wall. Brunetti pulled on the gloves, a size too large for him. He picked up the oar and slipped it into the *fórcola*, tilted it and ran it knife-like through the water. The length and weight were familiar; without conscious effort on his part, his feet and knees adjusted to the boat. He turned to see where Casati was in his stroke, waited until Casati lifted his oar from the water for the next stroke and did the same. It took Brunetti a few strokes to adjust to the rhythm set by the other man, but when he found it, he relaxed and entered into the steady rhythm set by the man behind him.

Brunetti looked forward, lining his sight with a distant object and aiming for that so as to keep in a straight line. 'Bit to the left,' Casati said, and the boat followed the words. Brunetti didn't have to be told when the curve was finished; his whole being sensed when it was time to sight another object and row straight for it.

As he rowed on, he began to feel the muscles in his legs and back react to the strain. As his hands ground against the wood of the oar, he felt a roughness inside the glove just at the bottom of his right thumb. To smooth it out – and he wasn't sure whether it was the stitching or the beginning of a blister – he would have to take his hand off the oar. He rowed on.

Bend forward, pushing the oar to the back, twirl it out of the water and bring the blade forward while straightening a bit, cut the oar into the water again, bend into the forward thrust, twirl the oar and lift it out.

He thought of Levin in *Anna Karenina*, the scene where the city slicker goes out to cut hay with the peasants. Urban, out of shape, body howling with pain, but on and on Levin went, swathe after swathe, hands covered with blisters, seeing how effortless it is for the peasants, and when, dear God, can I have a drink of water?

Levin had been harvesting hay, so the work he did made a visible difference. Brunetti, instead, saw only water, sky, marshland, more water, the occasional cloud. No colour, no sound, just a flat, dull horizon and endless water, always the same.

Behind him, Casati said, 'I think I'd like something to drink. How about you?' He felt the slowing of the boat and heard the thump of Casati's oar being set in the gunwale. He did the same, took the opportunity to look down at the shirt that clung to his body, and saw that the front was a darker grey all the way to the bottom. He stood up straight but was careful to do it very slowly, warning his spine what he was doing.

He turned and looked at the other rower, and when he saw how small what he took to be Sant'Erasmo seemed, off in the distance behind Casati, Brunetti realized how far they had come. The older man pulled something from a wicker basket beside his feet and tossed a bottle of mineral water to Brunetti. He forced himself to open it slowly and gazed around before taking his first sip. How enormous the *laguna* was. No safe pavements, streets, places with names: only the veins and arteries of the *laguna*, disappearing with the tide, returning when it withdrew.

The sun was his only sure way to tell direction: if it beat down on his left shoulder, they were heading north. He tried to remember the excursions he had made with his father, but his memories – not only of the geography – were no longer to be trusted.

Burano had to be off to the left, he thought. He turned to look and, indeed, it was there, but farther off than he thought it would be.

He tried to take small sips, but thirst overcame him and

he finished the water, put the top back on the bottle and wedged it into the space in the gunwale. If that was Burano and they were heading north . . .

'Are we in the Canale di San Felice?' he asked Casati, hoping his memory was right.

'Very close. It's the next one to the east,' Casati answered, pulling a handkerchief from his pocket to wipe his brow. He wore no hat. Real men. 'This is Canale Gaggian.'

Brunetti shook his head to show he didn't know it.

'It goes north, too.'

Brunetti shrugged his shoulders to show he still didn't know the canal, then smiled to say it didn't make any difference to him.

'It goes to l'Isola di Santa Cristina.'

'Ah,' Brunetti exclaimed, recognizing the name. 'It's private, isn't it?' he asked without thinking.

'Yes,' Casati answered after a moment, and then, 'But I know someone.'

When he realized that this was the only explanation he was going to get, Brunetti said, 'So we could go back the other way, past Torcello?' He tried to sound conversational and completely at home out here.

'Yes. Good,' answered Casati and looked at his watch. 'Let's go. The tide's changed, so we have about two hours before the water will be too low.'

At the thought that they might be back at the house in two hours, Brunetti felt guilty relief. He had taken his watch off so as not to be conscious of time and calculated that they had been out for an hour and a half. So that meant they were more or less half done. Thank God.

He put his oar back in place and waited for Casati's stroke. When it came, he dug his oar into the water and headed for l'Isola di Santa Cristina.

As the canal narrowed, they saw spoonbills ahead of them, waving their beaks from side to side in the mud as they searched for food. Instinctively the two men pulled in their oars and approached the birds silently, but one of them must have made a motion, for the two birds took wing and were gone in an instant. They continued and before long Casati hissed to Brunetti as they glided past four fledgling black-winged stilts, long-legged and fluffy, pecking into the mud at the edge of the canal. At their approach, the birds slipped under the overhanging vegetation and instantly became part of the reeds and stalks of dry grass.

Some time later, Brunetti saw what looked like a clump of low trees to their left. 'Is that it?' he asked.

'Yes,' Casati answered and gave a hard stroke which turned the boat in that direction. They ran along a low sea wall behind which stood a thick row of trees. About ten metres farther on, Casati stopped rowing and dug his oar into the water to slow the boat.

'Pull in here,' he called to Brunetti, who helped turn the prow by digging his oar into the water; they glided up to the side of the canal. Near the edge was a large cement block with a metal mooring ring. Brunetti pulled in his oar and tied the boat to the ring.

Casati stepped on to the island and moved ahead to Brunetti. 'I'm going to see my girls,' he said with a broad smile. 'Would you like to come and see them?'

Without waiting for an answer, Casati extended his hand and helped Brunetti step up beside him, then turned away and walked towards and then into the small clump of trees Brunetti had seen from the water.

Brunetti saw no girls, no matter where he looked. On the other side of this small island – they could have crossed it in minutes – was a house with closed shutters. Within and under the trees, they were surely invisible. As still were the girls. He saw a flash of white to his left and took a quick step away from it. But with a flurry of wings it moved faster and farther away: a duck, perhaps, but not a girl.

In a small clearing at the centre of the small clump of trees, Brunetti saw a row of three wooden boxes similar in shape to the plastic ones he had seen from his room: red, white, green: *evviva Italia*. And then he heard the girls: buzzing and whizzing and filling the air with their low noise. Brunetti stood stock still, afraid of the bees.

Ahead of him, Casati reached into the pocket of his corduroy trousers and pulled out a large chip of wood and a cigarette lighter, then stopped and set the wood alight. After a moment, a small column of smoke rose from the chip. Casati waved it around them like a magician's wand, and the bees slowed in a hovering trance. Casati turned to him. 'Come on. They won't bother you. Give me a hand,' he said, his voice blurred by the sound of the bees, which intensified as they approached the hives.

Casati moved off, and Brunetti followed, certain that the other man must know what he was doing. And indeed, the bees encircled them but ignored them. Casati continued to wave the smouldering chip, creating a safe path for them as the bees flew away from the trail of smoke, leaving it to the two men to follow the cloud of smoke through the tunnel of their whirling sound. Casati handed the chip to Brunetti, who continued to wave it around them in the same drifty manner.

Slowly, the way Brunetti had seen drugged people move, each motion an arabesque, a caress of the surrounding space, Casati removed the top of the first hive and set it upright on the ground. He reached in and pulled out a wooden frame covered with bees: crawling, walking, slithering, insinuating themselves under and over one another, each touching the others in a harmony of gentleness.

Casati waved Brunetti closer. His fear in abeyance, Brunetti moved beside him and looked at the wooden frame in Casati's hand.

'Do you see her?' Casati asked.

'Who?' Brunetti asked. Bees, he knew, were female, so these were his girls. But which could be the Girl?

'Look for the blue dot,' Casati said, and for a minute Brunetti feared the older man ought to have worn a hat under the sun. 'On the back of her head. That's the Queen.'

Brunetti, fear banished by curiosity, bowed closer to the thronging mass and hunted for a blue dot, but all he saw were hundreds of bees; he understood now what the word 'swarm' meant. And then he saw it, an iridescent blue dot, a bit bigger than the head of a pin. She hauled herself along in zigzag progression, nudged, pushed, caressed and cleaned by other bees, all of them unmarked and smaller than she. She dived into one of the hexagonal wax cells, pulled herself out only to move forward a bit, then back up and insert her tail part into the empty cell.

'Is she laying an egg?' Brunetti whispered, almost speechless with the majesty of what he was watching.

'Yes.'

'And the others?'

'They clean her and feed her and smooth her passage.'

Brunetti bent closer; he'd forgotten danger. Their motion never stopped: gliding up and over one another, circling the Queen, following in her train. The movement seemed random, yet it was all perfectly synchronized.

'What's in those?' he asked, pointing to rows of closed cells on the lower part of the wooden frame in Casati's hands.

'Eggs – as you saw – and then they're larvae, and then pupae, and when they come out they're bees, full grown,' Casati explained, slipping the frame back in place and pulling out another. He studied it quickly, slipped it back inside. He pulled up another and ran a finger along the bottom, smoothing off small beige globs. He tasted it and smiled, then held the frame out to Brunetti.

'Try it,' he said.

Brunetti switched the still-burning chip to his left hand and ran his right forefinger along the bottom of the frame, detaching some of the globs. He put his finger in his mouth and prodded the honey free with his tongue. Sweet, faintly grainy, sweet again, chewy, more sweet, more bliss.

Casati took the frame back and inserted it in the hive. When Casati opened the second hive, Brunetti saw more bees, more motion, almost all of the cells full and covered, and always the same buzzing rush that was no longer menacing, though it had grown even louder.

Brunetti, fascinated, waved the smouldering chip, which refused to burst into flame and produced only a steady stream of smoke. The noise had become an incantation. His thoughts flew to Aristotle, who had written – he no longer remembered where – about having once experienced 'one glimpse of celestial is-ness'. It was a phrase Brunetti had never understood. Until now.

The sound diminished as they approached the last hive. 'One more,' Casati said and took the top off the green hive. When he pulled out the first frame, Brunetti saw that there were almost no bees on it, and the few left crawled slowly and apparently without purpose. He saw no Queen.

'What's wrong?' he asked.

Casati shook his head in answer and balanced the frame on the hive. He stooped down and pulled out a drawer at the bottom of the hive. Brunetti saw the bodies of bees lying there, too thick to count. Casati pulled in his breath when he saw them. He removed a plastic ziplock bag from his back pocket, opened it to remove a slim leather case and took from this a plastic vial and a pair of tweezers.

'They shouldn't die in the hive,' Casati whispered. Brunetti had no difficulty hearing the other man because the buzzing noise had grown much softer near this hive.

'When they're sick, they're supposed to fly away so they won't infect the others,' Casati said, sounding puzzled.

Carefully, he used the tweezers to pick up a few of the dead bees; he dropped them into the vial, capped it, and slipped it and the tweezers into the case, which he returned to the ziplock bag and put back in his pocket. Then he closed the drawer, took the top of the hive and put it back in place. 'This isn't supposed to happen,' he said in a voice Brunetti associated with the stunned victims of violent crimes.

'What's wrong?' Brunetti asked again.

'The test will tell,' Casati answered, then almost consciously shook himself loose from his shock. Looking at his watch, he said, 'Come on. We've only got about twenty minutes.'

Casati hurried back the way they had come and clambered down into the back of the *puparìn*, leaving Brunetti to step down to his own place. He untied the rope and they were off.

'We turn around,' Casati said, and did it quickly, effortlessly, in four strokes of his oar. The sun was now pounding on Brunetti's right shoulder, so they were heading south. He glanced to the side and saw how the embankments had grown higher, and then he understood Casati's need for haste: natural embankments were emerging from the water on both sides of them as the tide went out, leaving them rowing in ever-shallower water.

He felt the sudden increase in Casati's rhythm and met it. They'd be stuck there overnight or until the tide changed again. He thought of the mosquitoes arriving at dusk, shoe polish or not, and he rowed.

This was not open water. 'Left,' Casati called from behind him, and Brunetti did as ordered. After about twenty strokes, Casati called out 'Right,' and an obedient Brunetti joined him in turning the boat, following a path that he could not discern. Plants grew towards them from both sides as the retreating tide exposed the grass that had been hidden under water when they came. Something slid roughly along the bottom of the boat, and both men froze. Casati cried out, *'Forza!'* and quickened his pace. Again the scraping sound came. Brunetti's oar hit something hard.

And then the waterway in front of them broadened with no warning and they emerged into a large patch of open water. Casati slowed his rhythm, and Brunetti was happy to match it. 'This is the Canale di Sant'Antonio,' Casati said, a fact which conveyed no meaning to Brunetti. But the slower rhythm did. 'We can take it easy now.'

Ahead of them Brunetti saw buildings and rooftops and the telltale bell tower. 'Is that Burano?' he called back to Casati.

'Yes. Would you like to stop for a coffee?'

Brunetti would have liked to stop and have other rowers take him home. But he called out, 'Good idea.' Real men.

8

The coffee was followed by two glasses of water, and then another, and after that Brunetti felt as though he might be able to make it from Burano to Sant'Erasmo. Two men came into the bar and said hello to Casati, who introduced Brunetti, explaining he was a friend who had come out to visit. That led the two men to offer them a drink, but Casati refused, saying they had rowed too much and needed to get home before even thinking about a glass of anything other than water.

He and Brunetti walked back to the boat, and the men came along, one of them saying the *puparìn* was the most beautiful he'd ever seen, and if Casati ever decided he wanted to sell . . .

Casati laughed and sat on the *riva* – so much had the water gone down – to lower himself into the boat. Brunetti did the same, untied the boat, called up farewells to the two men, and bent again to his oar, wondering if this was what it was like to be a galley slave. But slaves had no leather gloves and certainly did not stop for coffee in the afternoon.

Casati told him that there was a shortcut but that he didn't trust it at low tide, so they went out to the Canale di Burano, where the depth was certain, and rowed to the Canale di Crevan and to where they had started. They silently pulled into their docking place, and Brunetti tied the boat to the metal ring. Casati untied the grating and lifted it on to the *riva*. 'My great-grandfather made it,' he said proudly. 'I use it as an anchor, but I never leave it in the boat.'

It was only then that Brunetti noticed the forged swirls and arabesques that still survived among the pieces that had been broken off over the years. As so often happened with Brunetti, knowledge of the object's age added to its beauty.

Casati was quickly up the three steps, holding his oar and *fórcola*, and asked Brunetti to hand him up his. Casati set them all down and leaned over to offer Brunetti a hand, which he was not at all ashamed to accept. Once on land, Brunetti took both oars and put them over his shoulder.

They walked side by side, Brunetti with the oars and Casati with the two *fórcole* lying on the grating. They turned right on to a dirt path at the far end of which stood a small stone house, the tiles on the roof and the new window frames speaking of a recent restoration. Before Brunetti could ask, Casati said, 'The Contessa restored the house for us. But then . . .' His voice trailed off, and Brunetti saw the life go out of his face for an instant. 'I live here with my daughter and her family now.'

Casati turned into an even smaller path that led to a narrow wooden shed at the back. He led the way inside, placed the grating against the wall, and helped Brunetti set the oars and *fórcole* on pegs on the wall.

'Thank you for the lesson,' Brunetti said. He pulled the gloves from his pockets and held them out to Casati. 'And thanks for these.'

'Keep them for tomorrow, why don't you?' Casati suggested.

'What time?' Brunetti asked casually, trying not to show signs of his delight.

'Seven-thirty,' Casati said straight-faced. 'That way we can get where we're going and back before the real heat begins.'

'I'll be there.' Brunetti shook Casati's hand, and started back towards the larger house. From behind him, Casati called, 'Federica will bring you fresh bread,' and Brunetti raised a hand in the air to acknowledge that he had heard.

He looked at his watch as he entered and was surprised to see that it was almost six. They must have spent more time in the bar than he thought or gone farther than he was aware of. He went up the stairs to his room to get his *telefonino*, and on the third step felt reports begin to arrive from various parts of his body. Calves tight, back sore, neck shooting pain up into his skull, hands bruised, thumb flaring, feet chafed raw on the soles. He couldn't wait to tell Paola about it.

She, as it turned out, was sympathetic but not impressed. She expressed Zerlina-like concern for his various injured and exhausted parts, but not having been out on the *laguna* with him, she could not feel the immense relief of being free of the city, of people and the noise and demands they made.

How to explain to her, Brunetti wondered, how to make her feel the triumph of exhaustion? Instead, he told her that Casati's daughter – he'd already told her how warm his welcome from Casati had been – had left dinner in the fridge for him.

'Surely you're not going to eat now,' she exclaimed.

'No, I'll read for a while and then eat. I'm too tired to do anything else.'

'Good,' Paola answered promptly. 'That's why you're there, after all. Loaf around, eat, go to bed, and I hope tomorrow is even better than today. Did he say where he'd take you?'

'No. But it doesn't matter where it is or where we go. It's wonderful: you don't have to think about anything except putting the oar in the water. And the bees, Paola; you can't believe how wonderful they are. And the honey. I wish you could have tasted it, and you should have seen the Queen, crawling around and laying eggs.' Brunetti knew that, no matter how much he babbled, he was incapable of conveying the magic of the scene. 'If you come out . . .'

'Maybe next week, Guido. You said you needed to be away from everything. And I'm a thing. We can talk about it in a few days.'

'You're spending all your time reading, aren't you?' he asked, pretending to sound like a jealous husband and succeeding only in sounding like a real one.

'I've decided it's time to reread Jane Austen, and I've spent the day with *Emma*. Laughing out loud.'

'It's unlikely that Pliny will have the same effect on me,' Brunetti said. They exchanged wishes for a pleasant evening, then he hung up and went to find Pliny.

Brunetti walked around the lower rooms of the house, a bit like Baby Bear, testing all of the chairs in the large sitting room until he found the one that was kindest to his aching body: a sway-backed easy chair low enough to allow him to cross his legs comfortably with a view through the garden to the sky. Beside it hung the portrait of a man with a strong nose and wide-set eyes who might have been a member of the Falier family. He wasn't much in the way of company, Brunetti thought, but then he recalled that he had wanted solitude, and this was what solitude felt like.

He opened the *Natural History* to the eleventh book, curious to learn what the ancient world had thought about bees. He learned that they worked assiduously and, if caught too far from the hive by the fall of night, promptly lay down on their backs so as best to preserve their wings from being dampened by the dew, the better to jump up for work at the first sign of dawn. Brunetti had spent much of his reading life amidst the minds and convictions of people who had lived thousands of years ago, and he had learned not to laugh at their ideas but to try to understand why they thought the way they did. After all, his own world lived in constant discovery of its own ignorance.

Brunetti had read about people who believed the universe had been created on Sunday 23 October, about 6,000 years ago. He always forgot the year, but he found the precision of the date so charming that he had no difficulty in recalling it. What are bees sleeping on their backs when compared to that?

Pliny also believed that bees have the gift of foreknowing the wind and rain, and if the day is fine the swarm issues forth and immediately applies itself to its work, some bees managing to load their legs from the flowers while others fill their mouths with water.

This suggested to Brunetti that he might want to fill his mouth with something other than water. He went into the kitchen and opened the refrigerator. Ah, Pinot Grigio. Perhaps he could fill his mouth with that?

He took an exploratory look farther in and saw an enormous cellophane-covered platter of *frutti di mare* and, beside it, what looked like a bowl of salad, in which he saw slices of avocado and pear.

Taking the bottle and a glass with him, Brunetti returned to his chair, his book, and his bees.

And learned from Pliny the Elder that 'honey comes from the air; during its fall from a great height it is dirtied and is stained with the vapour of the earth; when the bees collect it, it is fermented and purified in the hive.' Brunetti looked up from the book and studied the sky: cloudless and growing dim with the passing of the day. No doubt the honey would soon begin to fall.

What a strange, optimistic, single-minded man Pliny must have been, impassioned to collect and record all aspects of nature, ceaselessly investigating everything, and ultimately a victim of his own scientific curiosity.

Wanting to see at first hand the eruption of Vesuvius, he set out to have himself rowed towards the beach below it in a quest for knowledge, but changed course to go and save the wife of a friend. Burning pumice and searing ash fell into his boat, yet he sailed on. He went to great lengths, according to the letter his nephew wrote to describe the circumstances of his uncle's death, to set at rest the fears of everyone he encountered. But then his luck, and his time, ran out and he was overcome by the ash-laden air and suffocated to death.

Brunetti woke with a start some time later and was surprised to find that he was sitting in semi-darkness. He pushed himself to his feet, turned on the light and, keeping his book in his hand, made his way into the kitchen. He set the platter and the bowl on the table, found a plate in the cabinet, knife and fork in a drawer. There was a loaf of bread on the counter; he cut off a few slices. He refilled his glass.

He pulled out a chair and went to get a towel; he folded it and propped it under the back of his book and opened it to find his place. He took his eyes from the page and studied the tiny creatures on the platter: shrimp, baby octopus, mussel, clam, canocchie, *latticini di seppia*. The day's exercise had caught up with him, and he decided to eat from the platter, the better to soak up the olive oil with his bread. There was more salt than he was accustomed to and less parsley. Brunetti made two trips to the counter, one to cut more bread and one to fill his glass.

He continued reading after he'd finished everything on the platter and wiped it clean with the last piece of bread. Soon what he read began to grow confused: honey from isolated places, bees flying with small stones balanced on their backs to keep them from being blown off course by the wind. He took a few deep breaths and paged back to an earlier chapter, thinking it would be easier to read entirely new material. Here he discovered that hedgehogs, to prepare food for winter, rolled on apples to stick them to their spines, carrying them to a safe place in a hollow tree, to be eaten during the winter.

'I think it's time you went to bed,' he said to no one in particular. And obeyed.

9

Fortunately, there was an alarm clock beside his bed, or Brunetti would have slept past his meeting with Casati. Unfortunately, the man who rose from the bed lacked the vigour and ease of limb of the man who had arrived on Sant'Erasmo the previous day. A long, hot shower, two coffees, and breakfast improved things considerably, and by the time Brunetti reached the boat, he was almost restored to his former self.

Casati was already there and lowering a soft Styrofoam container into the boat. Brunetti said good morning, stepped into the boat, and moved to stand below Casati to help with the container, which he stowed in the back.

Casati passed Brunetti the two oars and the two *fórcole*. The older man lowered himself into the boat. He opened the wooden box in the back, and both of them slathered on the beige goo. He put the tin back in the box and placed his oar on the gunwale, then signalled Brunetti to untie the boat. Together they pushed the boat from the sea wall and stood upright, wobbling for a moment, then gaining their balance and feeling the first heat of the day coming from in front of them.

'I want to go out and take a look at some of the others,' Casati said, and Brunetti assumed he meant bees. 'They're farther away: it'll take us about two hours. But we can have a swim when we get there. All right with you?'

Brunetti smiled back at him and nodded: he didn't care where they went. 'Tell me one thing,' Brunetti said, reluctant to call Casati by his first name but using the familiar *'tu'*, as two rowers would in their boat. 'Why do you want to see them?'

'Ah,' Casati said, drawing the sound out. 'You saw yesterday. They're dying. My girls are dying.'

'What from?'

'It might be varroa,' Casati explained.

'What's that?'

'Mites. Tiny mites that suck the blood from the bees and weaken them.' His disgust showed on his face.

'Not kill them?'

Casati made a noise. 'If they're weak, then other things can kill them,' he said. 'Too little food, viruses, pesticides, herbicides.' Casati picked up his oar. 'Man's turned against them,' he said.

Brunetti looked around and ahead of them and saw only salt water and salt marshes. 'All they have is salt water. Doesn't that harm them, too?'

Casati smiled. 'Did you have time to eat breakfast?'

'Yes,' Brunetti said, thinking of the fresh bread, jam and honey he'd found on the table, the butter in the refrigerator.

'How was the honey?'

'Delicious.'

'It didn't taste strange?'

He thought of what Pliny had written about honey, the different places from which it came, and that honey made from thyme was good for the eyes and for ulcers. 'No, it tasted fine,' Brunetti said, knowing now what was coming.

'It's from here,' Casati said, jutting his chin out to encompass the vast expanse of water that surrounded them. 'Emilio's family always made honey. And now I do, too.'

Deciding that it was time to row, Brunetti inserted his oar, waited for the sound from behind him, and joined Casati's rhythm. Today he wore the same trousers as the day before and an old cotton shirt he'd had since university. And a hat he'd found in a drawer, a faded orange baseball cap he could not have worn anywhere but here, where there was no one to see it. And the gloves, still. At least, he told himself, he'd wear them for the way out to wherever they were going. His hands felt faintly bruised and roughened after yesterday's rowing, but there was no sign of blisters.

They went the same way they had the day before. There was almost no traffic on the Canale di San Felice, broad and studded with houses on the Treporti side. Brunetti had a vague memory that this part of the *laguna* was completely enclosed by land and thus isolated from the Adriatic, which explained their near solitude on the water. They continued slowly ahead, soon working into a rhythm that suited them both. As had happened the day before, Casati sometimes called Brunetti's attention to a bird rendered almost invisible by the tall grass or to a current that might cause them trouble or help them along. He seemed easily at home in what to Brunetti was an amorphous, uniform grey-green expanse. No buildings, no bright flowers, no shadow, no points of reference: Brunetti was as lost as any stranger in the streets of Venice.

A group of buildings and fields appeared on the right, a few boats, and soon after, the canal veered to the left, and they followed. It began to narrow, and they came to a fork, where they took the unmarked, even smaller, canal to the left. Brunetti had a good sense of direction, and he felt that they were not far from where they had seen the bees the day before.

Suddenly he heard a soft 'shhhh' from behind him, and Casati's oar rose from the water and stopped. Brunetti lifted his own free of the water and turned to the man at the back. Both hands on his oar, Casati raised one finger and pointed to the right. Brunetti looked in that direction but saw nothing. He squinted to cut out some of the sunlight and then he saw them: along the side of the canal floated a duck with five tiny ones behind her, all of them absolutely motionless and, Brunetti assumed, doing their best to look like floating leaves.

The momentum of their last strokes carried them forward, and in no time they were beyond the ducks. Brunetti turned to see what the ducks would do, but the mother must have enjoined silence for not one of them moved, and then they disappeared as perspective hid them behind drooping grass.

Casati's oar slipped back into the water, and they continued ahead. Brunetti rowed on in the growing heat and light and wished he had thought to bring sunglasses or to put on sunscreen. At least the sleeves of today's shirt were long, and he was wearing gloves.

How long had they been rowing? Again, he'd left his watch behind, equating timelessness with freedom. A field of cultivated land sprang out of the reeds on their right, but Casati did not slow their rhythm. Brunetti consoled himself with the thought that the slaves in the galleys had not had long-sleeved shirts nor baseball caps. He rowed on, conscious of thirst and his tight shoulders and tighter back and little else.

'We can pull over here,' Casati said suddenly. Brunetti stopped rowing, leaving it to the man behind him to decide where to pull in and moor the boat. Casati gave a few more strokes, and the boat slid up to the left bank. Brunetti heard a thud behind him and looked to see Casati sitting on the rowing platform, knotting a rope to one of the corners of the frame of the metal grating. He stood and tossed it on to the land, where it sank into the tall grass and would serve as an anchor.

'Here. Catch.' Brunetti turned just as Casati threw him, as he had the day before, a bottle of mineral water. This time Brunetti opened it immediately and began to drink. So immersed in pleasure was he that he heard nothing, and when he looked back, all he saw was Casati's naked back and short trousers disappearing over the side of the boat. But in that flashing moment Brunetti had seen a broad trail down Casati's back. Red, darker than red, almost black, covering both his shoulders and running down to his waist, the mark covered most of his back. Scar or birthmark, Brunetti wasn't sure.

Brunetti watched the other man swim away from the boat. Silence returned; the heat and sun assaulted him. He capped the bottle, set it upright against the planking, and untied his shoes. He stripped and piled his clothing on the board behind him, set the baseball cap on top, and rolled over the side of the boat into the water. He frog-kicked away from the boat into the centre of the channel. He dived, and when he surfaced, he was entirely alone in the *laguna*. He swam back to the boat.

Brunetti started off the way Casati had gone but stopped after twenty strokes or so and swam back to the boat. Then he did the same distance in the other direction. To his surprise, the motion relaxed his arms and shoulders and allowed him to begin to hope that he would be able to use them again. He went back and forth until, head raised from the water as he turned, he saw Casati swimming towards him with an awkward, one-armed breaststroke, his other hand held above his head.

Brunetti swam to the side of the boat and draped an arm over it, treading water. As Casati approached, Brunetti saw what he held in his hand: a small plastic vial with a green plastic cap like the one he had used to collect the dead bees the day before.

Casati swam up to the stern and leaned over to set the vial on the top of his folded shirt, then draped both arms over the side, visibly winded from the swim.

Brunetti pointed his chin at the vial. 'What's that – more bees?'

Still breathing deeply, Casati answered, 'No, it's mud.'

'No bees?'

'They're all dead,' Casati said, and pushed himself abruptly away from the boat. He swam to the side of the grass island and pulled himself up on to it, then walked gingerly to the back of the boat. He stopped to remove his trousers and wring them out, shake water from them a few times, and put them back on. He stepped into the boat, reached under the horizontal board at the back, and pulled out two towels, tossed one on to Brunetti's place, and began to dry his calves and chest with the other. Brunetti saw only flashes of dark red when the other man turned round.

Seeing no easier way to get back into the boat, Brunetti swam around to the front and climbed on to the island. Stubbly grass poked at his feet, and he looked down to avoid the sharpest patches. He stepped into the boat and used the towel to dry himself, then put his clothes back on, leaving his feet to the sun.

When he looked at Casati, the older man was dressed and sitting on the towel folded on the back bench, staring off into the distance. There was no sign of the vial. Casati bent and began to wipe his feet, then slipped them into his frayed old sneakers. He stood and spent an inordinate amount of time folding and unfolding his towel and then draping it neatly over the side of the boat. 'It took a long time, but we finally killed them,' Casati surprised Brunetti by saying, sounding as if he included Brunetti in the crime by virtue of his humanity. 'First we killed her, and now we're killing the bees. Next it will be Federica and her children, and your children, too.' He nodded a few times to emphasize his certainties.

Brunetti sat, wondering if too much sun had driven the older man beyond strength and patience. He said nothing and tried to remain motionless, telling himself to become part of the wooden board he was sitting on, to turn himself into one of the planks on the bottom of the boat. Brunetti tried to imagine what it would be like to become a piece of wood. What did Daphne feel as her limbs became branches, her toes roots? She was soon invisible in the forest, just as he now half hoped to become invisible out here in the *laguna*. Flotsam? Jetsam? Brunetti didn't care which, just so long as Casati stopped raving.

Suddenly Casati leaned towards him, but Brunetti, protected by his now-treelike nature, did not move. In the sort of speculative voice in which Brunetti's moral theology professor had posed the rhetorical questions that always preceded his lectures, he asked, 'Do you think some of the things we do can never be forgiven?'

Brunetti looked down at his dry feet. 'I don't know,' he answered calmly, as he had so often done in class, hoping it would force the professor to make things clearer. Then, reluctant to do so, he said, 'I'm not sure I know what you mean.'

Casati gave this long consideration and finally said, 'Let me ask Franca if she thinks I should tell you.' To hear Casati refer so casually to his wife in the present tense made the hair on the back of Brunetti's hands rise, but before he could say anything, they were surprised by the sound of flapping wings, and three herons rose from the water ahead of them.

Casati slapped his hands on his knees and pushed himself to his feet. 'Well,' he said amiably. 'We should start back, I think.' He reached over and pulled the improvised anchor across the rough grass, hauled it in and set it on the bottom of the boat.

He picked up his oar, obviously waiting for Brunetti to do the same. When Brunetti did, Casati poked his oar into the embankment and shoved them out into the channel again, and then they were off.

To his own surprise, Brunetti felt refreshed, either by the swim or by Casati's sudden return to reality. He was ready to row to Trieste if Casati asked him to.

Brunetti rowed, musing on what Casati had said but failing to make sense of it. In the distance, planes continued to take off and land, so far away that Brunetti was never certain it was the planes he could hear and not the motors of far closer boats. He glanced to the west and saw what he thought was Santa Cristina.

His oar hit something submerged in the water and he pitched forward, but before he could fall over the oar, it slipped free and tore itself loose from the *fórcola* and from his hands and slid into the water. Brunetti danced around in the bottom of the boat until he regained his balance, then lowered himself to sit on the gunwale until his heart stopped pounding.

Eyes closed, Brunetti could feel the boat slow and stop, and then he heard a solid, banging noise from Casati's direction. When he opened his eyes, Brunetti saw the older man leaning over the side of the boat, poking his oar in the water.

'What did I hit?' Brunetti asked in what he struggled to make sound like a normal voice.

Casati remained bent over the side for some time, gazing into the water. He sat back on his heels, one hand wrapped around his oar, and looked at Brunetti. He muttered something that, to Brunetti, sounded like 'my past', but that made no sense. After a moment, Casati stood, looked into the water again and said, in an entirely natural voice, 'Out here, it could be a submerged root, or a piece of rotten wood that got carried out by the tide.' Setting his oar on the bottom of the boat, he reached to grab Brunetti's, which was floating in the water, and placed it beside his own. He looked at his watch, glanced at the sun, then turned and looked back to where they had come from. Casati pulled up the top of the storage box to rummage around in the space below it. His hand emerged with what looked like a *telefonino*, the old type, with the cover that had to be opened. Casati pushed a button, then another one, then closed the device and placed it back in the box before shutting the lid.

'What was that?' asked Brunetti.

'A GPS,' Casati told him. 'Tells me exactly where we are.'

'Why?'

He stared at Brunetti for a long time before he said, 'No special reason. But I always like to know where I've been.'

Without comment, Brunetti pushed himself to his feet and bent to slide his oar closer. As he did so, he looked into the shallow water at the side of the canal and saw something that looked like a metal circle, about the diameter of an inner tube.

'What's that?' Brunetti asked, pointing at the object.

Casati leaned in the direction Brunetti indicated. 'Could be something that came loose from a boat. Lots of things wash up around here.' He straightened and put his oar in the *fórcola*. 'Let's start back,' he said.

Brunetti had no idea how much time passed before they stopped again: it could have been twenty minutes as easily as forty, and they could have been anywhere in the waters between raised patches of tall grasses.

'One more visit, and then we can have lunch,' Casati said, reaching into the box under the platform but this time pulling out the by now familiar leather case.

'Bees?' Brunetti asked.

'Yes, I want to check them. These are the farthest out up in this part of the *laguna*.'

'May I come along?' Brunetti asked.

'Certainly. There's nothing illegal about what I'm doing,' Casati said, sounding unnecessarily defensive.

'I'd hardly think that,' Brunetti said with a laugh to show how absurd the idea was.

'Only secret,' Casati went on.

He tossed the makeshift anchor up on to the grass, and they climbed out of the boat. There was no trace of a path to follow in the rough grass, but Casati set off purposefully, heading due north. Brunetti, glad that he was wearing long trousers, followed him through the grass, which in places was sometimes high enough to rub itself aggressively across the back of his hands.

The earth seemed softer out here. It offered little or no resistance and seemed to provide his feet with a cushion at every step. The first squelch explained all of this to him: the rising tide had permeated the sandy soil.

Casati quickened his pace. 'The water normally rises to two centimetres here,' he said. Brunetti hurried to keep up as Casati led him across the grass, directly towards a large, sloppy-looking bush beside which stood a raised wooden platform holding three beehives, each with a different-coloured stripe on the front.

As they approached the hives, Casati stopped to set fire to a chip of wood and handed it to Brunetti; then they set off again. The bees surrounded them in fact and sound: they flew at them and around them, occasionally landing on a hand or shoulder to explore a bit. But then they left and went back to their peaceful business; the buzzing soared and lowered, now absolutely unthreatening to Brunetti.

The older man removed the top of the first hive and set it against one of the legs of the platform on which the three hives rested. Carefully, moving like a man under water, Casati checked all three hives and seemed pleased with what he found. When he was finished, he took the still-burning piece of wood from Brunetti and tossed it to the ground, then carefully ground it into the wet earth with his toe. Brunetti turned to leave, but when he failed to hear Casati's steps behind him, he stopped and looked back, only to see Casati stoop down to pick up the piece of charred wood and place it in a plastic ziplock bag he pulled from the leather case. He stooped and shoved some of the wet grass over the place where it had been, removing all trace.

They walked back side by side; Brunetti watched the rising water devour their footprints the instant they lifted their feet. When they got to the boat, Brunetti looked back to where they had been. He saw nothing but a meaningless hump in the middle of the *barena*.

10

It was easy to fall into a routine: Brunetti made himself coffee a little after dawn, read for a time, showered, then ate the breakfast Federica had left for him. Some mornings, he persuaded her to at least have a coffee with him while he ate. She was in her early thirties, tall and slender, an attractive, dark-haired woman, with a soft voice and very like her father in the way she moved her hands when she spoke. She had a ten-year-old son who wanted to be a fisherman when he grew up and a seven-year-old daughter who wanted to learn to row a boat. Federica was shamelessly proud of both of them. She smiled and shook her head in wonder at what life could bring a person.

She had lived on Sant'Erasmo since she was a child, had married a fisherman, Massimo, who had lived four houses away, and had known happiness until her mother's sickness and death. During their conversations, which sometimes continued when she brought him half an apricot cake in the afternoon, Brunetti learned that her father had still not fully recovered from her mother's death and probably never would.

'I think he feels guilty about it,' she'd said towards the end of the first week, trying to explain this to a curious Brunetti.

'People always want to save the people they love, don't they?' was the only thing Brunetti could think of to say.

'It's more than that. I told you: he blames himself for her death.' She had taken a few breaths, then asked, 'But how could he save her?'

Uncomfortable at hearing this and having no answer, Brunetti had reached for another piece of cake and changed the subject.

He and Casati set out early each morning and rowed in the *laguna* for much of the early part of the day. If they were going to be out longer, Casati told him the night before and brought an abundant lunch with him the next morning. Sometimes they'd meet friends of Casati's and then often didn't get back until late afternoon. Everyone they met insisted on giving them fresh fish.

When Brunetti remarked on the generosity of the fishermen they met, Casati said fishermen were always generous, far more so than farmers. To Brunetti's question, he explained that fishermen knew their catch would last no more than a day, so it was easy for them to give it away: give it away or watch it rot. Farmers, however, could store what they reaped and so had a tendency to keep it or even hoard it.

When they returned to the villa in the afternoon, they stored the oars, *fórcole* and grating and then Brunetti went to the villa and sometimes read for an hour or so. Or else he walked down to the more inhabited parts of the island, where he was perfectly happy to say hello to the people he passed on the street, and nothing more. He did not phone Lucia Zanotto; not for any reason he could think of, but only because he was out there to be alone, and alone he wanted to be. Somehow, Casati didn't count.

Casati had told him there was a bicycle in the shed and suggested he ride down to the trattoria at the other end of the island, where he could eat fish that was fresh and vegetables from the island. He called Paola every night and told her where they had been in the *laguna* – even though he usually didn't have even the name of a location to give her – and what he had eaten for lunch and dinner. When she asked him about books, he confessed that he had little time to read during the day and at night was so tired he turned out his light after ten minutes and had no memory in the morning of what he had read. He invited her to come out for the weekend, even offered to come in the *puparìn* and get her at the boat stop, but she said she wanted him to do his full two weeks of solitude and reflection.

After she said this, they spoke for a few minutes, and when he hung up, Brunetti realized his feelings were hurt. It did not occur to him that it had been his decision to come out here and to live separated from his family because he suddenly didn't like his job, nor did he consider the fact that his decision was the result of his own heedless behaviour. No, it was his feelings that were hurt when his wife said she did not want to come out to an isolated house at the end of an island to spend her weekend either being rowed around the *laguna* under a fierce July sun or, if she chose not to go with him, sitting alone in a house that was not her own, waiting for her husband to come home.

On the second Friday, ten days into Brunetti's stay, when they docked in front of the house in the late afternoon,

Casati said that he would not be going out on Saturday or Sunday because he had remembered something he had to do. He seemed embarrassed to be telling Brunetti this, so Brunetti did not remind him that he had said the day before that they'd go out both days. Making the best of it and aware of how much he owed Casati for the days he had spent with him, Brunetti said he wouldn't mind two days of resting and then remarked awkwardly that they had the advantage of deciding when they wanted a weekend off.

Casati smiled and said he'd see him at the usual time on Monday. They'd had a relatively easy day and had stopped on Burano for a long lunch, and Brunetti was restless when he got back. After Casati was gone, he took the bicycle from the shed and rode around the island for a long time, stopped at the bar for a coffee and a glass of water, and then went back to the villa to lie on the sofa and read. Later, as the light was fading, he rode back to the trattoria to have salmon trout with butter and almonds, then went slowly back to the house in the darkness, glad of the lights at the front and back of the bike. How he wished Paola could see the red sky fade to pink and then transform itself into this strange darkness, so different from the over-lit streets of the city.

Saturday passed quietly. Instead of rowing, Brunetti contented himself with going into the water just in front of the house, although he chose to walk in from the steps rather than dive. Once in the water, he did dive down and look around. He saw countless small fish he thought were baby rombo, and an unsettling number of what looked like jellyfish. He swam for an hour in the morning and another in the afternoon, and by dinnertime he was exhausted. When Federica came by in the late afternoon to ask if he'd like her to prepare dinner for him, he told her there was no need; he'd take care of himself. That meant he made himself pasta and salad and read while eating.

Sunday started out in glory; the sun launched itself into the sky and shot down bolts of heat, intent on driving all life – human or animal – into the shade or into shelter. The humans managed, and the goats huddled under trees, following the slow course of the shade as the sun rose ever higher. The dogs simply disappeared. After making himself a large portion of spaghetti with *aglio, olio e peperoncino* for lunch, Brunetti decided to go to the bar for a coffee. He pedalled past two mules lying stiff-legged under a fig tree and feared they were dead of the heat until one of them waved a languid tail. Though he wore the baseball cap and long sleeves and had slathered on sunscreen that Paola seemed to have hidden in his suitcase, by the time he reached the bar at the other end of the island, he felt as though he was himself a single tight-skinned blister.

Inside, he asked for a coffee and sat down at a table to read *Il Gazzettino*, which he had not seen for more than a week. The city, it appeared, was surviving his absence. He read the paper from front to back, even the ads, and found no mention of Ruggieri; not that he had expected to. The *passarelle* for *acqua alta* at Rialto had finally been replaced, and it seemed that this time they fitted properly. No work was being done on the MOSE tide barrier other than maintenance and repair; how many years had he been reading this headline? The new mayor had made another dismissive remark about culture in general and, this time, 'professors' in particular. Brunetti wondered what it was His Honour objected to. That they could read and write?

Brunetti suddenly realized his head had been moving closer and closer to the page as he read and wondered if his glasses had ceased to work, but when he looked up, he saw that it was because the windows behind him had ceased to provide any light. He folded the paper closed and went to the door. It faced in the general direction of Venice, somewhere there beyond the horizon, no doubt still washed in the golden sunlight of late afternoon. He stepped outside and was surprised to find it had grown cool. After a few paces he turned to face the sea, visible through the Porto del Lido. It had shrunk, or so it seemed. At some incalculable distance offshore, an immense dark curtain had been pulled down from heaven to water, slamming a door in sight's face. He stood and watched the wall of clouds that seemed to be rolling closer. He was distracted by the sound of an approaching boat, heard it boom as it slammed against the dock with unnecessary force – sloppy pilot. But when he looked towards the dock, there was no boat; then the booming came again, louder this time and coming from the direction of that cloud curtain. Another boom and a sudden excess of light.

Brunetti saw that the curtain had moved closer during the few moments he had turned away from it. Another boom, and this time he saw the flash of lightning, straight out of the cloud, pounding down on the surface of the sea. Instinct drove him to take a step backward, and his right hand rose to his eyes, as though it wanted to fend off the lightning.

Brunetti calculated the time it would take him to get back to the villa, hurried inside, put a Euro on the counter, and waved to the owner. Outside, he yanked the bicycle away from the wall and pushed off in the direction of the house. The wind from his right was powerful, forcing him to pull the handlebars constantly to fight it. After a few minutes, he started to calculate his speed in relation to the wind that was driving the cloud towards him: who would get to the villa first? Who would win? He put his head down and pedalled, but even this expense of energy could not keep him warm in face of the plummeting temperature. A flash of lightning to his right drove away all thought as he waited for the crash of sound.

After four seconds it came, blasting across him with a shock he could feel, thudding into his ears. He moved forward, chilled with the temperature or with fear.

The next bolt of lightning shut his eyes for him. His grip on the handlebars tightened, but the road was straight and smooth and he managed to fight the wind that tried to force him off to the side. When he opened his eyes, he saw he was still heading down the middle of the road. A clap of thunder and a cascade of rain descended at the same instant, causing him briefly to lose control of the bike. He swerved to the left, unable to see through the rain. He squeezed the brakes and came to a stop, and what seemed like a wave washed across him. Soaked, he started again and pedalled madly, guided only by the intermittent white stripes on the road, hoping that any of the rare motorists who might be approaching from the other direction would see him.

He swerved through the gates and up to the front of the house. He dropped the bicycle, pounded up the steps and inside. Like a character in a horror film, he slammed the door behind him and leaned his body against it, eyes closed, pulling in rasping breaths of panic and relief. Behind him, as though following the same script, the monster banged on the sky three times, each thud followed by a long, low growl.

When his heart calmed, Brunetti went up to his bedroom and changed into dry clothing, took the sweater from his bag and pulled it on. He rubbed some warmth back into his feet, pulled on socks and shoes, and went over to close the window, though no rain was coming in. Then he walked around the top floor, checking the rest of the windows. On the side facing the sea, the rain pounded almost horizontally at the glass, making it impossible to see anything.

Back downstairs, he turned on the lights in both sitting rooms, found his phone, and dialled Paola at home. Surely, with a storm like this, she'd be safely inside.

It rang unanswered for a long time. He disconnected and dialled her *telefonino*. Even before she could speak, he asked, 'Where are you?'

'At my parents',' she said.

'Is it raining?'

'Here?' Paola asked.

'Yes.' As he spoke, another enormous clap of thunder rang out, followed by the long tail of deep sound.

'What was that?' she asked, startled.

'Thunder,' Brunetti said calmly, speaking easily now that he was inside and safe from the lightning.

When the noise had ebbed away, he went on. 'We're having a terrific storm here. If it turns, it'll be over the city soon.'

'Good,' Paola said.

'What?'

'Good,' she repeated, this time a bit more loudly. 'You should see the streets, Guido. They're disgusting. It hasn't rained for weeks, so God knows what we're tracking into the house every day.' She paused and then added, 'I never thought I'd wish *acqua alta* on the city, but at least it would clean them.'

'If this storm makes it there, the streets will be clean enough, my dear,' he said. Then, 'How are your parents?'

'Fine, both of them. My father is going to Mongolia on Wednesday.'

'To buy it?' Brunetti inquired lightly.

'Ha ha ha,' Paola answered, utterly without humour. 'Well, he is going to buy a little bit of it.'

Brunetti waited.

'Copper. It seems they have masses of it, still in the ground. And the people who own the mine don't want to sell it to the Chinese, so they've asked my father if he'd be interested.'

Then, casting off the subject, she asked, 'How are you?'

Sensing that it was not a pro forma question, Brunetti said, 'I'm busy all day with rowing or riding the bike so I don't have much time to think. Well, to think seriously about anything, that is. And I like it.'

'Stay another week, and you'll come back a mindless fool,' Paola said, laughing.

'But with muscles like steel and the sparkle of rude peasant health in my eyes.'

'I'm glad I'm sitting down, Guido. You make my knees go all wobbly.'

'I do feel better, though,' Brunetti said, suddenly serious. 'I'm hardly drinking at all, get eight hours of sleep, and I'm moving and busy all day.'

'Will I recognize you?' Paola asked.

'It would break my heart if you didn't,' he said, unaware until he said it how true it was.

When they hung up, Brunetti realized it was no longer raining and the thunder had moved away from the island. He looked out the front windows and saw fat white clouds reflecting the glow of evening light. He walked to the corner of the property, still glad of the sweater, and looked to the south-west, but there was no sign of the storm, only the same soft evening light coming from the direction of the far-off city. How could a storm that fierce simply have disappeared without a trace? He'd have to ask Casati tomorrow.

He looked at his watch and saw that it was after seven, and yet the day was still with him, vibrant with life. He shoved his hands into his pockets and walked to the *riva* and stood for a while, watching the light on the fat clouds pass from red to rose and then fade away entirely. After a long time, he went back into the house to prepare his solitary dinner; well, solitary save for the company of Gaius Plinius Secundus, dead for nearly two millennia but very much present to Brunetti.

11

Brunetti awoke in Paradise. Birds chirped, the sun prised with rosy fingers at his eyelids, an invisible cow mooed in the distance, the heat was bearable, and his cotton bedspread welcome in the early morning. He lay still and listened to the silence, didn't bother to tease himself, as he had every morning since he'd arrived, with looking to the left side of the bed to see if Paola had slipped in during the night.

Instead, he went downstairs and into the brick-floored kitchen to make coffee, surprised by how cold the floor felt under his feet. He noticed that Federica hadn't brought the bread. He glanced at the clock above the sink and saw that it was still not yet seven: surely he had enough time to make coffee and have a shower before meeting Casati.

He drank the coffee standing at the counter, set the empty cup in the sink, and went back upstairs, where he shaved carefully. The job the days of rowing had done on his muscles relieved him of the need to represent his manliness with a few days' stubble; besides, he felt better with a shaved face.

The morning chill was still present, so he put a sweater over his shoulders before he went downstairs. Still no sign of Federica. Friday afternoon she had brought him his washed and ironed clothing, insisting that Signor Emilio had asked her to see to this. It made him uncomfortable, and that made him wonder why it didn't bother him in the least to receive the same treatment in his own home. Clean, ironed shirts, he knew, did not float into his closet every night while he slept, neither here nor at home, yet they might as well have done so, for all the attention he paid to them.

As he left the house, he saw Federica turn into the walkway that led to the front door. '*Buon dì,*' he said as she drew closer.

Ignoring his greeting, she asked, 'Have you seen my father?' She looked behind Brunetti, as if she suspected him of hiding her father in the house.

'No. Isn't he at the boat?'

She shook her head. 'He didn't come down for coffee this morning, and when I went upstairs, he wasn't in his room. I saw him in the morning yesterday, but not since then. He wasn't at dinner.' Then, after a pause, 'And he didn't sleep at home last night.' She was puzzled, not worried, so it sounded to Brunetti as though it was not such an unusual event. This made sense, he supposed. Casati was still a very handsome man, his age impossible to judge, but his vigour evident. As though she'd read his mind, Federica added, 'In the past, he's always called when he wasn't going to come home.' Aware of this comic reversal of roles, she gave an embarrassed smile.

'And the boat?' Surely, Casati must have moved it to a safer place yesterday: no boat owner would ever have left one tied to a stone wall, fender or no fender, with a storm coming right at it.

'There's a small marina where a lot of us put our boats when there's bad weather. But I haven't had time to check.'

'Where is it?' Brunetti asked.

'Come with me,' she said, already moving back the way she had come.

He caught up with her and they walked along side by side, silent. They followed the pavement until, up ahead, Brunetti saw a large L-shaped cement *molo* sticking out into the water, boats docked at the inner sides. They studied the boats as they moved closer, but the familiar *puparìn* was not there. These boats floated in full tranquillity. Only one, its tarpaulin sagging in places under the weight of rainwater that had not been bailed from it, showed signs of the passing of the storm.

'That's very strange,' Federica said, running her fingers through her unkempt hair. 'A boat can't disappear.'

'Did he take it out yesterday?' Brunetti asked.

'I told him not to, not with a storm coming this way,' she answered, trying to disguise her anger. Then her face relaxed. 'But maybe he did and had to sleep in the boat because he couldn't get back.'

It was when Brunetti heard her grasping at this straw that he began to worry. Didn't Casati have a *telefonino*? The storm had stopped twelve hours before: surely a man as familiar with the *laguna* as Casati would have found his way home, even in the dark. Without thinking, he turned back towards the villa, the only place he could think of going. After a moment, Federica caught up and fell into step with him.

'Do you have any idea where he might have gone?' Brunetti asked.

Federica kept her eyes on the ground as they walked, although she must have been as familiar with the route as with the floors of her own home; then she slowed and stopped. She said, 'My father . . .' then paused and pulled her lower lip between her teeth. She cleared her throat to make it easier and said, 'My father goes to see my mother every week, usually on Sunday.'

'I see,' Brunetti said in what he tried to make an encouraging voice.

'He goes to talk to her, to tell her what's happening and to ask her what she thinks.' She looked at Brunetti, as if she were a student pausing during an exam to see how things were going.

Brunetti nodded.

'He's done it since she died, so I'm accustomed to it.'

Brunetti nodded again; he could remember his own mother doing the same.

'So that's probably where he went,' she said.

She stood still and looked at him, and he saw that her sea-blue eyes had the same wrinkles at the corners that her father's had. 'That must be what he did.' She looked away from Brunetti and across the water towards Treporti.

She kept her eyes on the distant fields, letting whole minutes pass. A small boat chugged past, a dog, gap-mouthed with joy, facing forward on the prow.

When the noise of the engine had disappeared, she turned to Brunetti and said, 'My father said that he liked you. And trusted you.'

'Trusted?' Brunetti asked.

'He said he could see who had taught you how to row

and that you were reliable.' She nodded, as though to confirm her memory.

He wondered if she knew and said, 'He and my father won the regatta once.'

She smiled. 'It's not the first time I've been told that.' In response to Brunetti's unasked question, she added, 'It's one of my favourite stories. I've heard him describe every turn and twist, and I know the names of the men in the first four boats to finish.' After a pause, she added, 'It's the only time he won.'

She started walking again, back towards the villa. When Brunetti joined her, she turned to him and said, 'I can't tell you why I think this, but he seemed nervous, or excited, as if there was something he was impatient to do.' After a moment, in a softer voice, she added, 'I thought it was something he wanted to tell my mother.'

There was still no sign of the boat. 'Have you called him?' Brunetti asked, knowing it was a stupid question.

'Since early this morning,' she answered, pulling her phone from her pocket and hitting the redial key. She held it towards Brunetti, who heard a quick, insistent beep until she poked it off. 'I don't know what to do.' Her voice was rough.

Brunetti was at a loss. On land, if a person went missing, one called the hospitals and the police, but he was the police, and they were kilometres from any hospital. 'What about the Guardia Costiera?' he asked. 'Or the Capitaneria di Porto?' One of them, he was sure, had to be in charge of searching for someone lost at sea.

Yet, was he sure? Casati had been missing less than twenty-four hours, and there must be many possible explanations for that. But somehow a disappearance this close to the sea – especially in the wake of a storm like yesterday's – seemed far more serious than one on land, where the person could easily have got on a train and gone to Ferrara for the day or simply not bothered to call. On the mainland, there were so many places a person could go; out here, there was little choice but to come home.

'Massimo has a friend in the Capitaneria,' she said. 'I'll ask him to call.'

She turned and stared out over the waters of the *laguna*, as if only now aware of the vast expanse in which they would have to look for her father.

'Is there any place where he might have gone?' Brunetti asked again when they got back to the mooring place in front of the villa, thinking it better to be absolutely sure about this before a search was launched.

Federica gave this a lot of thought until she finally shook her head; it looked as though she'd dismissed a possibility, not found one. 'He's never been gone overnight before. Without telling me, that is.'

'Is your husband still at home?' Brunetti asked.

'No, he went out this morning. At four,' Federica said, glancing at her watch.

'Do you want to call him and ask him to contact his friend?'

'Yes, yes.' She pressed another key and, while she waited, again studied the empty horizon. Brunetti looked down and saw how cloudy the water was, as though whatever the waves had whipped up from the seabed yesterday had not yet had time to filter back down. He watched what might have been fish move about in quick spurts, then heard a man's voice answer Federica's call. She moved away a few steps and turned from him to continue the conversation.

Brunetti headed for the villa, reluctant to seem to eavesdrop. Casati had told him on Friday that he had something he had to do at the weekend, although the day before that he had told Brunetti they'd go out. Plans change, Brunetti knew: things happen. It could be anything.

The light had bloomed and the temperature had risen. Brunetti felt the sweat on his chest. He looked towards Burano and, beyond it, Torcello, but the reflected light was too fierce and he turned south-west to look towards Murano. How different it seemed from this side rather than from Fondamente Nove. Point of view changed everything, as it had with the idea of why Casati might spend a night away. Brunetti, a man, had seen it as understandable in someone still so youthful and vigorous, but he doubted that Federica would view it the same way. Would a woman understand another man's participatory triumph at the thought of Casati's having spent the night with a woman? Hardly, and particularly not if she were his daughter.

But someone like Casati would have called if he had known he was going to be away all night, even if he had to lie about the reason. The storm made it even more imperative.

His musings were interrupted by Federica, who was approaching from behind. 'Massimo said he'd call his friend when we hung up,' she said as she reached him. 'The Capitaneria handles this.'

All of a sudden, Federica put both of her hands over her face and made a low sound that had nothing to do with words or thought: it was fear made audible, nothing more. 'I don't want this,' she said in a tortured voice.

Brunetti took her arm and spoke her name a few times before she stopped. She uncovered her eyes and stepped back from him. Casati's daughter nodded, tight-lipped, and told him she was all right, then continued walking towards the villa.

Brunetti paused to find the number and called the Capitaneria di Porto to tell them he was a police commissario who was now on Sant'Erasmo with the daughter of the man who'd been reported missing and would like to speak to the person in charge.

He thought the officer he spoke to would request some proof of identity, but he did not. Asking Brunetti to wait a moment, he transferred the call to Captain Dantone, who was in charge of search and rescue at sea. The Captain said that they would search with boats immediately, starting near Sant'Erasmo and expanding as the boats covered a fixed order of quadrants. Finally, in the event of continuing failure, the Vigili del Fuoco and the Guardia Costiera would be asked to add their boats to the search. If still no sign of man or boat was found within half a day, the Carabinieri would be requested to do a flyover with a helicopter.

Brunetti thanked him, said he'd be remaining on the island, and asked the Captain how long the search would continue.

'Until we find the boat,' the Captain answered, then asked if there were more questions, and hung up when Brunetti said that there were not.

Until they found the boat, Brunetti repeated to himself.

12

When Brunetti went to tell Federica what he had learned about the search, he found her in the kitchen of the villa, making coffee. As he entered the room, he saw that there were two cups and saucers on the table; he pulled out a chair and sat to wait for the coffee.

When it finished boiling up, Federica brought the pot over and poured them each a cup. She sat and put two sugars into her coffee, slid the bowl towards Brunetti, and stirred the sugar around before taking a sip. Brunetti did much the same.

'The Capitaneria will send boats. So will the Guardia Costiera and, if necessary, the Vigili del Fuoco,' Brunetti said.

'And if they don't find anything?'

'Then the Carabinieri will send a helicopter.'

She considered this, stirred her coffee again. 'And if his boat sank?'

'It's too light to sink,' Brunetti said, although he was far from certain. 'The man at the Capitaneria told me they divide the area into quadrants and search back and forth.'

'They're from the South, usually,' she said to Brunetti's utter confusion.

'Who?'

'The people there.'

'Many of them, I suppose,' Brunetti conceded. 'But they've been trained to do this sort of thing.'

'The *laguna*'s very big.'

'Federica,' he said, stopping himself from reaching across the table to touch her arm, 'let them do their work, and then we'll see.'

She got up and collected their cups and saucers and set them into the sink. 'I think I'll go back home,' she said. '*Papà* might try to call.'

'Of course,' Brunetti said and got to his feet.

When she was gone, he called Paola.

'I saw the flashes of lightning from the terrace,' she said, 'but we still didn't get it here. Just some rain and not even a lot of it.' Then, abandoning the storm, she asked, 'Will you have anything to do with the search?'

'The only people who know I'm a policeman are Federica – her father told her, and he knew because Emilio told him – and the officer at the Capitaneria. To everyone else, I'm just some relative of Emilio's who's come out to go rowing.'

'If he was such a good boatman, why'd he go out in that storm?'

'I don't know that he did. All Federica said was that he seemed excited, or nervous, at breakfast, but she couldn't give any reason for thinking that, except that she knows him so well.'

'It could be that she's saying it now that she doesn't know where he is. Retrospective memory.'

'Perhaps,' Brunetti said. 'But she seems a sensible person.'

'All the more reason for her to try to make sense of what's happened. Or to find some sort of reason for it.'

'You've been reading too many books,' Brunetti said in an attempt at lightness.

'Probably,' Paola said quite amiably. 'Tell me what happens,' she added and then said goodbye.

After she was gone, Brunetti was swept with sudden longing for her presence, for the comfort her spirit provided to his own. Just talking to her for five minutes had calmed him and made him feel he was a better man.

He shook himself free of introspection and went up to his room, where he tossed his sweater on the foot of the bed and changed to his jeans. He was surprised by the way they hung at his waist and took the belt from his shorts and slipped it into place. There was a mirror on one wall, but Brunetti didn't look. Instead, he went outside, took the bicycle and started down to the bar at the other end of the island.

No respecter of human emotions, the day continued perfect. The rain of the previous evening had brought down the temperature, and though it was bound to rise during the day, the air now was still a caress on the skin.

Brunetti rode slowly, noticing the small puddles that remained in the fields. It had been a long time since the last rain; the plants looked relieved to have had it, and he was happy for them. The thought of Casati crept back into his mind, and he felt a moment's embarrassment at having so easily given in to the seductions of nature.

As he rode, he tried to recall his conversations with Casati and his remarks about the bees, his girls. Brunetti had read no more than the average person about bees and knew that the phenomenon of their mass deaths was worldwide, but he had never cared to find out more than that, even though Chiara often talked about them knowingly, insisting that bees were the canaries in the mine and a good gauge of how poorly things were going for the planet.

He thought of the dead bees Casati had brought back to the boat, saying that they had to be tested. Brunetti had given it little thought at the time, but if they were dead, then the only thing it made sense to test them for was what had killed them. Brunetti wondered what his friend the pathologist Rizzardi would think if he knew he was now concerned with the deaths of bees.

He saw motion to his left and automatically slowed the bike. A man stood in a tree-filled field, waving at him. He recognized one of the men who played cards in the bar in the afternoon, a retired fisherman who now farmed his land and often said how sweet it was to sleep late in the morning, by which he meant six.

'Hey, Guido,' he called. 'Come and give me a hand.'

Brunetti stopped the bike and lowered it into the grass at the side of the road, then walked across the field to the man, whose name he thought was Ubaldo. The wet grass, uncut for weeks, brushed at his ankles, a not unpleasant feeling. Four or five white plastic buckets surrounded the man, and all of them were surrounded by the trees. Brunetti stopped a few metres from him and asked, 'What is it?'

'Apricots,' Ubaldo answered, waving a hand towards the ground, where Brunetti noticed small orange ovals hiding in the grass.

'What happened?' he asked.

Instead of answering, Ubaldo pointed to the trees, whose

leaves glistened with last night's rain. Some fruit still clung to the branches, but it was evident from the slaughter at their feet that the wind and rain had had their way with the fruit.

'What would you like me to do?' Brunetti asked.

'Get one of those pails, fill it up and take it home with you,' Ubaldo said, bending down to pick up two apricots and setting them gently on top of the ones already in the bucket next to him. 'Go ahead,' he insisted, handing Brunetti another of the white pails.

'But there are too many,' Brunetti objected.

'That's why I want you to take some away. There's too much for my family.' When Brunetti still hesitated, Ubaldo said, 'Please. It's a sin to throw food away – my mother always told us that – so I want people to take them. Please.'

Brunetti remembered what he'd been told about fishermen: when they found themselves with an excessive catch, they chose to give it away rather than watch it rot. He picked up the pail and began to fill it. 'Just take the good ones,' Ubaldo said. 'I'll send the grandkids out later to get the bruised ones. My wife can make jam.'

Ubaldo's admonition gave Brunetti the right to be picky, and he was, careful to select only fruit that had no sign of bruises. After five minutes, the bucket was half full. He quickly filled it and asked Ubaldo if he would like some help with the rest.

'No,' the former fisherman said, pausing to wipe his face with a vast white handkerchief. 'It gives me something to do.'

Brunetti carried the bucket over to the bike. When he had the bike upright, he slipped the bucket over the handlebars and wheeled the bike closer to Ubaldo, who was still busy picking up the fallen fruit.

'Have you seen Davide?' Brunetti asked in mild inter-rogation.

Ubaldo stood upright, placed an apricot into the bucket, and said, 'No, not for a few days. Anything important?'

'No, I wanted to ask him something about the boat. But it can wait.' Brunetti smiled, rose up with his foot on one pedal, and took off. He called his thanks to Ubaldo and continued down towards the bar.

When he went inside, the three men at the long table looked up at him, their faces filled with curiosity they saw no reason to disguise. One of them waved him over to their table and pushed out a chair for him. 'Have they found him?' the first one, Pierangelo, asked, not bothering to explain how they knew Casati was missing.

Brunetti called over to the barman and asked for a coffee before taking his seat. He raised both hands in a gesture of surrender and said, 'I have no idea. I spoke to Federica; then she called her husband, who spoke to the Capitaneria.' Since arriving on the island, Brunetti had spoken only Veneziano with everyone he encountered; his use of the dialect had, he hoped, logged him into the confidence of those who took him to be one of themselves.

The oldest of the men, Gianni, wore a threadbare suit jacket as evidence of his former employment as a book-keeper for a glass factory on Murano; he had somehow come to take on the role of leader and said, 'They'll find him. If anyone can, they will.'

Franco – Brunetti had never been given their surnames and knew him only as the tall one with the arthritic hands – said, 'I heard he was over on Burano with that woman. He probably tried to come back in the storm.'

Brunetti happened to be watching Gianni when the other man spoke, so he noticed the way his face tightened when he heard Franco say this. Brunetti glanced away. A moment passed before Gianni said, 'Davide has more sense than that. He probably went out to see that his bees were safe.' He gave an enormous shrug, as if to indicate that there was no understanding the strangeness of human behaviour or the efforts to which a person would go for things they had at heart.

Pierangelo sipped at his wine and said nothing, which were his usual contributions to any conversation. He did, however, cast a long-suffering look at Gianni and shake his head.

The barman brought Brunetti his coffee, saying, 'That storm was nothing for someone like Davide. Remember the one when Claudio Mozza was lost? *That* was a storm. How long ago was it – seven, eight years?' He pulled over an empty chair and braced his hands on the back, looking around the table for help. The man who never spoke said, 'Eight,' and that was that. Perhaps he was their collective memory.

'That's right,' the barman said. 'Just two days ago, Davide said the *orate* were running two kilometres out from Treporti. He told me all he had to do was put a net in the water, and they fought to swim into it.' He chuckled at the memory and went on. 'I bet that's where he went.'

'And this other person, Mozza? What happened to him?' Brunetti asked. He looked from the barman to Gianni, to Franco in search of an answer.

'They never found him,' Gianni said. 'They were out there for three days, even sent out a helicopter.' He looked around, and the other men at the table nodded in confirmation. 'They found his boat. Down by Poveglia. No one ever understood how it got there.'

'Will they do the same thing now?' Brunetti asked innocently.

'There's no need,' the barman insisted. 'As soon as they start looking, Davide will show up and ask what all the fuss is for.'

The barman released the back of the chair, picked up three empty glasses from the table and, without asking if they wanted anything else, went back to the counter and started to wash the glasses.

'What he said about Davide is true: he's one of the best,' Gianni said to Brunetti, looking in the direction of the bar, 'but the wind last night was bad, and he's not a young man.' The men near him nodded at this.

Brunetti thanked them and went over to the bar, where he paid the bill for the table and said he'd go back to the villa and see if there had been any news.

13

In deference to the sudden rise in temperature that had taken place while he was inside, Brunetti pedalled slowly back towards the villa, regretting that he had forgotten his sunglasses and the baseball cap. Life inside a city was life within the shadow of walls; out here, the sun was unrelenting and cruel.

When the bucket banged against the frame of the bike, he recalled the apricots, reached in and tested them by squeezing, pulled out a soft one and took a bite. It exploded in his mouth, filling it with sweetness such as he had not tasted since – yes – since he and his friends had come out here to steal the same fruit. He finished it with another bite and tossed the pit to the side of the road, then wiped his chin with the back of his hand. And then he ate another and another and another until he told himself to stop. Up ahead he saw water running from a public fountain. He slowed and veered over, stopped but didn't bother to get down from the bike. He rinsed his hand, wiped his mouth and chin clean, then rinsed his hand again and wiped it dry on his jeans.

He pushed off and, consciously ignoring the ripe fruit, continued back towards the villa. From his left, he heard the approach of a powerful boat, moving fast. He turned and read the words on the side: 'Capitaneria di Porto'. There appeared to be four men on board. He increased his speed, though the boat left him behind very quickly.

He pedalled furiously for the remaining distance and arrived at the villa to see the boat bobbing in the water near the steps. A uniformed man stood at the wheel, another one next to him. A third was tying the boat to the metal ring in the sea wall, while a fourth was just starting towards the villa.

Brunetti braked when he reached them and got off the bike. He propped it against the wall surrounding the villa. 'Capitano Dantone?' he called to the man walking towards the villa, recognizing the two bars on the shoulders of his uniform jacket.

'Sì,' the man responded, turning towards Brunetti. He gave Brunetti a careful look and did not seem suspicious, though he might well have been of a man in jeans and faded shirt, wearing a pair of shabby old tennis shoes and holding a bucket of ripe apricots. Dantone was, Brunetti thought, at least ten years younger than he and seemed both confident and calm. He had close-cropped light brown hair, light-coloured eyes, and a nose so thin and fine that it might well have been a woman's, had not his heavy brow and sharply angled jaw laughed at that suggestion.

Extending his hand, Brunetti introduced himself and explained that he was the man who had called.

'Do you have identification?' Dantone asked in a normal voice. Brunetti failed to identify his accent.

'Yes, it's in my room. Would you like me to get it?' At Dantone's nod, Brunetti went upstairs. He brought back the plasticized card and passed it to Dantone, who looked at it closely, then flipped it over and studied the back.

'Thank you, Commissario,' he said as he handed it to Brunetti. 'Could you tell me why you're here?'

'My wife's aunt owns this villa, and I've come out for a while to row,' he explained.

'I see,' Dantone said. 'You know Signor Casati?'

'Yes. I've been rowing with him since I've been here.'

'How long has that been?' Dantone asked.

'Ten days.'

'And all you did was row together?' When Brunetti nodded, the Captain asked, 'How good a rower is he?'

'Very good.'

'Even in a storm?' Dantone asked.

'I'm sorry, Capitano, but I'm no judge of that. I'm only an amateur. You'd have to ask someone who's had more experience and who knows Signor Casati better than I do.'

Dantone nodded and was about to speak when they were interrupted by a squawky noise from the boat. Dantone walked over, stepped back on board, and picked up what looked like the receiver of a telephone. He spoke briefly, then turned to ask the pilot something. The sailor who had been standing beside him went down into the cabin.

Dantone spoke into the phone for a longer time, listened to the other voice, and hung up. He called over to Brunetti. 'Would you like to join the search, Commissario?'

Brunetti agreed immediately, then asked, 'May I get some things from my room?'

'Of course,' Dantone said, then continued talking to the pilot, who moved to the left of the wheel and pointed to a screen on the shelf in front of them. The man who had moored the boat reached to untie the rope.

Brunetti hurried up to his room, grabbed his sunglasses and sweater, then stuffed the baseball cap into his pocket. He was at the door when he remembered to go back and take his *telefonino* from the table beside the bed.

He heard the engine roar to life, ran down the stairs and outside, slamming the door behind him. He stepped on to the boat and remained on deck next to the pilot. The water appeared to be lower than it had been that morning.

The pilot took them up the same canal that Brunetti and Casati had used the first two days. Each time they passed what appeared to be a smaller canal, the pilot slowed the boat, and the two sailors studied the tributary through binoculars. Brunetti moved around the pilot and Dantone and looked at the screen on the shelf in front of them. He recognized the map of the Laguna Nord that showed a red dot moving to the north-east; it took him only a moment to realize that they were the dot.

The pilot tapped a few keys, and horizontal and vertical red lines divided the entire area into square segments. Small dark rectangles appeared on the right of the screen, and when Brunetti looked to the shore on the right, he saw the corresponding buildings.

To Casati, the mudflats and canals were as familiar as the *calli* of Venice were to Brunetti. Casati had seemed automatically to factor in tidal patterns and their twice-daily elimination and subsequent recreation of canals and *canaletti*; just so would Brunetti move about the city during *acqua alta*, adjusting his choice of *calli* to the rising and lowering of tides.

Brunetti pulled himself free of his reverie and saw that they were moving north. Reeds and tall grass were visible on both sides of the canal; as they proceeded, the grasses seemed to creep towards them from the sides of the narrowing canal. Finally the pilot slowed and then stopped the boat. 'No more, Capitano,' he said, 'or we'll run aground.'

Dantone, who was speaking on the phone, nodded and pointed back the way they had come. He kept talking while the pilot reversed and began the slow retreat from the canal. The grasses backed away from the moving boat until the pilot found a side canal wide enough to reverse into and emerge heading back towards Sant'Erasmo.

Brunetti had eavesdropped all along: Dantone was in contact with two other boats, represented on the screen as two more red dots. One was somewhere between Torcello and Burano, while the other was in the Canale di Treporti. All he heard was Dantone's telling them which canal they were to enter and then giving them permission to retreat when the water grew too shallow.

To cut the glare, rather than to protect himself from the sun, Brunetti put on the baseball cap and was glad to have brought it.

After an hour, none of the smaller canals could be entered. Listening to Dantone's conversations, Brunetti understood that the same was true of the areas the other boats were patrolling.

Dantone, after telling the other boats to go west and have a look, if they could, at Canale Silone and Canale Dese, pulled out his *telefonino* and punched in a number.

'*Ciao*, Toni,' he said, and Brunetti assumed it was a personal call. 'The tide's on the way out, so we're not going to be able to do anything for the next few hours. I'd like you to send out the helicopter, all right?' Dantone listened for a while and then said, 'I don't care what the procedure is. It doesn't matter who I call: Vigili del Fuoco, Guardia Costiera. No boats will be able to go into the canals for hours. You saw the moon last night: the tide's low. So do me a favour, would you, and just send it up?' Again, a long silence, and then he said, no longer bothering to disguise his irritation, 'Maybe in a kayak, but not in the boats we have.' There elapsed another long silence, and then Dantone said in a much more conciliating voice, 'I know, Toni: we've got the accountants screaming at us all the time, too. But this guy might be hurt and lying in his boat somewhere. And we aren't going to find him this way, not from the boats.' His voice grew more friendly and he said, 'Do it and I'll buy you a drink the next time I see you.'

Dantone said nothing for some time, and Brunetti began to think they'd have to wait until the tide made it possible for them to resume, but then the Captain said, 'Thanks, Toni. Just pray it works.'

He put his phone in his pocket and turned to Brunetti. 'I think there's nothing for to us to do but have lunch.'

They went to a place Brunetti knew on Burano, though he had not been there for years. Inside, the décor – or what passed for décor – was the same and, mercifully, so was the food. The service was as he remembered it: brusque to the point of rudeness and no one encouraged to linger over the meal. Perhaps this is what's kept the tourists at bay, Brunetti thought. Pity more restaurants don't emulate them.

Dantone said little during the meal save to remark that the storm had been *tanto fumo e poco arrosto*, much smoke and little roast. 'It must have looked frightening out here,' he conceded when Brunetti protested, 'but most of it was heat lightning, and the rain didn't last very long at all.'

Then, before Brunetti could contradict him, Dantone said, 'I know, I know, but I talked to our meteorologist before we came out here, and she said that's what the radar showed.' Then he added, as though to put an end to any doubts Brunetti might have about his competence, 'I've been here twenty years, and I've spent most of my time in the *laguna*.'

Their waiter appeared and set down three plates of chicken roulade with carrot and onion, went back and returned with two more, saying nothing and apparently not very pleased to be serving them. Conversation ceased as they started to eat. How could something as banal as chicken breast taste so good, so sweet? Maybe it was the addition of the carrots that sweetened things.

They all heard it at the same time and raised their heads simultaneously, as if they could see through the ceiling and the roof of the building to what was approaching above them. The noise put an end to their lunch, and all of them stuffed the last bites into their mouths before getting to their feet. Dantone put fifty Euros on the table, finished his glass of mineral water, and turned towards the door. Brunetti reached for his wallet, but the Captain waved his hand at him, saying, 'That's more than enough.'

Thinking it impolite to resist, Brunetti thanked him and followed them back to the boat. Above their heads, a helicopter headed towards the north-east. The men walked to the boat, their sense of urgency quelled by the tides, which knew little of urgency and came and went in their own methodical fashion. They stepped on board, the lowest ranker cast off from the dock, and they headed straight north.

Dantone picked up the boat's phone and pressed some numbers, waited, pressed again. Suddenly, all of them heard the sound of the rotors and a man's voice giving their location. Dantone looked at the map of the *laguna* on the screen and said, 'I'd like you to go up the Canale di Sant'Antonio and over to Valle La Cura and l'Isola di Santa Cristina.'

The voice from the helicopter said something Brunetti could not understand, though Dantone apparently did, for he answered, 'All right. Good. Follow Canale Gaggian back down.' He touched the shoulder of the pilot, and the boat slowed and pulled over to the right side of the canal and stopped.

Dantone turned to Brunetti and shook his head. 'Nothing,' he said. From ahead of them, the motor of the helicopter drifted into audibility, and then they saw it, perhaps ten metres above the ground, coming slowly towards them, though still at some distance.

Dantone looked down at the map on the screen and spoke into the phone again, tracing a course with his right hand. 'We got as far as where you are now, so start up San Felice, up to the top of Canale Cenesa and then back down Canale Balolli.' There was a pause and then Dantone said, making no attempt to disguise his irritation, 'Do what I tell you. I know the tides.'

Only Dantone could hear the pilot's answer, but they could all see the helicopter swing around to the right and move off to the north-east. It maintained its height above the grass fields, growing smaller as it moved away from them.

'What now?' Brunetti asked, knowing it was a stupid question.

'We wait for them to call in.'

'And if they don't find anything?'

Dantone gave a small smile. He pointed to the screen

that showed a detailed map of the *laguna*. 'I've read the meteorological reports and looked at the tide charts. There are very few places in the Laguna Nord where he could have gone. Or been driven.' He spoke with the assurance with which men of the sea referred to winds and tides, the same assurance with which Casati had spoken, and Brunetti believed him.

He noticed that the noise of the helicopter had vanished, or at least diminished to the point where it was difficult to tell if what they heard was the engine or the dim hum of wind. Dantone's phone rang, and the Captain answered immediately. He listened for a moment, then asked, 'What? Who? Who is he?' He was silent for a long time: there was no sound of the helicopter.

'Is he sure? But who is he?' Another silence, and then he asked, 'On the back side, where they're building? What was he doing there?' Dantone bent to look at the map in front of him, and said, 'We'll go and have a look,' broke the connection and put the phone back in his pocket. He put his hand on the pilot's arm to capture his attention and said, 'That was Minniti. They've had a call. Some guy from Murano was out rowing and just called to say he saw a capsized boat out behind the cemetery. I want to go and have a look.'

Brunetti turned from gazing north at the vast expanse of water.

'Behind San Michele, where they're expanding the island,' Dantone added.

The pilot had already turned and was heading, at speed, back down Canale Scomenzera. As they approached Murano, the pilot hit the button on the dashboard that unleashed the siren. He veered around a small sailboat, dashed down Canale Ondello, and soon emerged into the wider canal in front of Murano.

The Island of San Michele was just opposite them. A man stood in a *sanpierota* and waved his arm as they approached.

'Can you get to him?' Dantone asked the pilot.

'I doubt it, Capitano. The water's very low out here, and I don't want to risk getting any closer.'

'All right,' Dantone said. He went over to the railing and with a sweeping gesture of his right arm summoned the man in the other boat to come nearer.

Without acknowledging the signal, the man put his oar back in the *fórcola*. He came towards them with surprising speed, slid up beside them, and back-stroked neatly to bring the small boat to a stop.

Not more than twenty, he had the sun-burnished look of a boatman; not that Brunetti, after a look at him, was in any doubt about this.

Captain Dantone introduced himself.

'Bartolomeo Penna,' the young man said, adding, 'At your service, Capitano.' The smile with which he said it removed all hint of irony from the remark. He was a man of the sea, giving an officer the respect due to him.

'Where's the boat?' Dantone asked.

Penna turned around and looked back towards the piles of rubble visible at the edge of the island. It was obvious that construction was under way: boards and stones and the ripped shells of paper sacks that had once held cement were all heaped together, some held in place by crossed boards and wooden building panels.

'Over there,' Penna answered, pointing in front of the mound of refuse.

'I don't see anything,' Dantone said.

'The piles of junk hide it,' Penna said. 'You have to be closer.'

'Can we get there?' Dantone asked.

'Not with this,' Penna said, bending to give the side of the larger boat an affectionate pat, as if he were a polo pony giving a nuzzle to the neck of a Clydesdale.

'Can you take us over?' Dantone asked him.

'Of course, Capitano,' the young man said and moved to the back of the boat to clear a space for them.

Dantone turned to Brunetti, said, 'Come on,' climbed over the railing and lowered himself to stand at the centre of the boat. Brunetti moved along the deck and lowered himself just behind him.

Penna put his oar back into the water, and they started towards the cemetery.

14

Brunetti tried to fight the sense that this was going to turn out badly. Where else would Casati have gone than to the cemetery to talk to his wife? Who else could he tell about the death of his bees, his girls? Brunetti said nothing.

Arrow-straight, they headed towards the largest pile of soil and stones. Ten metres before it, Brunetti felt the boat slide across something that resisted its progress. Penna instantly turned them back towards the deeper water, but after only a few strokes he curved to the right and moved them forward again. Four more strokes and he stopped, turned his oar sideways in the water and drew the small boat to a halt.

Ahead of them Brunetti saw, capsized in the water, the bottom of a small boat.

From behind him, Dantone asked, 'His boat is a *puparìn*, isn't it?'

'Yes.'

'Penna,' Dantone asked. 'Can you get us any closer?'

'I'd like to,' the young man said eagerly, 'but a lot of rubbish has been dumped into the water around here, and I don't know what we'd run into.' Then, in a voice he tried to make encouraging, Penna added, 'It's really not very deep here, sir, not much more than a metre.' He hesitated for a moment and then continued, 'But there's been some dredging.'

Brunetti had turned to face the back of the boat, the better to follow their conversation. Dantone acknowledged the news with a shrug, looked at Brunetti and asked, 'You coming?'

'Yes.'

Dantone set his hat upside down next to Penna's feet, slipped off his watch, removed his *telefonino* from his jacket pocket, and put them inside the hat. Then he removed his jacket with what Brunetti thought was a sigh and placed it beside the hat. As casually as if he were just going to take a dip in the pool, he sat on the side of the boat, lifted his still-shod feet over the side, and lowered himself, fully clothed, into the water. It came, as Penna had predicted, only a bit above his waist.

By the time Dantone turned back towards the boat, Brunetti was leaning forward to place his own watch and phone inside the capsized hat and then just as quickly swung his feet over the side and lowered himself into the water. When he felt the mud shift and squiggle under his feet, Brunetti was glad of his tennis shoes.

The Captain moved off in the direction of the stationary boat floating about ten metres from them.

Brunetti followed, his feet sinking into the mud and resisting his efforts to pull them free, occasionally stepping on hard or – worse – soft objects. All of a sudden, Dantone gasped a loud 'Oh' and disappeared. Brunetti lunged and grabbed, but all he found was the Captain's hair. He pulled and managed to bring the Captain's head above the water, but his body refused to rise. Dantone's arms shot up and waved in the air, his body thrashing from side to side in panic.

To try for a better purchase on him, Brunetti stepped forward and stepped into nothing. Instinctively, he released Dantone and hurled himself backwards in the water. His feet scrambled about below him, and again one foot descended into nothingness. He pulled it back until both feet were firm in the soft mud, then leaned forward and grabbed at Dantone again, this time finding an arm. He stepped back, locked both hands on the arm, and shuffled backwards, dragging the Captain with him.

The Captain continued to resist him, rising and then falling as though pulled under by some other force. Finally, in a grotesque imitation of birth, Dantone pulled free and slipped forward into Brunetti's hands.

Dantone coughed, vomited up water, and coughed some more. When he stopped coughing, he leaned forward, hands on his hips, and breathed in deeply for a long time. 'A hole,' he finally said. 'There's a hole down there. My feet kept slipping on the sides.' He took more deep breaths and waited until both their hearts were beating normally. By common consent they locked arms and started moving gingerly, testing every step, towards the boat.

Thus joined, they came near to the upturned shell of a rowing boat, algae and barnacles clinging to the exposed bottom, floating there about three metres from the land. Brunetti's foot stepped into nothingness and he plunged into a hole, slipping free of Dantone's arm. He did not think; reason was lost to him. He sank and thought of death. His feet hit the bottom and sank into muck. Panic straightened his body, his head rose above the surface of the water, and he could breathe again.

Dantone had his shoulders in his grip, and yanked Brunetti towards him. He floated free of the hole, he knew not how; Dantone pulled him back and upright. Terror – though Brunetti would later call it instinct – stopped him from moving, filling him with the sensation that he was about to experience something strange and un-pleasant and dangerous. But then Dantone pulled him to the left, and they started off again, more carefully, more slowly, this time circling the boat and drawing no closer. Brunetti shook his terror away as they continued around the boat. He stopped and put a restraining hand on Dantone's shoulder. 'It's a *puparìn*,' Brunetti said.

'What do we do?' Dantone asked. 'Turn it over?'

The policeman in Brunetti answered. 'I'd rather not disturb it until we've seen more.' He thought of all the places he'd been where the evidence had been contaminated by too-hasty curiosity, and then he wondered why he was thinking of evidence. Of what?

'I want to take a look underneath,' Brunetti said. It made little difference if they were out of the water or in it: they were a pair of filthy amphibians by now. In response to Dantone's nod, Brunetti sucked in as much air as he could hold and jackknifed in the water, heading under the boat. Eyes open, he slipped beneath the edge, but there was no light and nothing to be seen. He ran his hands over the invisible curve of the inside and worked his way around to the other side, but he felt nothing except the smooth sides and gunwale. He swam back to the other side and out of the entrapping space, up to the surface.

He bobbed up not far from Dantone and said, 'Nothing to see. No light.'

'What now?' the Captain asked.

'If we pulled it up on shore, maybe we could turn it over and see if it's his,' Brunetti said, wondering why he refused to believe that it was. He latched his fingers under the edge of the capsized boat and started walking towards the shore.

Dantone moved to the other side, and together they hauled the boat nearer to the land, where they found no easy access but a sudden, sharp drop-off of almost a metre. Abandoning his hold on the boat, Brunetti climbed up on land, followed by Dantone. Both of them leaned over and pulled in deep, rasping breaths, then turned back to the boat.

It was easy enough to drag the prow up on to the land and haul it forward for a quarter of the boat's length, but they quickly realized there was no way they could turn it over or drag it entirely free of the water. There, on the left side of the prow, Brunetti saw the long streak of blue: Casati had told him about his close call some weeks before with a delivery boat's drunken pilot. 'It's his,' he said.

He walked around to the other side of the boat and saw that a rope was hanging taut from the ring at the back. He bent and pulled on it, hoping to free the anchor and bring it on to land, for surely the boat would have to be taken back to Sant'Erasmo. He pulled on it a few times, but it must have been caught on something on the bottom.

'Could you give me a hand, Capitano,' he called, surprised that he still didn't know Dantone's first name.

'Andrea,' Dantone said as he walked over. 'And you're Guido, right?'

'Yes,' Brunetti said, then, 'There's a metal grating on the end of the rope: it must be stuck on the bottom.' He passed the rope to Dantone, who moved to stand opposite him.

Together they pulled at the anchor. Brunetti felt it come

loose from below the surface and looked across at Dantone in satisfaction.

They pulled together, slipping hand over hand as the anchor moved along the bottom and the rope that they pulled ashore coiled once upon itself at their feet.

Brunetti looked at the place where the rope entered the water, wondering if Casati had decided to use something heavier, more secure than the grating he knew. He bent over and peered into the water, and that's when he saw the hand.

15

Perhaps he lost his balance; perhaps a loop of the rope had caught around his ankle and pulled at one side; or perhaps it was the sight of the hand that brought Brunetti to his knees. Whatever the cause, he found himself in the mud, his knees poked and scraped by stones and tile shards, still holding the rope but afraid to put his hand in the water with that other hand.

Dantone, standing behind him, looked to see what had happened. 'Guido, what is it?' he asked.

'In the water,' was the best Brunetti could manage. 'Look.' He was kneeling with his hands propped on the ground in front of him, fighting the impulse to be sick.

Dantone ran his eye down to where the rope entered the water. And saw it. 'Maria Vergine,' he whispered – an expression Brunetti's mother had used – his hands frozen on the rope.

The time that passed seemed endless, though it couldn't

have been even a minute. Finally Brunetti got to his feet and looked across at Dantone. 'We have to get him out of there,' he said.

Dantone nodded, as though there were no words he could find.

Together, hand over hand, they returned to hauling up this new, horrible, anchor. At first, Brunetti looked to one side of the rope, then steeled himself and looked at it and what was below: the top of a head, a shoulder, the other, and then the chest of the man that a quick glance down his face had told him was Casati, bobbing and turning in the water.

When he saw Casati's head float to the surface of the water, Brunetti said, 'I'll pull him out.' He looked at Dantone, who nodded and braced one leg behind him, his hands gripping the rope.

Brunetti let go of the rope and knelt at the edge of the water. He leaned down, grabbed Casati's body under the shoulders, and guided him to the place where the land dropped quickly into the water, but it proved impossible to lift the body.

He was about to ask Dantone for help when the other man was beside him, lifting, lifting. Together, they pulled the dead man from the water and laid him, face up, on the ground. Water ran from Casati's hair and clothing and quickly disappeared into the mud around him. His old shirt and loose trousers were slick to his body; one shoe was gone. The rope, like the body of a python, had coiled itself around Casati's leg, just below the knee, then moved down to dig a circle in the flesh above his ankle before being pulled straight into the water by whatever it was tied to. Dantone grabbed the rope and pulled until the metal grating broke the surface. He hauled it out and let it drop on the earth, not far from Casati's feet.

Brunetti leaned over the dead man and, not caring

whether he was destroying more evidence, covered Casati's eyes with his hands and pressed the eyelids closed. They remained that way for an instant, but then opened again. Brunetti pulled a cotton handkerchief, soaked and shapeless, from his back pocket; he shook it open and placed it, still dripping, over the dead man's face, then he sat back on his knees and closed his eyes.

Suddenly they heard footsteps, and soon after that one of the sailors from Dantone's boat appeared, slogging across the broken dirt and piled rocks, looking strangely out of place in his clean, white uniform. When he saw the dead man, he stopped. Dantone held up a hand to warn him to come no closer.

Brunetti pushed himself to his feet and looked down at Casati's body. How small he looked, this old man who had seemed so young, so vital.

'Where's the boat?' Dantone surprised him by asking, but he was speaking to the young sailor.

'Back there, Capitano,' the young man answered, turning to point behind him, where the angle of the cemetery wall cut off any chance of seeing beyond it. 'There's a dock.'

'You walked?' Dantone asked.

'The chart said the water's too shallow for the boat.'

Dantone, who had just pulled himself, and a man's body, from more than a metre of water, made an exasperated noise and got to his feet. He walked over to Brunetti. 'I'll bring the boat,' he said and started off in the direction from which the sailor had come. When the young man moved to follow him, Dantone stopped and said, 'Do you have your phone?'

'Yes, sir.'

'Call the Carabinieri and tell them we've found him. They can tell the helicopter to go back.' The officer nodded and started walking again, away from Brunetti and the dead man.

Brunetti looked out across the water, failing to find anything there but emptiness. He bent over the grating but didn't touch it. Had Casati been trying to toss it overboard in the storm to stop the boat from being carried into deeper water by wind and tide? Had the boat started to move away from shore? If it had happened during the storm, he would have been blinded by wind and rain, perhaps not seen where he put his foot, not seen the rope, coiling around his leg.

It would have happened quickly, but Casati was a fish: surely he would have tried to free himself by uncoiling the rope, even pulling up the anchor? It weighed no more than a few kilos.

Brunetti stared down at his friend, trying to work it out, and failing. All speculation ended there, at that coiling rope.

Brunetti looked over at the wall of the cemetery, where Casati had gone so often to speak with his wife, thinking of possibilities. After speaking with her, he had always returned to their daughter. But what if this time she had asked him to stay?

Dantone's shout interrupted his thoughts. 'Guido, Guido. We're here.'

Brunetti turned towards the voice and saw something that reminded him of a painting he had liked when he was a boy, of the Volga boatmen pulling a barge along a broad canal, a score of them on the shore, all hauling the same length of rope. This time, it was two uniformed sailors, in their long white buttoned jackets and black boots, pulling their boat slowly along the edge of the cemetery island, towards Brunetti and what was soon to be their cargo. The covering at the back of their boat was open, the motor tilted back free of the water. Dantone lay on his stomach on the prow, looking into the water and calling out orders to the two sailors.

When the boat stopped abreast of him, not far from the shore, Brunetti called to Dantone, 'Could you give me my phone?'

Dantone scrambled back and retrieved Brunetti's *telefonino*. He leaned far over the side with the phone in his hand, and Brunetti stepped without thinking into the water to lean out to take it from him. The phone was new, bought for him by Signorina Elettra out of the account for office supplies that she had been pillaging for years. She had spent some time showing him how to use the camera, and he thought he could do it.

Careful now to look where he put his feet, Brunetti went back to shore and approached the boat. He moved around it in a U, taking photos. He knelt and took close-ups from both sides of the rope coiled around Casati's leg.

Then he had no choice. He bent and removed the handkerchief and photographed Casati's open-eyed face from both sides and from straight above, then replaced the handkerchief and turned his back on the body to take photos of the disturbed earth, the abandoned grating tied to the end of the rope twisted around Casati's leg and ankle, the cemetery wall, and the horizon, anything to put new images into the camera and into his mind. He slipped the phone into the pocket of his shirt and looked off at the horizon.

The sailors helped Brunetti lift Casati's body; with no hesitation, they all stepped into the water and passed the body up to Dantone and the pilot, who lowered it slowly to the deck. Casati weighed far less than Brunetti had expected, as though death had removed something from him other than his life.

Then Brunetti climbed on board. The pilot disappeared into the cabin for a moment and returned with a woollen blanket, then lowered it slowly over Casati's body, careful to cover his face, from which the handkerchief had fallen. Brunetti nodded his thanks, and the pilot raised his hand to his forehead in salute, either to Brunetti or to the dead man.

Dantone said something to the sailors; Brunetti, standing beside him, heard the words but didn't know what they meant. The sailors picked up the ends of the tow ropes they'd abandoned on the shore and, after struggling for some time to turn the bobbing police boat around, began to haul it back the way they had come. Brunetti and Dantone remained on board with the pilot.

'I'll call the hospital,' Brunetti said.

Dantone and the pilot exchanged glances, and the pilot said, 'About ten minutes. Perhaps less. We just have to get back to deep water.'

Brunetti called Foa, the Questura's chief pilot, and told him what had happened, then asked him to organize a boat to come out to the back of the cemetery island. He described the boat that was dragged up on the shore, told him to bring plastic sheeting with him and, after turning the boat upright, to cover it and tow it back to the Questura, then find a place to keep it until the family could claim it.

'Are you on duty again, sir?' the pilot asked.

'Not really,' Brunetti answered shortly, repeated his instructions, and told Foa to get to it immediately.

'Yes, sir,' the younger man answered, sounding almost happy to be given a job, and was gone.

All this time, the two sailors had been towing the boat, but the scene was now deprived of charm. When they reached a point where the pilot said it would be deep enough for the motor, the men on shore walked to the boat and climbed on board. They lowered the engine into the water. The pilot turned the boat around and headed for the Ospedale Civile.

Brunetti reached over to Dantone's upturned hat, picked up his watch, and was surprised to see that it was almost six. What a strange thought to have, he told himself: Casati was lying dead at his feet, and he was worried about what time it was.

He found that the phone was still in his hand, found Federica's number, and called her. The motor drowned out her voice until he went down into the cabin and closed the door. He told her they'd found her father, and he was dead, killed in the storm. He was on the boat that was taking him to the hospital. Yes, he'd wait for her there. Reluctant to tell her that the body would be in the morgue, he told her to ask for Dottor Rizzardi when she got there, and he'd come and find her and take her to her father.

Her voice had fought off tears during their conversation, but at Brunetti's last words, she lost control and started to sob. 'Federica, can you hear me?' Brunetti asked.

'Yes.'

'Come when you can. Come with your husband. I'll be there.'

'What happened?' she asked with false calm.

'I don't know. Your father drowned.'

'Because of the storm?'

'Yes,' Brunetti answered, and promised again that he'd be at the hospital when she came.

She started to say something, stopped, and said only, 'No, no, he couldn't . . .' before hanging up.

He dialled the home number of Ettore Rizzardi, the chief pathologist.

After only three rings, Rizzardi said, with his usual dangerous politeness, 'Ah, Guido, how good to hear from you. In what way may I be useful?'

'*Ciao*, Ettore,' Brunetti said, knowing he was going to have to ask his friend for a favour but not certain how abrupt to be. 'How are you?' he temporized.

'At home at the end of a long and frustrating day, about to have a drink with my fair wife and then have dinner with some friends. Are you calling because you'd like to join us?'

'No, Ettore,' Brunetti said, incapable for once of falling into easy patter with Rizzardi. 'It's a friend. He died last night. Drowned. I'm asking you to do it.'

There was a long pause. Brunetti could hear the sound of other voices in the room.'Where are you?' Rizzardi asked.

'On a boat, bringing him in.' Brunetti looked out of the window and said, 'In fact, we're just arriving.'

'Where was he?' Rizzardi asked.

'At the cemetery.'

The doctor drew in a deep breath, then heaved a sigh that came down the line and wrapped itself around Brunetti. 'I'll leave now,' Rizzardi said, all joking fled from his voice. 'Twenty minutes at the most. I'll call and tell them you're coming and to reserve a place for him.'

'Thanks, Ettore,' Brunetti said and broke the connection.

He took three deep breaths and dialled his home number. Paola answered on the second ring, asking, 'How are you, Guido?'

'Not good. I'm on my way back to the city.'

'What's wrong with you?' she broke in before he could say more.

'I'm fine,' he said, 'but Casati's dead.'

'*Oddio*,' she sighed. 'What happened?'

'He was out in the storm last night. We found him an hour ago, trapped under his boat. Drowned.'

'Where are you?'

'On a boat. Taking him to the hospital.'

'But you're all right.'

'Yes, yes.'

'Will you come home?' she asked, then added, 'After.'

'Yes,' he said, not having given it a thought until now. Home. Of course. 'I don't know when, but I'll be home,' he said and ended the call.

Rizzardi must have called to give the order: three white-jacketed porters waited at the landing with a high-wheeled stretcher for the body. The boat glided up to the dock and slowed to a stop. The porters stepped on to the boat, bent to lift Casati over the side, and placed him on the stretcher. One of them straightened the blanket, making sure the face remained covered.

They nodded to Dantone – or to his uniform – and wheeled the body away. 'You can go back,' Dantone told the crew. 'I'll stay here until . . .' He finished with a shrug, no more clear than was Brunetti about what would happen or how long they would be there.

Brunetti knew the way and set off towards the morgue. Dantone caught up with him and walked at his side. 'What do you think?' the Captain asked as they crossed one of the inner courtyards. Heads turned to look at these two filthy men, no doubt to wonder what on earth they could be doing in a hospital.

Brunetti raised a hand. 'It looks like he drowned.'

'That's not an answer,' Dantone said in a casual voice.

Brunetti stopped, then moved to one of the brick paths that crossed the courtyard at the diagonal. 'You saw the rope,' he said to the Captain.

'Yes.'

Dantone studied Brunetti's face and looked away from him. 'I think we need a coffee,' he said.

While they drank it, pretending not to notice the stares they received from the barman and the other clients, they concentrated on getting caffeine and sugar into their bodies. Brunetti, after a full day under the sun, was beginning to feel feverish and didn't like the look of the back of his hands, which were the colour of bricks. He couldn't very well ask Dantone if his face was sunburned, but he felt as though he had a high fever.

After the coffee, he drank two glasses of mineral water, asked for a *tramezzino*, said he didn't care what kind, and drank a third glass of water with it.

Dantone insisted on paying, and Brunetti let him.

People who passed them in the corridors tried not to stare, but some of them couldn't resist. Dantone was a mess – his trousers looked like something he'd picked from the garbage; stained grey and brown, they had pieces of dirt and mud still clinging to them. His boots squished when he walked. Brunetti knew he looked no better, but at least his canvas shoes had dried out somewhat and no longer made any noise.

Brunetti knocked on the door of the morgue. An attendant he did not know opened it; when he saw the two men standing outside, he automatically made to shut the door in their faces, even though a closer look would have revealed that Dantone was wearing some sort of uniform. Brunetti stuck his arm out and stopped the door with his palm.

'Police,' he said.

The man, he noticed now, was tall and well-muscled, not the sort of person to be intimidated easily. 'May I see some identification?' the man asked. It was not a question, not really.

'Go and talk to Dottor Rizzardi and tell him Commissario Brunetti and Capitano Dantone are here.' Then, in a more reasonable voice, taking a step backward, Brunetti added, 'We'll wait for him out here in the corridor if you like.'

It must have been the willingness not to cause trouble that convinced the man, for he took his hands from the door and said, 'Please come in, gentlemen. I'm just doing my job.'

'I understand that,' Brunetti said. He looked at the raggedy Dantone, who nodded.

'Have they brought in the man who died in the *laguna*?' Brunetti asked.

'Yes. Dottor Rizzardi is with him now. It usually takes an hour, sir.' He pushed up his sleeve and looked at his watch. 'Not before seven-thirty, I'd say.'

'Thank you,' Brunetti replied.

'Is there anything I can get you?' the man asked, addressing them both.

Brunetti allowed himself to smile and said, 'We both could do with new clothing, but that's not important any longer. We'll wait for the doctor and see what he has to say, and then we'll leave.'

The attendant gave Brunetti a strange look, perhaps sensing the exhaustion in the two men. He turned and led them down the corridor. The waiting room was so cool that at first Brunetti thought there was air conditioning, but then he realized it was only because the walls of the building were so thick and because they were on the north side.

Brunetti and Dantone again told the attendant they wanted nothing and sat, leaving a chair empty between them. The attendant went away, closing the door after him.

For some minutes, neither of them said anything, and then Dantone asked, 'You know the pathologist well?'

'Yes. We've worked together for a long time.'

'Must be a lousy job,' the Captain said, careful to keep his face and voice neutral as he spoke.

Brunetti turned to look at him as he answered. 'He once told me he thinks it's miraculous.'

'What?' Dantone's shock was audible. 'What he does?'

'The body, not the autopsy,' Brunetti said. 'At least that's what he told me. He said it's perfect, the way it works and what it can do.'

Brunetti felt a debt to Rizzardi, who had come here on his free evening only because he had asked him to, and so he explained, 'He told me once that he sees how strong we are and how perfectly designed the body is for survival: that's what he thinks is miraculous.'

Dantone clasped his hands together and leaned forward to put them between his knees. He looked at the floor for a long time until he finally glanced sideways at Brunetti and said, 'Oh, I see. Yes.'

After that, the men sat in silence for some time until Dantone, driven by the growing cold, got up and began to pace the room. Brunetti crossed his legs, wrapped his arms around his body, and waited. There was a knock at the door and the attendant came in.

'Dottor Rizzardi said he'd like to talk to you.'

'Is he finished?' Brunetti asked in a voice he hoped would cover his reluctance to have the next conversation.

'Yes, he's back in his office. Do you know the way?'

'Yes,' Brunetti said with a sigh.

16

Brunetti led the way down the corridor to Rizzardi's office, where they found the door open. He stuck his head inside and saw Rizzardi, sitting in one of the chairs against the wall, bent over, tying his shoes.

'Ah, Guido,' Rizzardi said, getting to his feet. The doctor noticed Dantone, came over and shook hands with Brunetti and then with the other man while they exchanged names. He stepped back and looked at both of them. 'Was it you who pulled him out of the water?'

'Yes,' Brunetti answered for both of them.

'When?'

Brunetti looked at Dantone, who said, 'It was about four, I think, four-thirty. Does it make a difference?'

Rizzardi shook his head, put both hands on his tie to check the knot, and said, 'No, not really; I was simply curious. It was the only thing I wasn't sure of.'

'What are you sure of?' Brunetti asked.

'That he drowned,' Rizzardi answered. 'And in salt water. Some time last night.' He went back to his desk and leaned against it, as if he didn't want to sit in a chair and thus commit himself to staying there a long time. 'You said he was a friend of yours?'

'Yes, I think he was,' Brunetti said. 'Yes.'

'Why only think it?'

'I've known him only a short time,' Brunetti answered. 'A bit more than a week.' Rizzardi grunted to acknowledge this. 'But he knew my father,' Brunetti added, aware of how much this had warmed him to Casati. He waited a moment and asked Rizzardi, 'Anything else?'

Rizzardi nodded. 'There was water in his lungs as I told you. He was alive when he went into the water.' When neither man spoke, Rizzardi added, 'He had a rough time in the storm, I'd say: there were marks on his arms and on the left side of his forehead that would have become bruises.' Seeing Dantone's confusion, he explained. 'Blood stops circulating when a person dies, so bruising doesn't happen.' Rizzardi bowed his head to study his shoes, and added, 'I don't think the blows were very hard: just the usual things that happen on a boat in rough weather.'

'That's all?' Brunetti asked.

Looking up at them again, Rizzardi said, 'It looks like he had a rough life, too, at least when he was younger. There are scars and traces of fat in his liver: most alcoholics have them, no matter how long ago they stopped drinking. Same with cigarettes: he was once a heavy smoker, but he stopped.'

Brunetti was astonished to learn this. Who had he been, this mild, temperate man? His body had given up secrets that his tranquil life had not even hinted at. Brunetti noticed that the pathologist was gripping and releasing his hands from the edge of the table behind him, and

Dantone was turning his head back and forth as he and Rizzardi talked.

Rizzardi reached back across his desk to take his jacket from where it was draped over his chair. He put it on and asked, 'Do you have any other questions, Guido?'

'What about the scars?'

Rizzardi must have been waiting for the question, for he said, 'The injuries happened years ago, perhaps twenty, even more. They're not involved in his death.' Then, before Brunetti could ask about their cause, Rizzardi said, 'They're not the sort I'm used to seeing.'

'What does that mean?'

'They're chemical burns. Or acid. Something that causes the skin to melt. Flame leaves different scars.'

'The rope?' Brunetti asked.

'Yes, the rope,' Rizzardi said, running the fingers of both hands through his hair, something he did when preparing to end a conversation. 'It was tangled around his upper calf and then again around his ankle. The rubbing damaged the tissue in both places.'

That would have happened after Casati died, Brunetti thought, as his body was pulled about by the moving water, and would have caused him no pain. There was no consolation in that thought.

'I closed his eyes,' Rizzardi said.

Brunetti nodded his thanks but could not speak for a moment. Finally he said, 'I took some photos out there. I'll send them to you.'

'Thank you,' the doctor answered. When neither Brunetti nor Dantone spoke, Rizzardi suggested, 'Shall we leave, then, Signori?' and Brunetti liked him for not mentioning the dinner he had abandoned. The doctor led them into the corridor and turned to lock the door to his office.

Brunetti, remembering his promise to Federica, said, 'I told his daughter I'd meet her here.'

Rizzardi was startled into saying, 'Ah, I forgot; I'm sorry, Guido. Her husband called and said she's in no shape to come here. She collapsed after you told her. He'll bring her in the morning.'

Brunetti felt a wave of relief and then an even stronger wave of shame at his own cowardice. 'Did he say when they'd come?' he asked, hoping he could make amends if he was here when they arrived.

'Ten,' the doctor told him.

They walked towards the main exit together, all of them aware of how the temperature increased as they moved closer to the door. By the time they got to the *campo*, their bodies, like those of surfacing divers, had adjusted to the new conditions. The heat wrapped itself around them, and Brunetti thought he could smell his own clothing.

They shook hands just outside the main door to the *campo*, and Rizzardi went off in the direction of Strada Nuova and the vaporetto that would take him home. Dantone said something about going back to the Capitaneria and added that he and his men were available if and when Brunetti wanted to go into the *laguna* again.

'Thank you,' Brunetti said as they lingered in front of the hospital.

'Thanks for hauling me out of the water.'

Brunetti patted Dantone on the arm and said, 'Same to you.' The two men stepped down into the *campo* and went their separate ways.

Brunetti stopped when he got to the bottom of the bridge in front of the hospital and stared in front of him. How strange and closed-in it looked, this small *calle* lined with buildings on both sides. His view ahead slammed into a bridge and then another one, and then buildings, more buildings on both sides. Raising his eyes, he saw even more buildings and then rooftops, but there was no long, unobstructed view of anything. This is what it means to be in a city, he thought. This is what living with views to the open sea has done to me.

As he continued on the familiar way home, however, the strange sensation left him, and by the time he turned into his *calle* his sight had adjusted to a city perspective. He didn't have his keys, so he phoned Paola to ask her to open the main door. A few seconds later, the large door clicked open. Brunetti, covered with sweat and very conscious of the smell coming from his clothing, started up the stairs to the apartment. When he reached the third floor, he heard the door open above him and Paola's voice calling, *'Ciao, Guido. Bentornato.'*

Yes, it was good to return to his home, to this safe place they had created over the years. He paused on the last turning and looked up. She stood upright in the doorway, looking down at him, smiling.

'I'm a bit bedraggled,' was all Brunetti could think of to say.

'More than a bit,' she observed with a smile that failed to hide her surprise.

'Comes of being away from you for so long,' he said, starting up the last flight. Without Paola, his life was not only bedraggled, but dull, humourless, cool, joyless. He wanted to tell her this, but instead he said, 'I need a drink and a shower.'

He arrived on the landing and bent over to give her a kiss, careful to keep his filthy clothing from touching her.

She stepped back and looked him up and down. 'Could you reverse the order?'

When a scrubbed Brunetti, his clothing stuffed in a plastic bag to go out with the morning's garbage, came to dinner, only Raffi and Paola were there. Paola explained that Chiara had gone to spend three days at the home of a friend whose parents had a summer place on the Lido and hadn't returned yet. Brunetti's first thought was that she'd be in that water, but then it came to him that she'd be kilometres from the place where he had found Casati.

Raffi was happy to see him and spent most of the meal talking about what he'd done, he and his friends, while Brunetti had been away. One of them had been given a *topetta* for his eighteenth birthday, and he was letting Raffi come along for the lessons his father was giving him.

'The motor's tiny, only five horsepower, but it's great to be out there and go where you want,' he said, his enthusiasm so high that he forgot to eat for a few minutes, something that did not go unnoticed by his parents.

'You don't need a licence for a motor that small, do you?' Brunetti asked, spearing a piece of roast duck and using it to wipe up the rest of the orange sauce on his plate.

'No, so there's nothing illegal about it if they let me take the tiller,' Raffi said with obvious pride in his casual use of the term. 'Besides, Danilo's father's been with us all the time.'

'Good,' Brunetti said, beginning to feel haunted by all this talk of boats and the *laguna*.

As if she had read his mind, Paola broke in and said, 'Raffi, will you help me take the plates?' He got up to do so, and they carried them inside, leaving Brunetti alone on the terrace, where he indulged in an excess of long views. Though they extended over rooftops and were occasionally obstructed by bell towers, they soothed his soul as much as his eyes with their sweet assurance that he had returned to a safe haven.

Paola returned after about twenty minutes, by which

time Brunetti had retreated to the sofa in the living room, kicked off his shoes, and put his feet on the low table in front of him. She set down two coffees. Raffi had not seen the state his father was in when he came home, so the subject of Brunetti's experiences in the *laguna* had not arisen at dinner, and now Raffi had gone to the cinema with a friend.

'There's sugar in it already,' Paola said, sitting beside him. They drank their coffee silently. Brunetti, after more than a week of drinking only a single glass of wine with dinner, felt no desire for anything other than coffee; he surprised himself by wanting no grappa.

At no particular time in their long silence, Brunetti decided he would tell her everything he knew. Though it took some time, Paola waited until it was clear he had finished, when she asked, 'It's a strange thing to happen to someone who spent so much time on the water, isn't it?'

'Rizzardi said he must have been battered about by the storm. The anchor rope was twisted around his leg and pulled him in.'

'Ah,' Paola said. 'I'm sorry for his daughter.'

'Yes,' he said and pushed his cup and saucer farther back on the table.

He rested his head against the sofa and thought about the carefree days he had spent with Casati. In all of those days, he had not thought about Pucetti's impulsive gesture during the interview with Ruggieri, just as he had not heard from anyone at the Questura.

'I told you. He talked about his bees,' Brunetti said.

'Bees,' Paola repeated flatly.

Brunetti nodded. 'He kept bees out on the *barene* in the *laguna*, and we went out to inspect them.'

'To get honey?'

'No. It's too early for that. Not until the end of the summer.' Then he added, 'He said they were dying.'

'Yes,' Paola said and closed her eyes in thought for a moment. 'I've read about it: it's happening everywhere and they seem unable to stop it.' And then she asked, 'If he wasn't going to get the honey, what was he going out to inspect?'

'We went out to see them so that he could take samples.'

'Samples of what?'

'Once it was a few dead bees. He put them in a plastic tube, the sort they use for blood samples, to have them tested.'

'Once?'

'Another time, he came back to the boat with a vial of mud.'

'Could the mud have been killing them?' she asked.

'I doubt it,' Brunetti said after a brief pause. 'He told me people kept the same hives in the same places for generations. If the mud was going to kill them, I suppose it would have done so a long time ago.'

Paola closed her eyes for a time and finally asked, eyes still closed, 'Who would test them?'

Brunetti, who had been on the island for more than a week, didn't hesitate to answer. 'No one on Sant'Erasmo, that's for sure.'

'Then he'd have to send it somewhere else. How do you send something from Sant'Erasmo?'

'The post office, I suppose.'

Without a word, Paola got up and went towards the back of the apartment and her study. A few minutes later, she came back, saying, 'There's no post office on Sant'Erasmo.'

'Then what do they do?'

'Go to Burano, I suppose. That's the nearest one.'

Before giving it conscious thought, Brunetti said, 'Then I'll try the post office. I can stop on my way back to Sant'Erasmo.'

'You're going back?' Paola asked, unable to hide her surprise.

'All anyone there knows is that I'm a relative of Emilio's who's spending a few weeks in the house.'

Paola gave him a long look and waved her fingers in front of his face. 'Earth to Commissario Brunetti. Earth to Commissario Brunetti. Can you hear me? Can you read me, Commissario?' she asked in an otherworldly voice.

'What's that supposed to mean?' he asked, though he knew.

'It means that, by now, everyone on the island has heard about what happened. They know you went out on the boat from the Capitaneria, know you're a *commissario di polizia* – probably know the serial number on your warrant card – and know that you took his body to the hospital.'

'I'm still going to go back,' Brunetti insisted.

'Do you think people will talk to you?'

'If they think there's no risk if they do, and if I express the proper sentiments.'

'Which are?' she asked.

Brunetti had to think for a while about this but finally said, 'I spent almost two weeks with him, five, six hours a day. We talked about a lot of things while we were out there, though I never had the sense that I knew much about him except that he was a decent, honourable man, and now it pains me that he's dead.'

'I see,' she said.

'I'm sorry if that doesn't sound like much,' Brunetti said.

Paola leaned forward and put her hand on his knee. 'I'm glad you feel that way about him.' She sat back and gave him time to speak, but Brunetti could think of nothing more to say.

'What are you going to do?' she asked.

He slid down in the sofa and crossed his ankles. 'Go back and listen to what people say about him. See if he talked to anyone about his bees. Try to find this woman. And try to find out if he sent anything from the post office on Burano.'

'And what will all that tell you?' she asked with real interest.

'I have no idea,' he admitted. 'But I hope it will help me understand his death.'

17

The next morning, Brunetti was at the hospital at nine-forty-five. He waited a moment at the main entrance, but then it occurred to him that Federica and her husband, if they arrived on the 13 from Sant'Erasmo, would get off at Fondamente Nove, in which case they'd enter the hospital from the back or even from the entrance near the church. After what her husband had said about her reaction to the news, Brunetti was reluctant to phone Federica, so he sent a text message, saying that he would meet them outside the office of Dottor Rizzardi on the ground floor, in Area D. This spared his having to write 'Morgue,' a word he hated and that most people feared.

He had not bought a newspaper, thinking it would be disrespectful if they came upon him reading it, so he stood at the entrance to the corridor that led to Rizzardi's office and watched the people passing.

Brunetti thought of the rope around Casati's leg, and

that turned his thoughts to the living Casati. He remembered the older man and his delight in pointing out the wading and nesting birds in the *laguna*, and in the sheer explosion of life that was to be seen at every moment. He remembered the fledgling black-winged stilts Casati had shown him, perfectly camouflaged to blend in with the reeds and stalks of dry grass. Casati knew the names and habits of all the birds they saw and had had endless patience when pointing them out to the city slicker.

He remembered asking Casati, on one of the first days they went rowing, why his bees were so important to him. They had been up at the top of Canale Bussolaro at the time. The last words of his question had been dulled by the wind-borne thunder of a plane taking off from the airport behind them. Casati hadn't answered until it was quiet enough for them to speak again. 'They're the only thing that gives me hope, the bees.'

He'd stopped rowing then, and Brunetti'd pulled up his own oar and turned to look at the older man. 'Look at that,' Casati had said, pointing his chin to the left, and when that failed to encompass his meaning, he'd waved his left hand in a wide arc towards the mainland. 'Everywhere, we've built and dug and torn up and done what we wanted with nature. And look at this,' he'd said, turning to his right and waving out over the *laguna*, 'we've poisoned this, too.' His face had grown rough with anger.

Tight-voiced, he'd gone on. 'They've done what they wanted with nature, and our children will pay the price.' Immediately, Brunetti had thought of the MOSE, the tidal barrier that many people believed could not work, and realized that Casati's prophecy included Brunetti's own children. 'We've poisoned it all, killed it all,' Casati had said, turning back to Brunetti.

Then, in the midst of this catalogue, Casati's expression had softened, and when he spoke, his voice had grown calm. 'But the bees have had fifty million years, maybe more, to become what they are. My Queens lay two thousand eggs a day, Guido, each one of them, in every hive. More than their own body weight – just think of it – every day. So, hard as we try, we'll never manage to kill them all. They'll survive us and what we've done to them.' His smile had drifted away and he'd added in a softer voice Brunetti suspected he was not meant to hear, 'And what I did to them.'

When Brunetti realized Casati was finished, he'd asked, 'And they give you hope?'

The question wiped away the last remnants of Casati's smile. Sounding like the worst sort of Old Testament prophet, the older man had answered, 'Only the good deserve to hope.' Then, to show that the conversation was over, Casati had put his oar into the *fórcola* and started to row again.

For no reason, Brunetti's thoughts veered from this memory to the man in the bar trying to silence his friend when he mentioned the 'woman on Burano' that Casati had gone to see. Brunetti recalled as well his own masculine satisfaction that Casati might have found a woman, but now, satisfaction long fled, all Brunetti wanted was to find her.

His reverie was broken by the sound of a woman's voice speaking his name. He looked up and saw Federica, wearing a black skirt and grey blouse and holding the arm of a tall man with a high widow's peak and a thick nose that had been broken and badly set.

Brunetti approached them, and she opened her arms and embraced him. He felt her begin to sob and held his arms around her until she managed to stop and could move back from him, her face averted. Brunetti put out his hand to the man, who shook it a few times and presented himself as Massimo. That done, he stepped around Brunetti to take his wife's arm. There was protectiveness, but no claim of possession, in his gesture.

'Can we see him?' Massimo asked.

'Yes,' Brunetti answered. 'The room is down the hall. After, if he's free, we can talk to Doctor Rizzardi.'

'Is he the pathologist?' Federica's husband asked.

'Yes,' Brunetti answered. 'He's a good man,' he added, then wondered what difference this could possibly make to them.

Brunetti led them down the corridor and stopped at the familiar door. He knocked and the same attendant as the day before opened it. This time, the man stepped back immediately and allowed Brunetti to lead the others into the small viewing room where relatives and friends were taken to identify their dead. He muttered something soft and inaudible as they entered.

The room was as cold as Brunetti remembered it, shocking on this July day. The walls were a neutral grey, the floor enormous dark slate slabs Brunetti had always thought looked unfortunately like tombstones.

A wheeled stretcher stood in the centre of the room; a single window gave out on a courtyard in which a palm tree grew under the protective shade of a pine. He wanted to study the trees, but instead he studied the draped figure on the stretcher. There was the nose, and there, aslant, the feet.

The attendant approached the body and put both hands on the top of the cloth, the part covering the face. 'Signori,' he said softly, 'I am going to uncover his face. I'd like you to tell me if this is Davide Casati.'

Federica and her husband nodded silently. She wrapped her arms around her body, as if hoping to bring some warmth into the room. Her husband placed his arm around her shoulder again, pulling her slightly towards him.

The attendant moved the cloth. Casati's eyes were finally closed, and a sort of baker's cap was pulled down over his forehead. To cover the incision, Brunetti knew and hoped they did not.

Federica stiffened and turned to bury her face in her husband's chest. He coughed lightly once and said, 'Yes, that's Davide Casati.'

'Thank you,' the attendant said and covered Casati's face again.

Brunetti looked at the attendant, who nodded towards the door. Federica and Massimo turned and moved towards it, Brunetti behind them. Somehow the attendant got to the door first and held it open for them. Brunetti let the others leave and when they had started down the hall, asked the attendant, 'Can they see the Dottore?'

'I'm sorry but the doctor's started another autopsy.' Before Brunetti could protest, he added, 'It's a little boy. He had his tonsils out three days ago and was sent home yesterday.'

'He died?' Brunetti asked, hoping he had misunderstood.

'His parents found him last night.'

'That's horrible,' Brunetti said.

The attendant nodded. 'So they asked him to do it immediately. They need to know.'

Who did he mean? Brunetti asked himself. The parents? The doctors? The hospital administration? The police? Dear Jesus, keep my children from harm. He knew it was the worst sort of primitive superstition; he knew there was no-sense to it and no chance that it could help, but he could not stop himself from thinking this silent prayer. And let the boy's parents not be destroyed by this, he added, though he knew that prayer was useless.

Brunetti rejoined the others, saying, 'Dottor Rizzardi can't see you now. He's busy.' He thought it better not to explain.

Federica demanded, eyes wide, 'Does that mean we don't get any information? No one tells us what happened?'

'I spoke to him yesterday, very briefly,' Brunetti said. He led them out to the courtyard and around to the side where few people passed. He sat on the low wall and asked them to join him. He leaned forward so he could see them both and told them what Rizzardi had found: her father had apparently been caught by the storm and had somehow become tangled in his anchor rope and been pulled into the water by it.

Brunetti watched Massimo, who sat beside him, factor in the experience of a man who surely had found himself alone in the *laguna* with wind and rain howling around him. Ropes would be driven wildly along the floor of the boat, almost anything could be picked up by a random gust and tossed over the side. Brunetti saw him nod, accepting the possibility.

Federica, her hands clasped between her knees, stared at the pavement, silent. Brunetti saw her in profile and watched her mouth tighten and relax, tighten and relax as she struggled to understand, perhaps imagine, the scene. Her left hand sneaked from her lap and took Massimo's, and then she asked Brunetti, 'Did he say anything to you while you were out in the *laguna*?'

'He said a lot, Federica. We were together hours every day.'

'I know that,' she said shortly. 'I mean did he say

161

anything unusual? Strange?' Her eyes remained on the pavement.

Brunetti could think only of the times Casati had talked about his bees and the damage that had been done to the *laguna*, but he felt that their spirits had so mingled during those long days that he could no longer judge what the other man had said to be strange.

'No,' Brunetti finally said.

'Did he talk about my mother?'

'No more than to give me a sense that he missed her terribly.'

'"That he missed her terribly",' Federica repeated. She sat upright and Massimo's body blocked Brunetti's view of her, and then said, voice desolate and slow, 'Well, he won't any more, will he?'

Massimo's head whipped round to face her. A moment passed and the fisherman said, 'You told him not even to think about it, Fede.'

'But he went there,' she said with despair that left Brunetti's mouth open. She got to her feet. Massimo stood, as if in response to a current that had passed between them simultaneously. He pulled his lower lip between his teeth and covered his mouth with his right hand. 'Poor man, poor man.'

Massimo reached out his hand and shook Brunetti's. 'Thank you for your help.'

Federica wiped at tears with an inattentive hand, then took her husband's forearm in a strong grasp. 'We'll go now,' she said.

'Shall I go to the boat with you?' Brunetti asked.

'No,' she answered quickly. 'I think we'd like to be alone.' She turned and walked towards the door that led to the main exit, her husband beside her. After a few steps, she stopped and leaned against Massimo, who put both arms around her and held her for some time. Then she moved away from him, wiped at her face, and started walking again. Brunetti watched them go, certain now that he would return to Sant'Erasmo the next day.

Brunetti could think of nothing better to do than to go for a long, purposeless walk, which took up some hours of the afternoon, after which he went home and had a nap. After dinner, he explained the scene at the hospital, trying to make his vague feelings clear to Paola. They still sat at the dinner table, dishes stacked at the side of the sink, drinking their coffee.

'It's all grey, everything that happened,' Brunetti finally said. 'It might have been an accident; he could easily have stepped into the coiled rope – remember a couple of years ago, one of the crew of a vaporetto did that and it took his leg off him.' Telling that story was no help, he knew; every accident was different from all others, and there was no real connection.

'She asked if he ever said anything strange to me,' he told her. 'And whether he talked about her mother. If you'd heard her voice when she said he wouldn't miss her any more, your hair would have stood up on your head, believe me. *That* was stranger than anything Casati said to me.' If despair had a voice, in that instant Federica had used it, and if her father's death had been the result of his own despair, she would have reason for it.

'It could mean a number of things,' Paola said.

Brunetti agreed with her but said, 'Yesterday, before I found him, I was in the bar at the other end of the island, talking to some of the men he knew. One of his friends said something about his going to visit a woman on Burano, but the man he was talking to quickly turned the conversation away. It was nothing obvious, but I sensed there was something they didn't want a stranger to know. It was just a false note, and I didn't pay much attention to it at the time. But the islands are small places, and there are no secrets.' He set his cup on the table and got to his feet.

'If he'd gone to see this woman, it would at least be a sign of life, of still being in life.'

'And the daughter would have to feel jealousy, not despair?' Paola asked. 'Is that better?'

'Yes,' Brunetti declared. 'A thousand times better.'

'May I say something terrible?' Paola surprised him by asking.

'What?'

'The most interesting reactions are the most spontaneous ones.'

'But this is life, not a book,' Brunetti said, pretending her remark had not irritated him.

'As you will, Guido,' Paola answered.

18

The next morning, Brunetti called Vianello on his *telefonino* at eight and asked if he could perhaps call in sick and meet him at the Fondamente Nove *embarcadero* at nine-thirty and go out to Burano with him.

'Not in uniform, I assume,' the Inspector answered.

'No. We're just going out to ask some questions.'

It took the Number 12 more than half an hour to get to Burano, and during the trip, Brunetti explained what had happened to Casati and what they had been doing before his death. He told Vianello about the death of the bees and how much it had upset Casati, and how he had taken the samples of the dead insects. Vianello followed closely, nodding as he began to recognize the pattern of Brunetti's days.

Brunetti, halfway through his story, realized how weak it all sounded, at least as a reason to ask Vianello to come out to Burano with him. So he confessed: 'He spent much of his life on boats. It's hard for me to think he'd be so careless, but I want to exclude the possibility that he ... that he chose to go and join his wife.'

'And if you find he had a ... woman,' Vianello asked, 'would that be enough?'

'Yes, and for his daughter, too. I hope,' Brunetti said.

When Vianello made no response to that, Brunetti added, 'Maybe I just want to learn more about him.' As he said that, Brunetti realized that Casati had been the only man with whom his father had never quarrelled, the man his father had always considered his only friend. But he couldn't say this, even to Vianello.

'Let's do it, then. Besides, I've always liked Burano,' the Inspector said.

Brunetti nodded to acknowledge the remark and then asked, unable not to, 'What's happening with Ruggieri?'

'He says now that he remembers giving the girl two aspirin. She told him she had a headache, and he said he always takes them to parties in case he needs them.' Vianello's voice could not have been more dispassionate.

'How convenient that he remembered,' Brunetti observed.

'The people who saw him give something to the girl now say they might well have been aspirin. They're not sure any longer.'

'And so?'

'And so that's probably going to be the end of it,' was all Vianello said.

Brunetti looked out the window of the vaporetto and saw they were passing Mazzorbo. Many things passed. Eventually, Brunetti knew, all things do.

'What do you want to do when we get there?' Vianello asked at the sound of the slowing of the boat's engine. 'Try to find the woman?'

'Later,' Brunetti answered. 'I'd like to go to the post office and see if he was sending the samples from there.'

The boat pulled in and tied up, and the early crowd of tourists disembarked, going off in search of their Indonesian-made Burano lace and Chinese-made Murano glass, certain that, out here on a genuine Venetian island, they'd be sure to get the real thing. And at a better price.

Brunetti saw a café on the left, and they went in. The woman behind the bar smiled in welcome and asked what they'd like. Both of them had coffee and home-made brioche, which both of them complimented. When they were finished, Vianello took a twenty-Euro bill from his wallet. As he waited for his change, he asked, 'Signora, could you tell me where the post office is?'

'Don't you poor people have a post office in Castello?' she asked, hitting Vianello's accent right on the nose.

'Only in Via Garibaldi, Signora, or I can go to Sant'Elena if I want,' Vianello answered straight-faced, exaggerating his Castello accent to tell her he understood the joke in her question.

'It's easy to find,' she said. 'You know where Da Romano is?'

'Yes.' Vianello had eaten there many times, and always well.

'Turn into the *calle* just before it, and cross the bridge. That will take you right to it. It's open until two.' She gave Vianello his change with a smile, and the two men left the bar.

The post office stood on Rio Terranova, stuck between a *tabaccheria* and a shop selling masks and other souvenirs. They entered and found a broad wooden counter behind which sat two women. There were two old men standing in front of the first, two old women in front of the other.

Brunetti glanced around for some sign of an office and saw an open door just opposite the entrance.

Inside, a grey-haired man of about his own age sat behind a desk, talking on the phone and not looking very happy at what he was hearing. He saw Brunetti and Vianello, nodded but held up a hand, suggesting he'd be with them as soon as he finished the call.

They retreated from the doorway but not before they heard him say, 'But we need to stay open until two, Direttore. There's no way we can reduce our hours.'

There was no air conditioning, only one large ceiling fan that moved the air from place to place with no effect on the temperature. They stood and watched the old people collect their pensions or pay their bills, and Brunetti was struck by how slow each transaction was. On both sides of the counter, only first names were used, and there prevailed a sense of long familiarity. There was even a strong resemblance in body type and clothing. Indeed, they could all easily be members of the same family.

Ten minutes passed, and still one of the old women remained at the counter. Brunetti started towards the open door just as the man inside appeared on the threshold and waved them inside. Closer to him now, Brunetti saw the soft roundness of his face with an accumulation of flesh under his chin that was very soon to declare itself a separate entity. He wore a short-sleeved shirt and a strangely wide tie that attempted to conceal the straining buttons beneath it. When the man reached his desk, he turned and asked, 'Signori, how can I be of use to you?'

'Signor Borelli, a pleasure to meet you.' Brunetti, who had seen the sign to the left of the door, extended his hand and gave his name and rank. Then he introduced Vianello.

'We're here,' Brunetti said, 'about one of your customers.

Well,' he amended, lowering his voice and speaking more slowly, 'a former customer.'

'Yes?' the man inquired, apparently not connecting the term with Casati's death.

'Davide Casati,' Brunetti said.

'Ah,' Borelli breathed, 'I heard about it. Poor man.'

'Did you know him?' Brunetti asked.

'Perhaps,' he surprised Brunetti by answering. 'I see people in here all the time and recognize many of them, but I don't know the names of all of them. If he came often, then the women at the counter would know him. They're the ones who have direct contact with our clients.'

'In that case, I'd like to speak to them,' Brunetti said. 'If I might.'

'Nothing easier,' the Director said, moving towards the door. The old woman had disappeared and the two women were chatting amicably.

The Director walked over to the counter and said, addressing the woman on the left, who looked older than the other, 'Maria, these gentlemen would like to speak to you and Dorotea about someone who might have been one of our clients.' That captured their attention, and they both looked at Brunetti and Vianello to see what this might be about. 'I'll be in my office,' Signor Borelli said to no one in particular, nodded to Brunetti and Vianello but made no move to shake their hands or to explain to the women who they were. He went back to his office. This time he closed the door.

The women's eyes turned to Brunetti, then to Vianello, and the older one shifted some papers to the right, as if a clear desk would make it easier to answer questions. The one named Dorotea continued to look back and forth between Vianello and Brunetti, trying to assess which of the two men was in charge. To make it easier for her, Vianello took a step backward, leaving Brunetti in the front line.

'It's about Davide Casati,' Brunetti began. He could see that both of them recognized the name.

'Did you know him, either of you?' Brunetti asked, trying to sound like an insurance adjuster or a friend of the family.

The younger one raised her hand in a timid gesture, like a child in elementary school who had the answer but was afraid to speak until the teacher called on her.

'Did you, Signora?' Brunetti asked in his softest voice.

She cleared her throat and said, 'Yes.'

'Was he a client here?'

'Yes,' she said, then hesitated as though to signal that this was only half of the answer she wanted to give and Brunetti would have to question her to get the other half.

'Was he someone you knew, as well, not just a client?'

'Yes.'

'May I ask how that was, Signora?' Brunetti asked, tilted his chin, and smiled to show his innocent curiosity.

'I went to school with his brother's grandson,' she said. 'When we were kids.'

'Of course, of course,' Brunetti said, smiling at this happy coincidence. 'The islands are so close.' He might have been speaking of geography, but he might as well have been commenting on the fact that everyone knew everyone. And their business, and their private life. He nodded in satisfaction and he could see her slowly begin to relax.

'He married a friend of my sister,' she added, as if Brunetti had asked about her childhood friend and not Casati.

'I see,' Brunetti said and forced his entire body to relax. 'And Signor Casati, did you know him?'

She turned in evident distress to her older colleague, who took this as a request that she answer for her. 'Dorotea handles parcels, so she knew him. I take care of pensions.' Then, as if she feared being accused of having provided insufficient information, she added, 'We both can do pensions.' Having said this, she placed her hand on the pile of papers, as though taking an oath upon them.

'Ah, parcels,' Brunetti said, returning his attention to Dorotea. 'So if he received a parcel or sent one, he'd have had your help?' Even as he phrased it, Brunetti knew he would have to travel widely in the country to find anyone who would pose the question in this way when referring to the service doled out by the Ufficio Postale. But she smiled and nodded, so perhaps that was how she envisioned her work.

'Yes, I helped him a number of times,' she said proudly.

'Ah,' came Brunetti's polite expression of surprise. 'Did he receive a lot of parcels?'

'No, but he sent some, especially in the last few months.' She glanced aside at her colleague, who gave a small nod of approval, and went on, her voice taking on a confiding tone. 'He told me he tried to do it with DHL, but after he spent a half-hour on the phone without getting in touch with them, he gave up and decided to come to us.'

'I see, I see,' Brunetti muttered. Then, seeming to recall that they had been talking about parcels, he asked, 'Were they big things he was sending?'

'No. Small. Less than half a kilo. And as long as it's small, we're really much cheaper than DHL. And just as fast most of the time,' she added quickly, perhaps hoping that Brunetti had something small in his pocket he wanted to send.

Brunetti nodded thanks to her implied offer while he

tried to think of a country where the scientific testing of insects and soil might be done. 'Are those the ones he sent to Germany?'

'No, Switzerland,' she said. 'To the University. Of . . . it begins with "L", but it's not Lugano.' She stared down at the counter, as if trying to visualize the envelope. A smile blossomed. 'Lausanne.'

Her colleague, Maria, broke in, as though she could no longer contain herself, and said, 'It's terrible, what happened to him.' Then, pitching her voice in the range proper for discussing victims of fatal diseases or souls lost at sea, she said, 'May he rest in peace.'

Brunetti lowered his eyes to the floor and, along with Vianello, observed the seconds that propriety gave to the recently deceased.

While they were still silent, two people came in, about his age, obviously a couple. They paid three bills and left, saying very little, perhaps uncomfortable at the sight of the two strange men.

Vianello then asked, 'Did the University ever send him anything?'

Dorotea was quick to answer. 'No, not to him.'

Vianello smiled at the evasion and asked, 'Then to whom did they send it?'

Dorotea turned to her colleague, and they exchanged the glance that two people suddenly realizing they'd stepped into quicksand would give one another. 'Well,' Dorotea began. 'That is . . .' She looked to her older colleague, perhaps to ask for help in pulling her feet out of this.

'Some letters – return receipt requested – have come from the same university to . . . a person Signor Casati knows,' she said. Then, quickly, 'Knew.' Brunetti decided to let her tell him at her own speed, as though the letters were a minor detail in which he had little interest. He let the time pass.

'Patrizia Minati,' she finally said, but before she could continue, Maria interrupted to add an important element. 'She's a divorced woman.'

Brunetti gave her what he tried to make a knowing look, somewhere between disapproval and prurient curiosity, but when he saw Vianello's face he realized how poor his own effort was and returned his attention to Dorotea.

'She lives here?' Vianello asked, managing to sound as though he were just managing to stop himself from asking how she dared do so.

'Over by the church,' Maria added, as if this geographic liberty somehow compounded the offence of being divorced.

When it was apparent that she would say no more, Brunetti asked, 'Can't people get mail delivered on Sant'Erasmo?'

Again, it was Maria who answered. 'Of course they can. But these letters were addressed to her, not to him.' Then, just in case he might not have understood, she added, 'Since they came from the same university, they must have been for him,' she said and left it there.

'I'd certainly say so,' Vianello broke in to comment, his respect for her acuity audible in his voice.

Brunetti sensed that the women were growing restless, and so he said, 'Thank you both. You've been very helpful.' That brought satisfied looks to their faces, and Brunetti and Vianello used the opportunity to leave.

Outside, Brunetti saw that Vianello was busy on his iPhone. 'You trying to get her address?' he asked. Vianello nodded and pushed more numbers. Brunetti's lack of faith in technology in general and Telecom in particular led him to telephone Signorina Elettra.

'Good morning, Commissario,' she answered. 'How very nice to be in touch with you again. How may I help you?'

'Could you find an address for Patrizia Minati, on Burano?'

'Certainly,' she answered pleasantly. 'Would you like to wait?'

'Yes,' he said, looking over at Vianello, who was still pecking at the keys of his phone.

Brunetti looked around at the houses. The colours were cheap and garish and battered his eyes, flailing at one another in competition for his attention. No one would think of wearing any of those colours as clothing. Children, perhaps. Or lunatics. Red that made him think of the poisoned candies that were sold to children in Victorian London, green like Irish fields, blue the sky would never dare to wear. But as he considered it, he realized that fishermen who spent the entire day looking at the sea, either blue or grey or somewhere in between, and at the sky, either with or without clouds, would be glad to come home to colour, even this mad excess.

'Are you still there, Commissario?' she asked.

'Yes,' he answered.

'Calle del Turco, down at the end, last house on the right. I checked it in *Calli, Campielli e Canali*.'

'And could you have a look if there's anything we should know about her?'

'I've already started, Dottore.'

'Then take a look at Davide Casati while you're looking, please.'

'The man who died out there?'

'Yes: anything you can find. Any trouble with us' – though Brunetti very much doubted this – 'work history, health problems. You know what I mean.'

'Of course, Signore. And for Signora Minati, as well?'

'Please.'

'I'll get to it,' she said and broke the connection. At that instant, Vianello looked across at him and shook his head. 'Nothing,' he said, 'We'll have to go over to the church and ask people there.'

'Calle del Turco,' Brunetti could not prevent himself from saying. 'Last house on the right.' Vianello's expression made him laugh.

It took the Inspector a moment to recover, but when he did, he said, 'She should be mayor.' He considered this and corrected himself. 'She'd be wasted. A chimpanzee could be mayor.'

Brunetti's mind turned to local politics and he said, 'Indeed,' then passed to more serious things.

19

Nothing is very far from anything else on Burano, so they were quickly on the other side of the island, approaching the church of San Martino. Following the map provided by Vianello's *telefonino*, they cut through Campiello San Vito and over the bridge. Right, then left, then down a narrow *calle*, and they were in front of the door of the last house, the name Minati on the bell for the first floor. The house, a shocking yellow, seemed tri-polar: the windows on the ground floor were shuttered tight, with no sign that anyone had opened those shutters for years. The first floor had flower boxes on every windowsill, behind which crisp linen curtains rustled in the slight breeze; the floor above had the withered look of a house that was no longer occupied; the shutters were sun-cracked and dry as driftwood; weeds grew from the metal gutters.

They rang the bell, waited and rang it again. After a long time, they heard the slithering sound of curtains being pushed back. A woman a few years younger than Brunetti, with dark copper hair, leaned out of a window and asked, 'Yes?' She stood with her hands braced on the windowsill, arms stiff, looking down at them.

'I'm Commissario Brunetti, Signora,' he said, and gestured towards Vianello, saying, 'This is Ispettore Vianello, my assistant.'

'Brunetti?'

'Yes,' he answered, stepping back so that looking up at her would be easier on his neck. 'Are you Signora Minati?'

She confirmed this and asked, 'Police?' sounding uncomfortable. Brunetti nodded, although he thought she might not have seen the gesture from above.

'Why have you come?' she asked with nervous curiosity.

'I'd prefer to tell you that inside, Signora.'

'Ah,' she said, lifted her hands, and pulled halfway back inside the window. She ran the fingers of one hand through her hair, which she wore in a curly cloud around her head. Finally she asked, 'And if I don't want to let you in, Signore?' She asked it as a real question, one that required an answer.

'We could continue to talk like this,' Brunetti said mildly, glancing around at the other buildings, although there seemed to be no life in any of them. He backed across the street and propped his shoulders against the wall of the house opposite. This would be fine for him, he thought, though holding his neck at such an angle was already uncomfortable and would, he was sure, very soon begin to hurt.

'All right,' she said and disappeared from the window. A moment later, the door snapped open and they went in. The stairs were narrow and well-worn, a single window at the top of the first flight. They turned and continued up the second ramp, where the woman stood at an open door.

'Do you have identification, gentlemen?' she asked; it was only then that Brunetti heard the tremor in her voice. From outside, the angle and distance had prevented him from seeing her clearly. As he reached the landing in front of her apartment, he saw reflected in her face the tension he'd heard in her voice. She was very thin and almost as tall as he was. She had dark eyes surrounded by the deep wrinkles left by long periods under the sun.

Remaining in the hallway, they handed her their warrant cards; she looked at them carefully, glancing up to study their faces and compare them with the photos. Then she handed the cards back, thanking them in a calmer voice. She stepped back through the door and waved them into the apartment.

Brunetti saw four white easy chairs around a thick-legged low table made out of what looked like a carved shutter that must have come from the Middle East. On one wall were rows of tall, narrow framed pieces of Arabic calligraphy, two with what looked like a flamboyant signature at the bottom. Two other walls held framed pages in different sizes, all in a variety of Arabic handwriting. On the last wall were books, leaving the Arab conquest to the other three.

'They're beautiful,' Brunetti said, moving closer to take a look at one of the framed documents. 'What are they?'

'Land registry documents,' she said. 'The others are pages from the Koran.'

'Where did you find them?'

'I lived in Uzbekistan for some years. The municipal office in the village where I worked had records from past centuries. When they decided to get rid of them, no one was interested, so I asked for a box of them and they were happy to give them to me.' She looked across the room and observed, 'I've always found the calligraphy beautiful.'

'Where you worked?' Brunetti asked, ignoring her comment. Vianello, he saw, was walking from one to another of the framed pieces, studying the calligraphy, shifting back and forth to bring it into closer focus.

'For FAO,' she said, naming the Food and Agricultural Organization of the UN but not giving any further explanation.

'What were you doing for them?' Brunetti asked.

'I was an edaphologist.'

'What does that mean?' Vianello interrupted with real curiosity, looking away from the pages towards her.

If she was surprised that this had now become a double inquisition, she gave no sign of it and said, 'It means I tested the soil to see what nutrients were in it. Or were lacking. And the salt content.'

'In the soil?' the Inspector asked.

'Yes.' She looked at Vianello. At his nod, she continued. 'When we found out what there was too much of or too little of, FAO tried to find a natural way to rebalance the soil by rotating crops or planting something that would fix the nitrogen in the soil. Or encouraging the farmers to rely less on pesticides and chemical fertilizers.' She smiled, and Brunetti could see her relax even more. Straight-faced, she explained, 'I tried to convince them that cow-shit's the best.'

Vianello laughed and said right back, 'My great-uncle always said horse was better.'

'Was he a farmer?'

'When he was a young man, that's what most people in Friuli did.'

'I see,' she answered.

While the two of them were speaking, Brunetti had moved behind one of the chairs. When she saw this, Signora Minati said, 'I suppose we'd all better sit down.'

'When were you in Uzbekistan, Signora, if I might ask?' Brunetti said when they were seated.

'Until ten years ago. I was there a total of three years, at the ends of the earth; near the Aral Sea, in a small town called Moynaq,' she said with a small smile. 'We had electricity but little more, and even that wasn't very reliable.'

'How did you test soil?' Brunetti asked. 'Did you have a laboratory?'

She sat with her hands folded in her lap, paying careful attention to his questions. Instead of answering this one, however, she said, 'Before we continue with this, I'd like you to tell me why you're asking me these questions.' When Brunetti failed to answer for some time, she added, 'The only people who've been this curious about my work there were men from the Uzbeki Secret Service. They came to Moynaq to question me.'

'I should have begun by asking you if you knew Davide Casati,' Brunetti said and watched her response to the mention of his name.

She showed no surprise at all. In fact, she looked at him and smiled, deepening the wrinkles around her eyes, then said, 'I was waiting for you to ask about him.' She glanced away and, looking at the quiet motion in her curtains, said, 'He was a good man.'

'Did you know him well?' Brunetti asked.

'At least well enough to know that much about him. As I assume you did, as well, Commissario, if you spent much of the last two weeks rowing with him, unless Brunetti is a more common name than I thought.' She had the grace to smile again after saying this, removing Brunetti's suspicion that he had unknowingly had a computer chip placed in his ear.

Brunetti let a moment pass before asking, 'Could you tell me the nature of your relationship with him?'

'"Relationship with him"?' she repeated, putting ironic emphasis on the first word.

'Yes.'

'I did him favours and he gave me fish,' she said, showing the first sign of exasperation with Brunetti's questions.

'What sort of favours did you do for him?'

'You should know that, Commissario,' she said sharply. 'You saw him collecting the samples of his bees.'

'Yes, I did. The ones he took last week, of bees and soil.'

'He'd sent others.'

'I'd assumed as much,' Brunetti said. He thought of the vial of mud Casati had carried back to the boat. 'Did he want you to read the reports when they came back?' he asked, thinking it better not to mention their visit to the post office.

'Yes. And interpret them.'

'And what did they say?'

'The usual things: varroa, nosema, lack of nutrition, pesticides, chemicals. It's what's killing them everywhere.' Her voice changed and she asked, 'Why do you want to know this, Commissario?'

'Because he seemed troubled by what he found: the bees and the soil. So I'd like to know what the reports told him, if only to put my mind at rest.'

She appeared to think about this and then said, 'Davide came here a few months ago. He'd heard about me. This is a small island, and Sant'Erasmo is even smaller. In population, that is. There are no secrets on the islands. He knew that I'd worked for FAO examining soil, and he knew that

I'd come back here after Uzbekistan, and he knew the rumours that I'd been fired but still had a pension from FAO. My guess,' she said with a resigned sigh, 'is that everyone on the island knows that, and some might even know how much the pension is.'

'Are the rumours correct?' Brunetti asked. 'Were you fired?'

'Yes.'

'What for?'

'For causing trouble.' She pushed herself up straight in the chair, then returned her hands to the way she had been holding them in her lap.

'This was more than ten years ago. I went to Uzbekistan to study what the death of the Aral Sea was doing to the soil. Not to the people, or the animals, or the climate; only to the soil. For the first few months, I made myself ignore anything other than the soil: I didn't see the skin cancers, the dead animals lying in the fields, and I ignored the dust and salt storms. I dug up soil samples, before and after storms, and I ran some tests on them and sent carefully labelled tubes of earth back to the laboratory in Rome, describing the increased salinity.' She looked at the backs of her hands, as he had seen many guilty people do during questioning. Many innocent ones, as well, he reminded himself.

'But after a while, I couldn't pretend any more not to see what was going on. I started to add into my reports comments about the people and the way they were dying – the sea was already dead, so there was no use commenting on that – and the animals, and the crops that didn't grow, except for the cotton that was growing everywhere and that had killed the sea.'

Brunetti looked at Vianello and saw that he was listening to her story with rapt attention.

'I suppose my reports became somewhat uncontrolled, but death was all around me and in the salt that blew in everywhere and was on my body and in my eyes. And all this so that they could grow cotton,' she added.

Neither Brunetti nor Vianello spoke, so she went on. 'But then someone in Rome must have let them know – the people in Tashkent, or the people in Moscow – what was in my reports, or perhaps they quite innocently passed the information on to them. Or, more likely, everything was being read as I sent it. What I wrote was common knowledge to anyone living there, and to many scientists in the West, but the government wanted to be able to deny it.' Her voice suddenly tightened and grew impassioned. 'There are satellite photographs that let you see how much the sea has shrunk in the last years, but the government denies it's happening.'

She looked at them, one after the other, and gave an uneasy smile. 'Sorry, but it makes me wild that this can happen, that they can destroy a *sea*, for God's sake.' She stopped speaking for some time and then went on in a calmer voice. 'There must have been some sort of complaint from the government, so first the men from the Secret Service came to talk to me, and then the people in Rome decided that it was time for me to take early retirement. I understood what was going on, of course, so I decided to accept their offer. I couldn't stand to be there any more and was happy to leave. I'm not a particularly brave person. So I packed up my things and left. But I left the tiny laboratory there, with all the instruments, so the person who replaced me could do the same tests and see the same results.'

'And then what did you do?' Vianello asked, like one of the old men of Ithaca asking Ulysses to tell them what happened next . . .

'I travelled for a while and tried to find another job. But the word was out, I think, and I couldn't find one, at least not in my profession. So I travelled some more.' Again she looked at each of them in turn and said, 'They gave me a very generous pension.

'And then I came here and moved into this apartment; an aunt left it to me, ages ago. And here I live, a retired woman who putters around in the *laguna* in her boat or paddles around in her kayak, but who is known as the scientist who knows about nature.'

'I see,' Brunetti said. Then, impressed but not diverted by the ease with which she'd led them away from the reports on the samples Casati had sent to Lausanne, he asked, 'And Davide Casati?'

Her mouth tightened, as if in disapproval of his tenacity. 'We were almost friends, and beyond that, it's none of your business.' When she saw the effect her brusqueness had on them, she added, almost as an apology, 'Besides – if I might set your perfervid minds at rest – he was still in love with his wife, who died four years ago, a very ugly death from a very ugly disease.' Brunetti watched her debate whether to continue and decide to do so. 'He felt guilty that he couldn't save her. Many men do. When their wives die.'

After a long silence, she went on, only studied patience in her voice now, 'To me, he was a man from Sant'Erasmo who wanted to know why his bees were dying, and someone had told him to ask the woman on Burano who knows about science things.' Then, with what sounded like irritation but might as easily have been the truth, she added, 'I'm sure some of them think I'm a witch. I know spells and secrets and go into the *laguna* in my own little boat and don't tell anyone what I'm doing there.' Again,

Brunetti noted, she had pulled the conversation away from the reports she had read and interpreted.

'What *are* you doing there?' Vianello asked, surprising them both.

'I'm seeing how peaceful and beautiful it is, how lovely the birds are, how perfectly it has evolved,' she answered. And then, after a moment, she added, speaking far more slowly and in a lower voice, 'And I'm watching it die.'

'Could you explain this to me, Signora?' Vianello asked.

She raised a hand and waved in the direction of the water, then forgot about the gesture and her hand fell back into her lap. 'There are fewer birds – some species no longer come here to nest – there are fewer fish. I seldom see a crab in the water. The frogs are gone. The tides don't make any sense any more. And . . .' she began. A sudden tightness came into her voice as she said, 'the earth itself . . .' She stopped, appeared to play back what she had started to say, and turned her head to look out the window.

'What is it, Signora?' Vianello asked.

'Nothing, nothing. I tend to get carried away.'

Brunetti noticed her suddenly casual tone, as though all of this were happening far away and did not concern her. Like most honest people, she was a bad liar.

'"The earth itself" is what, Signora?' the inspector asked.

'Excuse me?' she asked, trying to sound confused but not managing to.

'It's what you began to say: "The earth itself", and then you stopped. I'm curious about what you were going to say.'

'Oh, I don't remember,' she said distractedly. 'It was nothing.'

'I thought, since you work with the soil, that you meant it literally, Signora, about the soil.'

Her face lost all expression, and he watched her repeat in her mind what he had just said. Then she smiled, as if she'd seen an open window through which she could fly. 'No, I meant the Earth, the planet. I suppose I was going to say it's gone mad.' She gave a self-effacing laugh and added, 'I often say that.'

'I think we all do, Signora,' Vianello said and gave her a broad smile. 'I try not to say it in front of my children, though. They're too young for that sort of thing.' Brunetti listened to his friend sounding forthright and honest, pulling her away from the scent that had alarmed her.

'How old are they, officer?' she asked, while Brunetti watched her hands.

'Seven and nine,' Vianello lied. What's more trustworthy than a man with two young children?

'Still so little?' she asked before she thought.

'Yes, I married late,' he lied again. 'I wanted to be sure.'

'And are you?' she inquired.

'Yes, absolutely,' the Inspector said and pasted a broad smile on his face.

Obviously at a loss for what to say, Signora Minati looked down at her hands and saw them, claw-like, grasping one another in a death grip. She stretched out her fingers and pressed her open hands against her thighs.

She looked at Brunetti. 'Will there be anything else?' she asked.

Brunetti got to his feet, quickly followed by Vianello. 'No, Signora, I think that's all. You've been very generous with your time.'

She preceded them to the door and opened it. Brunetti took his notebook from his jacket pocket and wrote in it. He passed her the slip of paper and said, 'This is my *telefonino* number.'

She took it and studied it as though she'd found it in her hand at the end of a magician's trick and had no idea what to do with it. She folded it in half and then again and put it into the pocket of her skirt, saying nothing.

Brunetti offered his hand. She shook it, and then Vianello's, then the two men descended the steps and left the building.

20

Outside, both of them aware that they would be visible from the window, they walked away from the building at a normal pace. As they did so, Vianello said, 'I wonder what she's frightened of. She's been away from Uzbekistan for ten years, so we can forget that.' He sounded certain, and Brunetti thought he was right.

'That leaves the reports that were sent to her,' Brunetti said. He continued walking, looking down at his feet. He stopped and turned to the Inspector. 'Or it could simply be that she's afraid of having two policemen come to talk to her.' Many people would be, he knew but didn't want to say.

They reached the *campo* that led to the boat stop, and as they stepped from the shadow the narrow streets provided, the sun pounded down on them, reminding them that it was July, the worst month. Both of them removed their jackets, Brunetti regretting his concession to respectability by having abandoned last week's cotton Bermudas and tennis shoes.

His thoughts veered towards Paola, and he found himself remembering that she'd once told him how gullible he tended to be about women, abandoning his normal suspiciousness and always willing to believe their moral superiority to men. He defended his normal suspiciousness, if only to himself, with the fact that he had asked Signorina Elettra to see what she could find out about Signora Minati.

As if serving as the voice of Brunetti's conscience, the Inspector observed, 'You weren't very hard on her, were you?'

'No,' Brunetti admitted. 'She seemed an honest person.'

Vianello wiped his brow with his handkerchief but said nothing.

Brunetti missed his baseball cap, regardless of how much it would have made him look like a tourist lost on the island. 'Is this what it's been like in the city?' he asked Vianello, hoping that last night's heat was not to be a constant.

'Yes,' Vianello answered. 'Worse. Here, at least there's a breeze off the *laguna*. There, nothing.'

They reached the *embarcadero* and went inside the covered platform to escape the sun. The air was close and humid and it seemed hotter than outside, but at least the roof had put an end to the sun's flagellations. They sat on one of the benches, leaving a space between them to encourage the reluctant air to circulate.

How had he managed to stay outside and row with Casati all day in this heat? Had effort and concentration transformed light into a caress and driven heat from his mind? Here, inside this airless trap, he found it impossible

189

to imagine that other world of endless space and limitless horizons.

'She never said anything about the results from the soil samples, only about the bees,' Brunetti said aloud. 'She talked about the diseases the bees have, and then she wandered away and talked about Uzbekistan. When she started to say something about the soil again, she stopped herself.'

Vianello nodded. 'When I asked her, she went all mystic on us and said she was talking about the whole Earth. Which I don't believe for a minute.'

'I'm not so sure,' Brunetti said, though he made himself sound reluctant.

'Why?'

'Some people think that way, that it's all a unit, a whole, all connected together.'

Vianello turned to him and asked, 'So?'

Brunetti suspected that little was to be gained from a discussion of the nature of the universe and answered, 'So we ask Signorina Elettra to call the University of Lausanne.' He took his *telefonino* from his pocket. That was quickly done. First, Brunetti told her when Casati was likely to have sent the parcel, then he explained Casati's strange remarks in the days before his death and his unending grief for his wife, although he stopped himself from saying anything about where this might have led.

'I'll call the university and ask about the parcel and the replies.' There was a pause, that, even over the phone, Brunetti sensed was important. 'What about the Vice-Questore? Should I speak to him?' Signorina Elettra finally inquired.

So long as the Vice-Questore was made to believe that Brunetti was doing no more than taking advantage of the fact that he was already on Sant'Erasmo to speak to the dead man's family and ascertain his state of mind before his death, Patta would cause no trouble. He might even be pleased to have time to prepare some glittering prevarication for the press about the concern the police took over every citizen's death.

'It might be better to say nothing to him at the moment,' Brunetti decided at last. 'After all, it's being treated as an accident.'

'"Boat accident during the storm",' she affirmed, and then she was gone.

When he turned to look at Vianello, he saw that his friend was leaning forward, his head in his hands, moaning.

'What's wrong?' Brunetti asked, fearing the heat had struck Vianello down.

The Inspector shook his head from side to side, then sat up and rested it against the partition behind him. Eyes closed, he said, 'The more I hear, the more I begin to believe that you are giving serious thought to the possibility that a man killed himself because his bees were dying.'

Sweat covered Vianello's face, and sweat had plastered his shirt to his chest. Brunetti looked around the *embarcadero*, but they were still the only people in it. 'The boat's coming, Lorenzo.'

Vianello opened his eyes and pushed himself to his feet. 'It's like trying to save Pucetti, only I can't explain how it is. It doesn't make any sense.' He glanced sideways at Brunetti and threw his hands up. 'But maybe it does.'

The boat pulled up and they got on. They moved to the shade and chose to remain outside to catch what breeze there was. Neither spoke during the trip to Sant'Erasmo.

As the engine shifted down, Brunetti said, 'I'd like you

to come with me to talk to Casati's daughter.' When Vianello didn't answer, Brunetti said, 'She's the only person who might be able to tell me what he was really like.'

'But you just spent ten days with him, didn't you?' Vianello asked.

'Yes. He taught me a lot about bees and made me see how wonderful they are, he showed me how to be a better rower, and he told me about the fish and birds in the *laguna* and the tides, but he never told me much about himself. Sometimes he'd say things that weren't clear to me, terrible things about death and destruction that I didn't understand.'

Brunetti took out his handkerchief and wiped his face, using it almost as if it were a towel. 'But I never really felt that I understood him,' he admitted, folded his handkerchief and put it back in his pocket.

The sailor pulled back the metal bars, and the passengers began to file off the boat, all of them involuntarily flinching away from the sun as they stepped into its rays. Vianello stood with his arms folded, looking off in the direction of Venice.

Saying nothing more, Brunetti walked past Vianello, following the others, his hearing and sense of space searching for Vianello behind him. When he heard the Inspector's footsteps and sensed his closeness, he felt relieved that he would not be alone when speaking with Federica and assessing whatever it was she said.

As they walked away from the dock, the sun did its best to pound them into the ground but managed only to exhaust and irritate them. After what seemed a long time, Brunetti turned into the path that led to the villa and held the door for Vianello. Inside, he led his friend towards the back of the house and into the kitchen.

Without bothering to ask permission, Vianello went to the refrigerator and pulled out a large bottle of mineral water. He opened a cabinet, closed it, opened another, and pulled down two tall glasses. He filled them both and handed one to Brunetti. After they'd emptied the glasses and set them on the counter, the Inspector asked, 'Where can I wash my face and hands?'

Brunetti pointed down the corridor. The sound of a door opening and closing drifted back into the kitchen. Brunetti poured two more full glasses and carried them back to the sitting room where he had taken to reading and sat in the chair he thought of as his. He saw Pliny lying face down on the table beside him and left him there. He crossed his legs, leaned his head against the back of the chair, and waited for his friend to join him.

When Vianello did, he handed him one of the glasses, and the two men sat silently for a few minutes before Brunetti said, 'He had terrible scars down his back. I saw them when we went swimming: horrible things. Burns. Rizzardi said it was chemicals, not a fire. I've never seen anything like them.'

'Did he ever talk about them?' Vianello asked.

Brunetti shook his head. 'No, and I couldn't ask. I acted as if they weren't there.'

'Of course,' Vianello said but didn't ask anything.

They sat silently, safe from the heat and sun, hearing nothing but the occasional buzz of a far-off motor or the squawk of a gull.

'You really think he could have killed himself?' Vianello finally asked.

Brunetti remembered the strange sensation that had overcome him as he first approached the capsized boat, although the nameless, formless sense of danger had burned away once he began to study the boat. Perhaps he was inventing the feeling, and it had been no more than the effect of hours under the sun and the delayed shock of having fallen into the sinkhole.

'He might have,' he said. 'He knew too much grief.'

Vianello looked around this room as if to savour the peace of it. 'He could walk out his front door and dive into the *laguna*. Where it's clean. He had his boat in front of his house. He lived with his family.' That was all he said, and Brunetti realized that, in modern times, these things probably didn't count for very much any more. But on Sant'Erasmo, they did.

'We should talk to his daughter,' Brunetti said. It wasn't an answer, but it might provide one.

They walked down the path to the little house, saw the fishing nets draped in the sun on both sides and, behind them on the right, a large trellis of grapes running towards the end of the garden, a small bicycle lying on its side beneath it.

Brunetti knocked on the screen door, and after a time Federica opened it. 'Come in,' she said in an empty voice and turned towards the back of the house. 'In here,' she said, opening a door at the end of the corridor. Chairs stood around a long wooden table with elephantine legs, probably used only for large family meals. There were three dark velvet easy chairs arranged in a circle near the window, but they wore plastic coverings and were thus unavailable for use.

Brunetti and Vianello sat on one side of the table, Federica on the other, facing Brunetti. 'What is it you'd like to know?' she asked. She was the same woman he had met almost two weeks ago, who had brought him his breakfast and prepared meals for him, with whom he had often spoken, the same woman he'd seen going into and leaving her home and then at the hospital the day before, but the light was gone: her eyes were sombre, her movements slow, her voice level and without inflection. He realized that her eyes reminded him, now, of something he had seen in Casati's, and the thought chilled him.

'Federica,' he began, 'my sorrow is nothing like yours. I know that. But I want to speak to you as a friend, as a man who thinks of your father as a friend. I say that because I want you – and need you – to trust me.' He spoke without thinking, with no anticipation of how she would react.

'What do I have to trust you about?' she asked in an uninterested voice.

'I want to know more about your father,' he said.

Her eyes shot to his, and her expression changed to the one he had seen on his own children's faces when he or Paola had to talk to them about something wrong they had done. He saw something stronger than the shifty trace of unspoken guilt in Federica's eyes. Her voice grew soft, almost fearful, and she asked, 'Why?'

'He wasn't the same, not with me, during the last days we went rowing together,' Brunetti said.

Federica looked at the surface of the table. After a moment, she swept her hand across it in a cleaning motion, as though there were dust or something dirty on the surface. Then she wiped it again, this time in an arc that reached farther from her body, then she folded her hands in front of her. 'Why are you telling me this?' she asked the surface of the table.

'Because I want to understand what happened,' Brunetti said.

Beside him, Vianello nodded but said nothing.

'What do you think happened?' she asked, glanced up at

him, then down at her hands. When Brunetti didn't answer, she said, 'You have to say it, Guido. I can't.'

'I think he might have given up on life, Federica. I've seen it in people before. They give up from sickness or from trouble, or from things other people can't understand.'

She closed her eyes and sat motionless for a long time. Finally she looked up at him and said, 'We tried. All of us. Massimo, the kids. But it wasn't enough, no matter what we did.'

Brunetti waited, leaving her to tell it as she could. 'When Mamma died, he went inside himself and didn't talk about it or about her. At first, I thought it would get better, but it didn't. All he said was that he was guilty for what happened to her. He watched her die – it took more than three years – and then when she was dead, all he'd say was that he killed her. Nothing more. Then, when his bees began to die, he said he was killing them, too. Nothing anyone said to him made any difference.'

She looked at them, as if to ask if they could understand such madness, but neither seemed capable of answering.

'Over the last few weeks, he became worse.' Her voice had changed, Brunetti noted: a rancorous note had come into it. 'It's that woman on Burano, I'm sure. Ever since he started spending time with her, he got worse. It was like she poisoned his life.' Gathering momentum, she went on. 'Every time he came back from seeing her ...' she began, and before he could ask, she said, 'I have friends there, and they told me when he went to see her.' She closed her lips and pulled them inwards, as though she wanted to prevent them from speaking.

'I tried to talk to him, but he wouldn't listen. Massimo wouldn't say anything to him; told me I was being foolish.' Suddenly her face softened as she said, 'Then you came and went out rowing with him, and he seemed his old self for a while, even though he kept seeing her. But then it stopped. And then this happened.'

She forced her hands to embrace one another in some sign of peace, and stopped talking, hands folded in front of her.

'Did he ever say anything that would lead you to think . . . ?' Brunetti asked.

She shook her head.

'He seemed very wise to me,' Brunetti heard himself say. 'But I always had the feeling that he had struggled or suffered to earn that wisdom.' He watched her face as he said this, realizing only now that this was indeed the opinion he had formed. 'I think he had to learn how to be good.'

Federica looked from him to Vianello and back. Then she turned and looked out the window that gave on to the garden and the trees, and, far beyond them, to the Dolomites, invisible now and waiting for the next rain to sweep the air clean enough to bring them back to visibility.

'My mother was much younger than my father,' she said. 'More than twenty years. He was forty when they married, and she was only eighteen. I was born when my mother was nineteen.'

Neither man acknowledged in any way what she was saying: they'd learned that this was the best way to behave once a person began to speak.

'When I was a little girl, we lived in Marghera because they both worked there. He worked in a factory and she worked in a warehouse. Then, when I was about nine, he was in an accident – he never wanted to talk about it, and my mother wouldn't tell me anything – and he was in the hospital for a long time. Months, I think. But I don't really remember because . . . well, I was a child, and children have strange memories. I remember that I went to live with my mother's brother then, in Castello, and went to school there.' Then, as though surprised at the realization, she said, 'I must have spent a long time there. Because I went at the beginning of school, and I stayed. When school finished, I didn't go back to Marghera but came out here to live. I remember because the day I came here from my uncle's was my birthday.'

'Were you happy to move out here to the island?' Vianello asked.

'My uncle's wife . . .' she began, and Brunetti found it interesting that she did not refer to her as 'my aunt'. Then, leaving that to stand alone, her face softened towards a smile and she continued. 'I liked having my parents again.' Did she sound hesitant when she said that? 'Yes,' she added, suddenly decisive, 'I did: I had my mother back, too. She'd stayed there and been with my father in the hospital. But then we all came here and could live together again.' It sounded to Brunetti like a child's recitation of a fairy tale.

'I had my *mamma* and *papà* back again, and I could go swimming all the time. And my father, when he came back from the hospital, started to fish and got the bees, and he didn't have to go to the factory any more and come home angry all the time.'

Because she was still concentrating on the garden, Brunetti and Vianello exchanged a quick glance but remained silent until eventually Vianello said, 'That's a big change.'

'Yes, it was. He was happier. Well, I thought he was happier. My mother was, too.' She continued to think about this and added, 'He was quieter, too; he never got angry any more, and that was wonderful.'

Brunetti broke in here to say, 'It's hard for me to imagine your father being angry at anything.'

'No, not after we came here, he wasn't.'

'And his bees?' Brunetti asked.

'Oh, he got them when he came here. First my parents rented a house, and then my father got the job as caretaker here, so we moved to this house and there were bees here already.' She stopped for a moment and then said, 'They're still there.' She put her hand to her mouth. 'Who'll take care of them?'

21

Silence descended until Brunetti thought to ask, 'Do they need much taking care of?'

His question seemed to trouble Federica, who took her hand away and closed her eyes. Brunetti noticed her left hand, gripped into a fist. He was afraid she was going to cry.

'I don't know,' she said in a broken voice. 'I never learned what to do. All these years, watching him and going out with him to see them, and I don't know what to do with them or when, or what to feed them in the winter. I never really paid any attention to what he was doing. He tried to explain, but I wasn't interested. I just wanted to eat the honey.' She took a deep breath.

It's always the odd, unpredictable things that set us off, Brunetti thought. Grief lies inside us like a land mine: heavy footsteps will pass by it safely, while others, even those as light as air, will cause it to explode.

When at last she looked at Brunetti, she said, 'Maybe I was jealous of them. Is that possible?' She tried to shake the idea away. 'Of bees?'

Brunetti smiled to show he understood what she meant. 'If they took his attention away from you, then it makes sense that you'd be jealous, especially when you were a child.'

She nodded, wanting to believe him. Then she sat straighter in her chair and folded her hands in front of her. 'What do you want to know?'

'I went swimming with your father, and I saw the scars on his back. Do you know anything about them?'

She shook her head, first confused by his question and then confused by her own response.

He watched as she sent her mind into the past. Her eyes contracted a few times, and then she said, 'It was the accident. He didn't have the scars when we were living in Marghera, but then the next summer, when we were out in the boat and going swimming, he had them. I still remember seeing them for the first time. I think I started to cry, they were so awful. But my mother told me not to be silly: if my father could forget about them, then so should I.'

'Did she tell you how your father got them?' Vianello asked.

'I asked her,' Federica said, 'and she told me that they were why he was gone for so long, because he had to get better from them.'

'Do you have any idea what work he did?' Vianello asked.

She must have anticipated this question, for she said at once, 'He was a pilot and moved things from the different parts of the factory.' She gazed into her childhood years, remembering. 'He used to draw me pictures of the boats he piloted and tell me about the canals that went around the buildings and out into the *laguna*.'

'This was before the accident?' Brunetti specified.

'Yes. He always loved the *laguna*, even when we lived on *terraferma*. I remember he told me about the tides – even if I didn't really understand.'

Brunetti watched as memory surfaced and she went on. 'After we came out here, he gave me a book about the birds that lived there.' She bowed her head and propped her elbow on the table so she could put one hand to her forehead. 'I still have it: *Uccelli della laguna veneta*. It was a book for grown-ups, but he read it to me and explained the things I didn't understand.' She took a few deep breaths and said, 'I read it to my children.'

'This was after the accident?' Brunetti asked.

Head still lowered and eyes shielded by her hand, she didn't reply at first. 'Yes,' she finally said. 'He didn't read to me before. My mother did, but he usually wasn't there when I went to bed.'

'Do you know where he was?' Vianello interrupted.

She lifted her hand and looked at the Inspector, who had spoken softly, as one would to a girl.

'My mother always complained that he was out with his friends.' She looked back and forth between them, as though to see which of them would be the first to accuse her of disloyalty to her father.

'Sounds like my wife,' Vianello said with a smile that suggested he was exaggerating.

'He really was,' she admitted. 'My mother would get angry, and they'd argue, and then he'd leave and come back after I was asleep.' That said, she rubbed her hands together and began to pick at one of her fingernails. 'I think he drank a lot. Then.'

She looked at the two men, and said, 'I remember that's the way he was before we came out here. But then it was as if we'd come to a magic country where people changed into the person you wanted them to be, and all of a sudden my father became quiet and patient and had time to read to me.'

'And your mother?' Brunetti asked, allowing himself to slip back into the part of good cop.

'Ah,' she said, dragging out the syllable. 'She was very happy for a long time. More than ten years. I finished school and found a job on Murano.'

'When was that?' Vianello asked.

'Oh, when I was nineteen. I took the summer off after school, and then I found a job in a glass factory, in the office there.' She thought for a moment and added, 'There was lots of work then. Not like now.'

'And later on, what happened?' Brunetti inquired.

'My mother was diagnosed with cancer,' she said flatly.

Silence settled into the room and forced itself upon them.

'I had just had my daughter when she was diagnosed.' She took a deep breath, shrugged. Then, with the ease of a schoolgirl pronouncing the name of a foreign classmate, she said, '*Mesotelioma pleurico polmonare.*'

Vianello broke in to say, 'How awful for you all.'

'Yes,' she said simply. 'My father disappeared after she died.'

'Do you mean he went away?' Vianello asked.

'No, but he might as well have done that. I'd get up in the morning and come over here – we still lived in Massimo's house then – with my daughter to at least have coffee with him, and I'd find breakfast ready for me on the table. Coffee made: all I had to do was put it on the stove.'

'And your father?' the Inspector asked.

'He was gone; so was his boat. After Massimo got home in the afternoon, I'd cook something to eat and come over here and leave some for him, and in the morning it was gone, and the dishes were washed and put away, and breakfast was ready for me. But sometimes I'd go a week without seeing him.'

'And when you did, did you ask him what he was doing?'

'Only once. He said he was in the *laguna*, looking for a reason not to kill himself.'

'*Oddio*,' Vianello exclaimed in a soft voice.

She got to her feet and went over to stand by the open window. There was no view of the water from there, but the sky was lightened by its reflection. Brunetti didn't know whether she was tired of talking to them or tired of being observed by them.

'How long did he do this?' Brunetti asked.

'Until April,' she answered. 'My mother had died in December.' She gave them some time to consider this, then said, 'Yes, all winter, and it was a bad one. He was out there, rowing, every day.'

'And in April?' Brunetti asked.

'One morning, when I came over for breakfast, he was sitting at the table, drinking coffee. He got up when I came in and put his hand on my arm and asked if we'd like to come and live with him. All he said to try to persuade me was that we'd have more space here. At the time, I thought it meant he was better, but now I think it meant only that he was lonely.' She barely managed to speak the last words.

'What happened then?'

'He started going out to fish again and selling the fish to people here and to restaurants in Venice. And then in May, when he opened up the hives after the winter, he began to make honey and sell that.' She took a few breaths and then continued. 'He talked less, but it was always my mother he talked to most, not to me.' Her attention during all of this was directed outside the window, as though she were speaking to the bird that was twittering away in the fig tree near the garden wall.

'Did he stay like that?' Brunetti asked.

He saw her nod her head and then shake it before she said, 'Until about six months ago,' and nothing else.

'What happened?'

She turned to face them and said, 'His bees started to die. At first he said it was part of the natural cycle, and then he brought home some medicine against something that sounded like "Verona". After about a month, he came home one day and told me he'd burned four of the hives he had at one place. He was shaking, like someone confessing to a terrible crime. He told me it's what some beekeepers do when the hives are infected and they can't get rid of the parasites,' she explained.

'Did it work?'

She shook her head again. 'Nothing did. They kept dying, all except three other hives he kept – I think they were out in the *laguna*, too. He didn't have any trouble with those, but all the other bees, he said, were sick with something he couldn't understand, and there was nothing he could do to stop it. They kept dying.'

'Is there anyone who could have helped him, anyone he might have told?'

'Not that I know of. No. He had some friends here, but he was the only one who kept bees. Besides, he never talked a lot.'

Brunetti thought back over his days in the boat with Casati and realized how little interchange there had been. He'd been told about bees and fish and birds, and how to build a boat, and how to navigate by the stars, but Casati had never explained why he had built his own boat, nor why he had chosen to live out there on Sant'Erasmo.

'Did he talk to you about the bees?' he asked. 'And what was happening to them?'

'I suppose he did,' she admitted. 'But I didn't pay much attention.' She bowed her head, and he feared she was about to make some confession of bad feelings between them. Then she admitted, 'We didn't talk much. I still missed my mother. It's been four years, but I still miss her every day. And I didn't want to tell him that.'

'I imagine he did, as well,' Vianello interjected.

'Of course he did,' she said, her voice unsteady. 'He didn't show he missed her,' she added, sounding angry. 'Except by going to the cemetery. But then he found someone else to talk to.' The last sentence could have been spoken by a different person.

'Do you mean Signora Minati?' Brunetti asked.

'Did you see her? Talk to her?' she demanded, the words tumbling from her mouth.

'Yes.'

Her look was fierce but strangely childlike: he had seen it on Chiara's face many times when she thought she had been unfairly treated. 'What did she tell you?' Federica asked.

'That your father asked her to interpret some laboratory reports for him,' Brunetti explained calmly.

'"Laboratory reports?"' she repeated, as though they were words from some other language.

Brunetti nodded; so did Vianello. 'He sent samples to a laboratory at the University of Lausanne, and when the analysis came back, he asked her to explain it to him.' Coming from Brunetti, and in that tone, it sounded like the most normal thing in the world.

'Is she a doctor?' Federica asked. 'Was something wrong with him?'

Brunetti smiled at this. 'Yes, I think she's a doctor, but not a medical doctor. She studies soil and what's in it and what can be done to change it. At least that's what I gathered from what she told us.' Vianello nodded again, but nothing could change the look of complete bafflement on Federica's face.

'I don't understand,' she said. 'I don't know what you're talking about.'

'He'd sent some of his dead bees to the lab, and some time later he sent a vial of soil. I was with him when he collected samples, but he'd been doing it for quite a while,' Brunetti said, then changed the subject. 'We had a drink in a bar on Burano. The men there seemed to know him. Do you know who they might have been?'

She shrugged. 'He knew a lot of people, but I don't think they were friends. You know how men are.'

'What do you mean, Signora?' Vianello broke in to ask.

'Men – you – don't have friends,' she said with quiet certainty. 'You have companions and pals and colleagues, but very few men have friends. If they do, it's usually women, sometimes their wife.'

When he heard her say this, Brunetti's masculinity took offence and he asked, 'That's something of a generalization, wouldn't you say, Federica?'

'Who's your best friend?' she asked right back. Then, turning to Vianello, she said, 'And yours?'

Brunetti was stunned by the audacity of the question and the prejudice that stood behind it. He was about to explain that Vianello was far more than a colleague when he chose the path of greater wisdom and turned her question into one of his own. 'Was your father still in touch with any of his old friends from Marghera?'

After a moment's surprise, Federica accepted what was obviously his offer of peace and answered, 'Zio Zeno. Zeno Bianchi.'

'Excuse me?' Brunetti said.

'He's my godfather,' she explained. 'He was my father's best friend at work.'

'Ah,' exclaimed Brunetti. 'Where is he now?'

'He's in Mira.'

'Do you mean he lives there?' he asked. It was close enough, no more than twenty minutes away from Piazzale Roma.

'Yes. Sort of,' she said.

'I'm sorry, Federica,' Brunetti said. 'I don't understand.'

'He's living in a kind of nursing home.' Then, in a slower voice, 'He's been there for a long time.'

'Why is that?' Vianello asked.

'Because he's old, and he's blind and has nowhere else to go.'

22

'My mother told me he got sick at about the same time my father had his accident,' Federica began. 'Some terrible eye disease they couldn't do anything about.' She called back her memory of those events, then continued. 'He used to come to dinner at the house in Marghera.' Finding something she was glad to remember, she added, 'Zio Zeno never married. He always told me he'd wait for me to grow up and then he'd marry me.' She smiled, as people always do at the thought of happy families and happy times.

'He was in a hospital – I think it was in Padova – for a long time, but it didn't help. And then some place for rehabilitation. My mother said he wasn't the same after it happened because he hated to be helpless, always needing other people.'

'But what could he do, poor devil?' Vianello said, his voice rich with concern. 'He couldn't work. You said he had no family.'

Federica interrupted in her turn and went on. 'And the state certainly wouldn't take care of him: they'd give him a miserable pension and put him in a nursing home somewhere and forget about him.' Shaking herself free of this reality, she continued. 'It was a long time ago, and things were bad then.' She looked from one to the other and added, 'Maybe they're better now,' although her scepticism was clear.

'Why did he go to Mira?' Brunetti asked, as though it were the end of the world.

'I don't know. No one ever said why.'

'Has he been in the nursing home all this time?' Brunetti asked. A nursing home in Mira, of all places.

Federica took a long time to answer, and Brunetti was afraid she was going to object to his continuing questioning, but she was merely trying to remember. 'I really don't know too much,' she said. 'My father called him once a month or so, always on Sunday afternoon. And he was always sad after they talked.'

'Did your father ever go to see him?' Brunetti asked.

She shook her head a few times, absolute negation reflected in the speed with which she did it. 'No. Zio wouldn't let him come because the place was so terrible. My mother told me he once said that sometimes there wasn't even enough to eat. He couldn't stand to have my father see him there.' She looked to make sure they understood a man's dignity, and then added, 'My mother told me he said he could hear Zio crying when he said that.' They sat in silence, thinking of the state-run nursing homes in which they had seen their relatives, perhaps their friends, put.

She started to speak, coughed, started again.

Brunetti heard the whish of cloth on cloth as she uncrossed her legs under the table. 'I never understood why he kept calling him. They hadn't seen one another for years, and still they talked once a month. What could they tell one another?'

Neither man tried to answer this question.

'Would you know how to get in touch with him?' Brunetti asked. 'Your Uncle Zeno?'

'I'm sure I have his phone number somewhere, and his address. 'I'll look for it. I know I have it.'

'Thank you,' Brunetti said and studied her face, which seemed less troubled than it had when they started talking. 'I have to go into the city again, but I'd like to come back and stay a bit longer. Would that be all right with you?' he asked.

'Of course,' Federica was surprised into answering. 'I'm glad you're here. With my father gone, it gives me someone to talk to.' While the thought ran through his mind that this was a strange thing for a married woman to say, Federica added, 'During the day, that is. Massimo's gone by four and doesn't get back for twelve hours. That's a lot of time to spend by myself.'

'Have you stopped working?' he asked.

'Yes. With two children, you know . . . Besides, there's much less work at the factory, so they don't need me any more. Most of the glass comes from China now: no one can compete – not when they put "Made in Murano" on it.'

'Can't you stop them?' Vianello asked.

She gave a resigned smile in which there was anything but humour. 'It's like trying to stop *acqua alta*,' she said.

They sat in silence for a moment, three Venetians, relatives at the wake of a city that had been an empire and was now selling off the coffee spoons to try to pay the heating bill.

Brunetti saw Federica prepare to say something, but then stop. He waited. She opened her mouth and this time she found the words, or the courage, to ask, 'Why do you want to know about Zio Zeno? He's blind and in a nursing home out on the mainland.'

'You said he was a close friend of your father's and spoke to him regularly for years.' Brunetti remembered what she had said about the friendships of men, then continued, 'So I'd . . .'

She started to interrupt him, and again stopped.

Putting on his softest voice, Brunetti said, 'What were you going to say, Federica?'

'I don't know if they were still talking to one another.'

'Why is that?'

'Recently, I asked my father how Zio Zeno was, and he said he didn't know. I asked him to say hello to Zio when they spoke, and he said he wouldn't be speaking to him again.' She glanced at them, and when neither of them commented, she said, 'They've spoken to one another once a month for ages, and suddenly they weren't speaking.'

'Did you ask him why?' Brunetti wanted to know.

She shook the idea away. 'When my father spoke in a certain way, I knew there was no use insisting or asking him questions. He'd made up his mind, and that was that.'

'No idea?' Vianello asked.

'None. You can ask Zio Zeno when you speak to him,' she said. 'I'll go upstairs and get you the number.'

After Federica's footsteps had receded into silence, Brunetti looked across at Vianello and asked, 'Well? What do you think? If they both spent months in the hospital, it would be in their employment and medical records, wouldn't it?'

'Even if it was so long ago?' Vianello asked.

'The ways of the computer are many and mysterious,' Brunetti answered in a falsely solemn voice.

'I have faith in the computer,' Vianello said, 'but not in the people who enter information into them.'

Brunetti swept his friend's doubts aside by saying, 'We need a date, and we need the name of their employer. Then we can begin looking. There's always something.'

'And this blind man, Zeno Bianchi?' Vianello asked.

'We go to talk to him as soon as we can.'

'About?'

'About his blindness and its cause and about why he and Casati no longer spoke to one another.'

Vianello put his palms together and turned them over to look at the back of his right hand, as though he sought there what he wanted to say. 'Guido,' he began but did not finish the sentence.

Brunetti was suddenly alert to the tone of Vianello's voice and suspected he knew what was coming.

'Yes?' he asked with studied mildness.

'Are you sure you know what you're doing?' Vianello's glance shot to Brunetti's face and as quickly away.

An idea had been growing in Brunetti's imagination since the time Casati had spoken about how 'we' had killed 'her' and killed the bees and would go on to kill his grandchildren and Brunetti's children. At the time, it had seemed nothing more than wild, raving talk, and to a certain degree it still did. But not entirely.

It took him some time to think of a way to answer Vianello. 'No, I'm not sure, not at all,' Brunetti said. 'But I'm doing what I want to do and what I think is right to do.' That was all the explanation he could give. 'Is that enough?' he asked his friend.

'Yes,' Vianello answered.

At the sound of Federica's returning footsteps, both men sat up straighter and turned to face the door. She entered, a small slip of paper in her right hand, walked over and placed it on the table in front of Brunetti. 'It's the number of his *telefonino*, and that's the name of the place where he is,' she said. 'It's all I have.'

Brunetti thanked her and put the paper in his pocket. 'Do you remember the name of the company where they worked?' he asked.

She glanced out the window and rubbed absently at her right cheekbone. Eventually, she said, 'It was named after the wife of the owner. M something: Maura, Mar . . . No, not that.' She pulled her lips together and said, 'M, M, M,' but it appeared to bring memory no closer. Her face changed in an instant, and she smiled. 'No, it's R. "Romina Rimozione". Her name was Romina, and the company removed things.' She turned to smile at Brunetti and tapped her finger on her forehead. 'It's all in there. Still.'

'Did Signor Bianchi live in Marghera, too?'

'Oh, I thought I'd told you. At San Pietro in Castello, in one of the apartments above the cloister.' Seeing Brunetti's confusion, she said, 'To the right of the church, there's that big doorway that goes into the cloister.

'He lived on the top floor,' she went on. Before they could ask, she explained. 'I never saw him there, but once when I went with my father into the city – this was after we moved out here – we took a walk down to San Pietro, and he told me that's where his friend Zeno used to live.'

'You said he never married,' Brunetti reminded her.

'No. And he was a handsome man. But then,' she began and paused briefly to think this through, 'I suppose all tall men who are friends of your father are handsome when you're a little girl.'

Smiling, Brunetti said, 'I certainly hope that's true of my daughter's friends,' and got to his feet.

Federica put herself between Brunetti and the door, trying to make the motion seem natural, and failing. 'When will . . .' she began.

She ran out of words, and Brunetti supplied them. 'I think the pathologist will give a release in a day or two.'

'Not before that?' she asked, stricken by the delay.

'I'm afraid not, Federica. I'll ask them, but these are things we – the police – don't control. I'm sorry.'

She nodded.

Brunetti bent and kissed her on both cheeks, and Vianello extended his hand and shook hers. Brunetti and Vianello started back towards the villa.

23

'Does it make any sense for us to stay here?' Vianello asked as they left Federica's house.

'No. There's nothing we can do here for the moment,' Brunetti answered. While he had been speaking to Federica, he'd seen a trail open up before him, a trail made seductive by the unexplained. Two men working for the same company had been hospitalized at the same time, and a long friendship had been ruptured soon before one of those men died. Brunetti knew himself enough to know he would not ignore this trail, just as he knew that to return to Venice would be to put the first foot on that trail.

'How do we get back?' Vianello asked.

'Same way we came: on the boat.'

Brunetti left a note for Federica on the kitchen table, explaining that he was returning to the city for a few days but would call her when he knew when he'd be back and would do his best to find out when her father's body would be released for burial.

There was nothing he had to take with him, aside from his keys; he went upstairs to get them and to close the windows and shutters, leaving it to Vianello to close the ones on the ground floor. They walked to the *embarcadero*, each wrapped so deeply in his own thoughts that neither reacted to the heat and humidity. During the ride, he called Signorina Elettra and told her that he and Vianello were on the way to the Questura, and while they were, he'd like her to try to find some record of . . . here he had to pause and look out the window to find a way to express what it was that might have happened. 'An accident in Marghera, at least twenty years ago, involving a company called Romina Rimozione. There are two men who might have been injured: Davide Casati and Zeno Bianchi.'

'Ah,' she exhaled, making the sound last a long time. She did not sniff, she did not wag her tail, nor did she pull at the lead, but Brunetti could sense her desire to be off in pursuit of what might be only a rustle in the grass but might just as easily be prey.

'The second one,' Brunetti continued as though he had not heard her sigh, 'spent months in a hospital in Padova. His problem was his eyes: whatever happened left him blind. The other was burned badly, though I don't know where he was treated.'

'Anything else, Dottore?'

'Have you had a response from the university?'

'No, nothing yet.'

'Is there any way you could . . .' he began and left the question unfinished, not wanting to be recorded suggesting to his superior's secretary that she break into the computer system of a university in a foreign country.

'I'm reluctant to do anything like that in Switzerland, Signore. They're very good at placing tripwires, and since the request was made through official channels, there will eventually be an answer. All that's needed is time.'

Brunetti knew that, but it did nothing to still his impatience.

'All right,' he said and pulled the paper Federica had given him from his pocket. 'There's a nursing home somewhere in Mira: Villa Flora. Could you have a look and see what sort of place it is? From what I've heard, it must be ... basic.' It seemed a neutral way to describe a place that could reduce a man to tears when speaking about it.

'Of course, Signore. If they have a website, I'll send you the link.'

'We'll be at Fondamente Nove in fifteen minutes. Could you ask Foa to meet us?' Brunetti asked. When she said she would, he broke the connection.

When they pulled up to the landing, Brunetti saw the police launch bobbing in the water a few metres to the right. As the passengers started filing off the left side of the boat, Foa pulled alongside the other, and the sailor pulled back the metal bar and saluted the two police officers as they stepped on to the smaller boat bobbing beside them.

Foa touched his hand to his cap and swung away from the Number 13 in a graceful pirouette that started them back towards the entrance to the Rio dei Mendicanti that would take them quickly to the Questura.

Brunetti studied the building as they approached and was surprised to see someone standing at the window of his office. He was even more surprised when, as they drew closer, he could discern that it was Vice-Questore Giuseppe Patta, who stood, like a whaler's widow, two steps back from the window, casting his gaze to left and right in the only directions from which his beloved could return.

He nudged Vianello in the ribs and said, 'Patta's in my office.'

It was with the exercise of enormous restraint that Vianello refused to look upwards, thus losing the opportunity some day to tell his grandchildren what he had observed with his own eyes.

Foa glided up to the dock, and the Inspector followed his superior off the boat, careful to raise his eyes no higher than Brunetti's head.

As they entered, the guard in the glass security booth raised his hand, then stood and came over to open the door. 'Commissario,' he said, leaning out. 'The Vice-Questore would like to see you in his office.'

Brunetti nodded his thanks, and both men went silently towards the stairway. At the bottom, Brunetti paused for a moment and said, 'Perhaps we should give him time to get back to his own office.'

'You'll spoil him if you're not careful, Guido.'

Brunetti allowed two minutes to pass before he put his foot on the first stair. Vianello veered off towards the officers' squad room. Brunetti walked towards his superior's office and into the small anteroom, where he found Signorina Elettra, who was that day lightening the burden of the heat with white linen. Her blouse threw beams of reflected light at Brunetti. It gave the impression of flowing looseness, as though the material had alighted on her shoulders while being wafted to some astral location. Anyone glancing at it would at first think it should be worn by a larger person. Until, that is, the viewer observed just where the shoulders ended and how the pleats slid open when she raised her arm to push back a strand of hair.

'How nice to have you back, Commissario,' she said, her face tossing a few more beams his way.

'One of life's oft-repeating joys,' Brunetti said.

'To come here?'

'In a word, yes.'

'The Vice-Questore has just arrived and is waiting for you.' With a sly smile, she added, 'Another joy.' Then, with an upraised hand, 'Perhaps I should tell you, Commissario, that he's not in the most tranquil of moods.'

'How unusual,' Brunetti said, passed in front of her desk, and went to the Vice-Questore's office. He knocked, a sound that was acknowledged by a bark.

'Good afternoon, Vice-Questore,' Brunetti said as he closed the door. He came across the room.

'Sit down.' Patta's eyes reflected quite a different light from that of Signorina Elettra's blouse. Brunetti had had years to learn the signs of Patta's irritation, and he saw immediately that the signals the Vice-Questore gave were mild. This, however, did not allow him to relax: Patta was as dangerous impatient as rabid.

'What's going on?' his superior demanded. Brunetti found it interesting that Patta had said nothing about his recent, prolonged absence from the Questura nor about his supposedly compromised health.

'If you're referring to the man from Sant'Erasmo who died while I was there, I know only what everyone on the island knows: he was caught in a storm, fell from his boat, and drowned.' Hearing this, Patta waved a hand, which Brunetti interpreted as an invitation to sit. Patta today wore a light tan linen suit, but this late in the afternoon, the elbows looked like accordions. Had he been doing push-ups while waiting for Brunetti to arrive? As was always the case in the summer – as well as after the two winter vacations he managed to afford himself – Patta was bronzed and as sleek as a well-oiled cricket bat.

'Actually, I was talking about the problems Avvocato Ruggieri has been having.'

Aha, Brunetti told himself. Of course, and what a fool I am. How could Patta be interested in a man's death when the son of a wealthy notary had suffered momentary embarrassment?

'I'm sorry, Vice-Questore,' Brunetti said, 'but I know nothing about that.'

'Then why are you here?'

'Because I found the body of the man who drowned, Dottore, I thought it correct to file a report in the hope that this would speed things along.'

Patta's eyes narrowed in a look so filled with suspicion that Brunetti feared he might soon be subjected to physical torture. 'Is that the truth?' Patta demanded in a voice he made deep enough to hold all of the menace he injected into it.

'Yes, sir,' Brunetti said. 'I haven't thought about that interview since it was interrupted,' he said, trying to look like a person who had recently suffered a collapse from a weakened heart.

Patta put his wrinkled elbows on the table, wove his fingers together, and rested his chin on the bridge formed by his fingers. He kept Brunetti under scrutiny for a few moments, like an entomologist waiting for a dung beetle to begin rolling up its ball of lies. Finally he said, 'I hope, Brunetti, that this isn't another one of your—'

A knock on the door cut Patta off.

'Come in,' he barked.

The door opened, and Signorina Elettra appeared. 'Ah, Vice-Questore, I didn't know anyone was with you,' she said, and gave every appearance of being embarrassed at having interrupted them. 'You said earlier that you wanted to send an email to the Prefetto.' Only then did Brunetti notice that she had a notebook in her hand. Was she actually going to take Patta's dictation? His superior was indeed a remarkable man.

Brunetti's face showed no expression as he got to his feet. 'I'll leave you to your work, Dottore,' he said with a small nod. He went slowly to the door and paused to allow Signorina Elettra to pass in front of him, then he went out and closed the door.

Her chair stood far back from her desk, as though she had pushed it away hurriedly. A page of text filled the screen of her computer, and a headset lay in front of it. YouTube? In the fashion of all good detectives, he decided to be sure, as if her choice in music would tell him something important about her.

He walked to her desk and, consciously ignoring the computer screen – which he considered taboo unless she showed it to him – picked up the headset, placed one of the earpieces to his left ear, and listened. 'No, Dottore,' he heard her say, 'I think it should go in a registered letter. An email is too informal.'

'*Oddio*,' Brunetti whispered, replaced the headphones quietly on her desk, and left her office.

24

As Brunetti walked back to his office, he asked himself why a place as modest as the one Federica talked about would have a website. The sort of place where patients were kept hungry would hardly cater to the computer literate. But then he recalled that even the shelter where the city sent lost or abandoned dogs had a website. Brunetti paused and reflected on the way one thought had suggested the other; the spontaneity of the comparison embarrassed him. He should take the hungry old man a box of chocolates.

He nevertheless clicked on 'Villa Flora, Mira', sure that the photos would attempt to make spare rooms look inviting or grim-faced patients happy. He prepared himself to view a cement bunker pretending to be home.

Where had that tremendous villa come from? Where that rose garden gambolling happily up towards it? He read the captions and learned that this was Villa Flora, Mira. There could certainly be only one home for old people named Villa Flora in Mira.

'An ambience where our guests will feel entirely at home.' 'Villa Flora offers only a change of address, not a change of life.' 'Why should retirement mean you're no longer special?' 'Well, well, well,' Brunetti muttered under his breath. 'America comes to Mira.'

Brunetti looked through the photos again, more slowly this time, and read the historical information about the building. Designed by a friend of Palladio, the villa – the information insisted – was very much in the master's style. Brunetti clicked back to the photo that served as the backdrop for the web page. Any influence by Palladio was from the architect's early years, Brunetti decided, for the building resembled nothing so much as the fierce, fortress-like Villa Godi, where Brunetti had taken his family years ago, mistaken in his certainty that the kids would love the archaeology museum in the basement.

He clicked to the photos of the separate suites on offer: there were nineteen of them. Each had a sitting room, a bedroom, and a bath: meals were served in the dining room, though they could be taken privately. Much of the furniture in the residents' rooms could easily have been taken from his parents-in-law's *palazzo*: spindly-legged tables, velvet-covered sofas, ornate gold-framed mirrors; while the bathrooms looked like those in a five-star hotel: twin sinks, shower heads the size of pizzas, gold fixtures.

The dining room was what he imagined cruise ships boasted: fields of white linen, glistening cutlery, three glasses at every place. Drapes were pulled back from the French windows; beyond lay formal gardens filled, at the time of the photo, with an excess of roses of every colour, each large section of the garden neatly enclosed by low boxwood hedges. And the staff? As Brunetti had guessed, they were described as 'top professionals in their fields', 'highly motivated to treat every resident as a guest', and were always aware that 'a guest is a member of our family'. Scrolling down, he saw many pictures of the staff, always smiling, always extending a hand to help.

He went back to 'Home' and looked for a key word that might be related to costs or prices, but nothing was to be found. He tried 'Services' with similar lack of success. Instead of spending more time searching, he dialled Signorina Elettra's number.

'Sì, Commissario?'

'I've got the website of Villa Flora in front of me,' he said, 'but I can't find any place that lists prices.'

'They're called "fees" now, Commissario,' she informed him in a voice that suggested reproach.

'Of course,' Brunetti answered, sounding suitably chastened. 'And these fees?'

'Two thousand Euros,' she said.

'But that's nothing for a place like this,' he exclaimed, having clicked back to the photo of the façade of the villa and remembering that this was the same sum he had paid for the nursing home where his mother had lived out her life.

'A week, Signore,' she added.

'Maria Vergine' escaped him. Where would a factory worker find more than a hundred thousand Euros a year to pay for a retirement home? From what Federica had told him, it sounded as though Bianchi had been reduced to tears by hunger.

'That's beyond belief,' he protested, without knowing why.

'Indeed,' she answered and said she had another call.

When she was gone, Brunetti considered tactics. Two

policemen arriving to question a blind old man, two men with their deep voices: did he want that? Someone had once told him that blind people could smell the difference between men and women; not because of perfume or aftershave but because of their different hormones. Women smelled sweeter, he had said, something that influenced even the sighted.

He dialled Griffoni's number; when she said she was not busy, he asked if she'd come up to his office. While he waited, Brunetti went and looked out the window and allowed anomalous information to move around in his mind: a few dead bees in a plastic vial, the Aral Sea, two thousand Euros a week, dark mud in another vial. If they were pieces on a board, would he be able to move them round so that they formed a picture?

Griffoni's knock pulled him back from these reflections. As soon as she came in, tall, blonde, and with the casual assurance of a woman who had always been aware that she was beautiful, he knew she was a better choice than Vianello, even if Bianchi would not see her.

'Claudia,' he said, 'I'd like you to help me.'

An hour later, Foa pulled up to the dock at Piazzale Roma, where an unmarked car was waiting. The driver, who was not wearing a uniform, got out to open the rear door when they approached, even snapped out a salute, which Brunetti attributed to the shortness of Griffoni's skirt.

During the twenty-five minutes it took them to get to Mira, Brunetti finished telling her the last of the story: the price of the retirement home.

'The accident happened twenty years ago?' she asked, ignoring the rows of stores that lined both sides of the highway and concentrating on what Brunetti had just told her.

'More or less. Signorina Elettra is still trying to find out what happened. Why do you ask?'

'Because if this man Bianchi's been there since then, he's paid them more than two million Euros.' She glanced away momentarily and then looked back at him and said, speaking with quiet emphasis, 'I can't even count how many years I'd have to work to earn that.'

They turned into a road that ran along the right side of the Brenta canal. Brunetti made no comment, waiting to hear more of what she thought. 'Someone's paying for him, then,' she said. It was a declaration, not a question. 'We can exclude the possibility of insurance,' she went on in the same tone. 'They'd drag something this expensive through the courts for decades before they'd pay.'

Brunetti nodded in agreement but said nothing.

She leaned back in the seat and turned away from him, watching the large houses and extensive gardens on their right. 'Who'd pay?' she asked in a low voice, as if speaking to herself.

After asking that, she turned to Brunetti and repeated, 'Who'd pay?'

By way of answer, Brunetti said, 'And if someone was paying, why weren't they also paying Casati?'

'Because he was hurt in the same accident?'

'I have no proof of that,' Brunetti answered. 'But it makes sense: they were hospitalized at about the same time and kept in touch for years.'

'Why was that, do you think?'

'No idea.' When Griffoni did not comment, he continued. 'All I know is what Casati's daughter told us: old times, old friends who had an argument, and the misery Bianchi lived in.'

At that moment, the car turned through the iron gates in

the fence that isolated Villa Flora from the rest of the world and headed up the gravel drive. The façade of the villa declared itself, upright and square and glowing warmly in the sun, the garden in front of it dappled with white and red roses.

Griffoni bent forward to see more of the building and garden. 'Misery,' she said and leaned back in her seat.

The driver stopped in front of the building, got out, and opened the door for Griffoni. Together she and Brunetti started up the steps. He raised the small brass lion head that served as knocker and hit it a few times against the metal plate beneath it.

After some time, the door was opened by a woman who wore a dark blue jacket and mid-calf skirt that might have been a uniform or merely a sober taste in clothing. In her fifties, she had a plump and amiable face that succeeded in making them feel welcomed by the smile she flashed at them. A plastic ID card was pinned to the right lapel of her jacket, adding to the argument that it was a uniform. It bore her photo and name: Anita Segalin.

'Welcome to Villa Flora,' she said. Her eyes were a deep brown and moved slowly from Brunetti to Griffoni and back again. Though neither of them answered, she flashed them another smile that resided exclusively in her mouth. The flash erased, her face returned to its normal passivity, her eyes continuing to move back and forth between them, assessing things. 'How may I help you?'

'We've come to visit one of your residents,' Brunetti said, choosing that word in place of 'patients', a word that seemed out of place in these surroundings.

'And who might that be?' she asked, stepping back to allow them to enter a long hallway illuminated by the sunshine that flowed in from the rooms on either side.

'Zeno Bianchi,' Brunetti answered.

A half-second before Brunetti spoke the name, Signora Segalin had flashed him another tight smile, as though both to encourage his memory and congratulate him for coming to see any resident of Villa Flora. 'Ah,' she breathed when she heard the name. 'He'll be delighted; he has very few visitors.'

'I'm sorry to hear that,' Brunetti said.

'And you are?' the woman asked.

'Guido Brunetti, and this is Dottoressa Claudia Griffoni.'

Signora Segalin's eyes widened slightly and she asked, 'Dottoressa?'

Griffoni put on her warmest, most disarming smile and said, 'Not of medicine, I'm afraid, Signora.' This time, she looked mildly relieved.

'Public Administration,' Claudia said, a half-truth, for she had taken a degree in this before taking another in Law.

'Is there some problem?' Signora Segalin asked, as though this were an official visit of some sort. The question was not followed by a smile.

'Nothing that can't be sorted out very quickly, I'm sure,' Griffoni said with easy confidence. 'The new regulations for persons with handicaps are very complicated, and I wanted to explain some changes to Signor Bianchi.'

Signora Segalin nodded, as though she completely understood this desire. Brunetti thought of the way Alvise's wife had spent the last six months going from office to office, trying to get a public health nurse to come to visit her grandmother, more than ninety, who had been confined to bed for the last four years. Perhaps the sort of people who could afford Villa Flora were accustomed to greater solicitude from the social services: certainly Signora Segalin appeared to find nothing untoward in their unannounced visit.

'I last saw Signor Bianchi in the gazebo,' she said, semaphoring her pleasure at the word, eager to help now that she knew these people had something to do with public administration, the broad group charged with visiting rest homes to see that the rules of patient care were being followed. 'I'll take you to him.' She turned and walked swiftly towards the back of the building; they followed, drawn along so quickly that they had little time to pause to look into the rooms on either side of the corridor.

Brunetti glanced through the first doorway they passed and saw an enormous bouquet of mixed roses standing on a narrow table, magazines and newspapers fanned out on both sides of it. From the next room floated what he thought might be a Chopin nocturne, badly played, but when he glanced inside, the view was too narrow to allow him to see anything but the curved back of a grand piano. At the end of the corridor, the woman paused and opened a thick wooden door. The door, Brunetti noticed, had a normal metal handle that was pressed down to open it, not the long metal bars of fire exits he was accustomed to seeing in nursing homes.

Outside, a gravel path led to a small gazebo covered with trailing roses, the sweetness of which he could smell at a distance. Signora Segalin stopped when they were still a few metres away and turned to flash them another smile. 'Let me go ahead to prepare Signor Bianchi. He has so few visitors.' She kept her voice low, as if afraid someone might overhear her.

She walked quickly to the gazebo and climbed its three steps. Brunetti watched her approach a man in a white wicker chair, a small dog sitting alertly at his side: he, unlike his owner, watched Signora Segalin draw close. One parent had apparently been a Jack Russell; the other was anyone's guess, so long as it was a dog with very long legs. The dog stood and went over to Signora Segalin, who bent down and scratched at one of its ears.

Brunetti and Griffoni exchanged glances: a dog in a nursing home. The dog turned his attention to the other humans and studied them as they studied the man in the chair. The man, too, had had at least one parent with very long legs, for his knees rose high in front of him, creating a slanted lap on which they could see an old-fashioned transistor radio in his left hand.

Bianchi, for this must be Zeno Bianchi, wore large dark glasses that covered his eyes and much of his upper face but failed to cover the slick red scar that began at the left hairline, appeared to trail under the glasses, then slithered straight down his right cheek and beneath the open collar of his shirt. There was another patch of tight red skin on the right side of his forehead, beginning at his temple and cutting a jagged line upward through his short white hair.

Brunetti knew him to be close in age to Casati, but he seemed years older, with deep hollows in his cheeks and a great deal of wattled skin to the left of the scar under his chin. Even in the cloying heat of July he wore a wool tweed jacket, white shirt, and tie. The upper part of his body curved forward, emphasizing the way his shoulders pushed at the shoulders of his jacket. A woollen plaid blanket bearing signs that it was shared by the dog lay across his lap. He wore light woollen trousers and dark brown shoes.

'Signor Bianchi,' Signora Segalin announced, 'you have visitors. From the social services.' She bent to the dog and said, 'Bardo, you have guests.' The dog wagged his tail at the news. Bianchi gave no response.

Brunetti and Griffoni approached the man and the dog.

Because Bianchi could not see them, Brunetti did not extend his hand, but Bianchi put his left one out in an entirely normal manner, and they both shook it; and, in turn, told him their names.

'Please,' Signora Segalin said, moving quickly to some wicker chairs and sliding two of them to face Bianchi. 'Sit down. Be comfortable,' she told them as they took their places in the chairs. 'I've got to go back to the office, but you can come and tell me when you've solved Signor Bianchi's problems for him.' Long experience with the blind man had apparently taught her not to waste her smiles on him, but she did give a small flash, really little more than a spark, to Bardo, who failed to see it, so eager was he to sniff the shoes and ankles of the new people.

'Is he behaving himself?' Bianchi asked, turning his face in their direction. His voice was weak and high-pitched; Brunetti wondered if he had breathed in fire all those years ago and damaged his vocal cords.

'Yes, he is,' Griffoni said, patting at her lap. Bardo needed little more than that and sprang up, turned a few tight circles before curling himself into another one, careful to place his head where he could keep an eye on Bianchi.

Absently, Griffoni put her hand on the dog's head and, as if milking a cow, began to pull at his ears. Bardo made a small noise and Bianchi said, 'He doesn't like to have his ears touched. Try his neck.'

When Griffoni did, the noise changed: it was surprisingly like the purring of a cat. 'Good,' Bianchi said. 'He likes that.' Brunetti heard a far-off woman's voice: perhaps there was someone walking in the rose garden behind them.

'What is it you'd like from me?' Bianchi startled them by asking.

Griffoni shot a glance at Brunetti; the remark had been made in a very curt voice. 'I'm afraid Signora Segalin confused things,' she said. 'I told her I'd taken a degree in Public Administration, and she drew the wrong conclusion.'

'And the right conclusion?' Bianchi asked, speaking above the woman's voice.

'We're from the police.'

Bianchi said nothing, and Griffoni returned to scratching Bardo's head. The purring noise started again, managing to block out the invisible woman's voice.

'And what is it you want?' Bianchi asked.

'We'd like you to tell us about your friendship with Davide Casati,' Brunetti said. Bianchi turned sharply in the direction of Brunetti's voice but turned too far: his sunglasses were directed to the left of Brunetti's shoulder.

Bardo shifted on to his side, exposing his neck. 'He likes to be scratched there,' Bianchi repeated.

'Most dogs don't,' Griffoni said.

After a long pause, Bianchi answered, 'He's very trusting.' Then, using the past tense to make it clear he was not talking about Bardo, he went on, 'We were friends for a long time. Best friends. I'm very sorry for his death.'

'His daughter told us you spoke to him often,' Brunetti said.

Bianchi didn't answer. He moved his hand a bit, and it was then that Brunetti realized the woman's voice was coming from the radio he held. He hadn't seen one like it for years: black, rectangular, the size of the old Walkman, with a small metal antenna poking out of one corner. As he watched, Bianchi brought his right hand out from under the blanket and used what remained of it to anchor the radio while he moved a dial with the intact fingers of the other hand. The voice of a woman speaking with militant cheerfulness grew louder: 'The Blessed Virgin asks us to join her in the worship of her beloved Son. By reciting the rosary together, we earn her grace and favour. Today we recite the Joyful Mysteries, so let us begin with contemplation of the Annunciation and declare that the time for the Incarnation is at hand.'

The maimed hand put Brunetti in mind of the front end of a crab, a hard pink carapace with two pincers made of thumb and pinkie. He tore his eyes away and looked helplessly at Griffoni: what could they do if Bianchi chose to have them listen to the recitation of the rosary? It began, a chorus of female voices murmuring the incantation he recalled from his childhood.

'That's Radio Maria, isn't it, Signor Bianchi?' Griffoni asked in a friendly, interested voice.

Bianchi's head swivelled until he was facing in her direction. His left hand moved again, and the voice lowered and almost disappeared. 'Do you know the programme?'

'Yes, of course,' Griffoni said with raw delight. 'My mother listens to it every day.'

'She's a believer?' the blind man asked.

'Of course,' Griffoni said again, strongly, proudly.

'Are you?'

Griffoni turned to Brunetti, raised her eyebrows, and shrugged. 'Yes,' she said, then added with audible regret, 'Perhaps I don't do as much as I should – Mass – but I believe.' Then, with sudden force, 'It's a good thing. I can't imagine how . . .' She let her voice fall off. Anyone who didn't know her would be entirely persuaded of her sincerity.

Brunetti heard a click, and the droning voice of the women reciting the rosary was silenced.

Bardo suddenly flipped himself upright, barked once at

Griffoni's face, and jumped to the ground. He ran down the steps of the gazebo, his nails clicking all the way, and disappeared into the garden.

'Will he be all right?' Griffoni asked Bianchi, quite as though he too had watched the dog run off.

'He's a dog, remember,' Bianchi answered. 'He knows his way around.' He lowered his head, then reached his good hand to the table beside him, felt its surface with his knuckles, and set the radio on to it.

'Signor Bianchi,' Brunetti said. 'We'd like you to tell us about the accident that you and Signor Casati were involved in.'

'What did he tell you about it?' Bianchi asked in a peremptory voice.

'We were swimming together, Signor Bianchi. He could hardly hide the results: I was curious about the cause.' When, Brunetti wondered, had he learned to be so mendacious?

He looked back at Bianchi's hands and saw that the old man had covered the stump with his left hand. Twenty years had passed, and Bianchi still thought of this. Brunetti remained silent, waiting to see how Bianchi chose to interpret his answer.

'Why do you want to know?' Bianchi asked.

Brunetti had thought about this on the way and answered putting a great deal of hesitation into his voice. 'His daughter, whom I think you know, is very upset at her father's death, to the point that she thinks it might not have been an accident.'

Hearing this, Bianchi put his good hand to his mouth.

'She's told me that,' Brunetti went on, 'in the last weeks of his life, he seemed troubled and nervous about something. She doesn't know what it was. She asked him, she said, shortly before he died, if anything was wrong, but all he said was that it was something from his past that troubled him.'

Bianchi's face tightened involuntarily. 'And that's enough to make you come out here to ask me questions?' he asked.

'It's enough to make us curious,' Brunetti said.

'Don't the police have better things to do with their time?'

Griffoni let out a guffaw and immediately slapped her hand over her mouth. 'I'm sorry, Commissario. I wasn't thinking,' she said, her voice partially muffled by her fingers. She turned her head to face Bianchi when she added, 'I shouldn't have laughed.'

Brunetti had been looking at Bianchi when she made the noise and had seen tension flee from his face at her words.

In a sober voice, Bianchi asked, 'And if you find nothing?'

'Then I could at least reassure your friend's daughter that it was an accident.'

Bianchi nodded a few times, then said, his voice struggling against what sounded like anger, 'It wouldn't be the first one.' Brunetti decided not to respond and held a hand up to stop Griffoni from speaking.

After a very long time, Bianchi asked, 'Did he tell you it was his fault?'

Brunetti tried to think of an answer that would disguise his ignorance yet make it sound as though Casati might have told him. 'He said that he acted without considering the consequences of what he did,' Brunetti began, watching Bianchi's face. When he saw the old man's lips tighten and his nostrils flare, he went on as though he'd only paused to find the right words to finish his sentence. 'He didn't want to say more than that.'

'No, he wouldn't, would he?' The anger had grown more audible, no matter how hard Bianchi seemed to struggle against it.

'Why not?' Griffoni interrupted to ask, sounding honestly puzzled.

'He didn't consider the consequences of what he did?' Bianchi repeated rhetorically, outrage finally unleashed to streak through his voice. 'Of course he didn't, the fool.' Because his eyes were hidden behind his dark glasses, only his voice and the mouth that spoke the words conveyed his feelings. The voice had grown rough and loud, and his left cheek was flushed almost as red as the scar above it. His good hand abandoned the stump and tightened into a fist.

'Did he tell you he smoked a cigarette in a place where it was forbidden?' Bianchi began but stopped immediately as though that were enough.

Before Brunetti could answer, Griffoni said, 'I'm afraid I don't understand, Signore. What happened?'

'He tripped,' Bianchi answered, turning towards her. 'We were in an area where barrels were stored. Some of them had leaked, but we didn't know that. We were supposed to roll them out to the trucks and boats, but Casati wanted a cigarette, so he stopped to light one.'

On the last words, Bianchi's voice veered out of control. He brought his good hand up, wiped the spittle from his mouth and rubbed it on the knee of his slacks. Brunetti saw a tremor run from his shoulders, down his arms to his two hands.

Bianchi took a few deep breaths and went on in a calmer voice. 'I tried to stop him, but he told me to leave him alone. He lit the cigarette.' As he said this, Bianchi's left hand moved as though he were trying to hold the cigarette while his right struck the match. 'Then he had to show me what a wise guy he was, so he put his head back and blew a line of smoke rings.'

Bianchi stared ahead, facing the past. 'There was a piece of pipe or hose on the floor, half covered in liquid, but he didn't see it. He stepped on it and it moved, must have rolled under his foot.' Bianchi raised his head, and if he could have seen, he would have been looking at the ceiling. 'That's when he fell. He must have dropped his cigarette because, all of a sudden, he was on the floor and there was this line of light moving away from him. Towards the barrels.'

Bianchi pulled his attention back from the ceiling and returned to facing forward, straight between Griffoni and Brunetti. 'That's what I saw, that line of light, and then there was an explosion and heat and more light and then I didn't see anything any more.' He lowered his head and used the fingers of his left hand to rub delicately at the skin on the back of the other, reduced hand.

Silence descended on the gazebo and expanded until they heard a clicking noise on the steps. Bardo had returned. This time he ignored both Griffoni and Brunetti and, as though sensing Bianchi's need, put his front paws on his knees and hopped on to his lap. He danced a few circles then settled comfortably and dropped his head on to his paws, eyes on Brunetti. Bianchi's good hand went to the dog's neck and began to scratch it gently.

'How did you get out?' Griffoni dared to ask.

Bianchi's hand stopped moving; Bardo turned his head and licked it back into motion. 'Davide carried me out of the warehouse before it burned down,' he said, his voice suddenly calm, almost solemn. 'I didn't know that until later. Weeks. They took me to the hospital. All I remember from that time is the pain. And the darkness.'

'How did you find out about what he did?' Brunetti asked.

'Someone from the company came to see me. He asked if I remembered what had happened to cause the fire. I said I didn't.'

'He did that to you and you lied for him?' Griffoni interrupted, making no attempt to disguise her astonishment.

Bianchi's chicken-like shoulders pushed the material of his jacket up, then let it drop back into place. With his index finger, he tapped Bardo on the top of the head a few times and asked the dog, 'He was a friend, wasn't he, Bardo? And you can't drop your friends in the shit, no matter what they've done, can you?'

The dog turned his head and licked at Bianchi's hand again, this time in agreement. Head still lowered to the dog, he went on, 'That's when they told me it was Davide who had got me out of the building and that he'd been hurt. A lot of people saw him coming out of the warehouse, carrying me in his arms like a child. That's what they said. That's when more barrels inside began to explode, the ones with flammable waste, and . . .' He stopped. 'I have some scars on my legs. It burned through the cloth.'

Bardo began to snore, a remarkably peaceful sound. The three of them sat there silently for a long time, listening to the smooth sound of the dog's breath.

'When did you speak to him again?' Brunetti asked.

'Not for months. He called me. I was still in the eye hospital in Padova. He called me and asked me if I'd talk to him.'

'What did you tell him?' Brunetti asked.

Bianchi turned his face towards Brunetti, who saw the man's brow furrow, as though he didn't, or couldn't, understand the question.

'I said of course I'd talk to him,' Bianchi said, and nodded at the simplicity of it.

'Why?' Griffoni asked.

The sunglasses turned to face her. 'I told you. Because he was my friend.'

25

'Of course,' Griffoni sighed. Brunetti remembered that she was Neapolitan and so might understand this more profoundly than many other people, or might be quicker to sense the unease in Bianchi's voice. 'And you remained friends?'

'We spoke last Sunday,' Bianchi said. 'The way we did every Sunday.'

Brunetti quelled his impulse to catch Griffoni's eye. From the beginning of his career, he had schooled himself to disguise his reaction to what he was told or what he saw, and so, even now, when there was no chance that Bianchi would gain an advantage by seeing Brunetti's response, he pressed against it and kept it from his face or voice.

'The way we did every Sunday,' Brunetti repeated to himself. Well, that was a lie, wasn't it? But why would he bother to tell it to the police? And in what way was it related to the lie about his being kept hungry here?

Brunetti's thoughts turned to one of the old sayings popular with his mother and her friends: *'Non c'è due senza tre.'* 'There are never two without three.' Bianchi had told them at least two lies already; what would the next one be?

'Why are you telling us what he did to cause the fire?' Brunetti asked, quite as though he believed the story.

Bianchi gave a slight shrug of one shoulder. 'It doesn't matter any more, does it? Now that Davide's dead.'

Hoping that Bianchi would not sense his suspicions, Brunetti turned towards him, and was prepared to offer some bromide when Griffoni held up a hand to silence him and said, 'How fortunate you are to have had a friendship that lasted so long, Signore.'

Bianchi lowered his head but had nothing to say, either to them or to the dog.

'And how fortunate to be able to stay in a place like this. It's so lovely.' Ah, the woman was a snake, undulant and sly and very dangerous. 'My grandmother was in a home for years, but it was nothing like this.' Then, before Bianchi could speak, she said, raising her voice minimally, 'Not that the place where she was had anything wrong with it. Not at all. It's just that this is so . . . oh, I don't know the right word. Elegant?'

Bianchi raised his head and, with a weak smile, said, 'I'm afraid I'm not able to see that, Signora.'

Hearing Bianchi's remark and seeing the expression of silent long-suffering he put upon his face, Brunetti realized that he was watching a chess game, played by masters. He thought of the chief tourist attraction of Marostica, a game of chess with humans costumed as the various pieces, played on giant squares in the medieval city centre. That game, however, was played out with identical moves every two years: here, each move was made in response to that of the adversary, and there was no question that they had become adversaries, Bianchi and Griffoni.

'How is it that you come to be in such a place, Signor Bianchi?' she insisted, voice dripping with wonder and admiration.

'It's what the insurance company suggested,' he answered. 'And, as I said, it doesn't make much of a difference to me, anyway. I can't see what the other people tell me about: the roses, the paintings, the fresh uniforms.' To a man with his disability, he left it to them to infer, they were meaningless frivolities, completely foreign to the poor victim of eternal darkness.

Brunetti watched Bianchi's mouth contract, as though he were trying to decide on his next move or if the last one had been correct. As Brunetti watched, Bianchi gave a tiny nod and said, 'Even the food, which everyone tells me is so good, tastes different if you can't see what you're eating.' He raised his hands in a gesture of acceptance, as though to emphasize that he spoke reluctantly, like someone forced to tell the truth about a party everyone else had enjoyed. At least he didn't tell them he was always hungry.

'Ah, that's too bad,' she sighed. 'But I can assure you that everything is perfect; it couldn't be lovelier, and the garden is a marvel.' Like every good actress, she continued the scene even as she prepared to step offstage and, sweet-voiced, asked Brunetti, 'Wouldn't you say so, Commissario?'

'Absolutely,' Brunetti affirmed and then immediately asked, 'And which insurance company is that, Signor Bianchi?'

'Surely you don't expect me to remember that after all this time,' Bianchi said, allowing irritation to sift into his voice.

'I'm sure the accounting office here could give me their

243

name,' Brunetti said, wondering if his easy certainty would make Bianchi squirm. Though the man gave no sign of being disturbed by Brunetti's remark, Bardo suddenly raised his head, opened his eyes, and whined, as though he'd been disturbed in his sleep.

Griffoni looked at Brunetti and raised her eyebrows.

'You said you spoke to Signor Casati every Sunday, Signore,' Brunetti began. 'Did he say anything to you recently that might have suggested that he was worried about something, the way his daughter said he was?'

Bianchi put his hand on the dog's head and patted it to calm him. Bardo lowered his head to Bianchi's knees and closed his eyes again. 'No, nothing that I recall.'

'Do you remember what you talked about the last time you spoke?'

Bianchi made a light, chuckling sound. 'Probably about football. Davide was mad for it.'

Brunetti injected some testosterone into his voice and said, 'And last Saturday Inter wiped the floor with Pescara, so if he was an Inter fan, he would have been especially excited.'

'Yes, that's what he talked about,' Bianchi said, sounding distressed. 'He always forgot how little I care about it now.'

As if in apology for his own enthusiasm, Brunetti said, 'I think we all get a little carried away when there's a victory like that: seven/zero. I can't remember the last time Pescara was beaten that badly.' He put a great deal of self-satisfied triumph into his last sentence.

'Yes, that's pretty much what Davide said.'

'Commissario,' Griffoni interrupted, 'I hardly think Signor Bianchi needs to listen to the football news again. Or,' she said, putting her hand on Bardo's neck and giving a small tickle, '*piccolo* Bardo, either.'

'Oh,' Bianchi said, smiling, 'He doesn't know he's small.' Then, turning his head towards the wall, he added, 'He's not small to me.'

Brunetti got to his feet and, looking down at the claw that rested on Bardo's back, decided not to try to shake hands with Bianchi again. 'I'd like to thank you for your time, Signor Bianchi.' He stopped there, not telling the other man whether he had been helpful or not.

Griffoni stood and said much the same thing, then bent down and patted Bardo on the head a few times as a way of saying farewell to both of them.

They went down the steps and crossed the space between the gazebo and the main building, both of them suddenly aware of the heat, which the shade and the plants inside the gazebo had lessened. 'Well?' Brunetti asked.

'Nice invention,' Griffoni said.

'What?' Brunetti asked, complimented but still embarrassed.

'The football game. Inter and Pescara play in different leagues; any idiot knows that. Even I do. Anyone does, even if all they do is read headlines.'

'Well, he doesn't read them or have them read to him, does he?'

'Apparently not, but apart from this he wanted us to believe Casati still called him on Sunday, and they chatted like old friends.' She stopped, and turned to Brunetti to say, 'Why would he do that?'

They started walking again, and at the main building, Brunetti held open the door to allow Griffoni to pass in ahead of him. Just inside, he paused, and when she turned to look at him, Brunetti said, 'Isn't it strange, the way we're so willing to assume that what handicapped people tell us is true? As if their suffering had made them honest.'

'You don't think it does?' she asked.

'Is he honest?' Brunetti asked with a flick of his head in the direction of the gazebo.

'I doubt it,' Griffoni said. 'But he loves his dog.'

Brunetti stared at her as if she had tried to interest him in a copy of *The Watchtower*. 'I beg your pardon,' he said.

'He's been blind all these years, and yet he can still love his dog.'

'It seems very little to me,' Brunetti said and turned away, starting back towards the main entrance, where he hoped to find Signora Segalin in her office.

Behind him he heard Griffoni's steps and then her voice: 'It's still something.'

Signora Segalin's eyes blinked out her delight in seeing them, these kind people who had come to visit Signor Bianchi. Without giving any explanation of why they wanted the information or with what authority they requested it, Brunetti managed to be given copies of the receipts for payment of Signor Bianchi's bills for the last year.

Casually, he slipped the folder under his arm, as if this were a mere formality, and shook hands with Signora Segalin, thanking her for all her help. She accompanied them to the door, where their car and driver awaited them. Signora Segalin seemed to give this no special importance: perhaps she was accustomed to guests who arrived in cars with drivers.

Beyond the gates, they turned on to the state highway and returned to the real world. 'But I still think he's manipulative and dishonest,' Griffoni said, as if she were finally completing her last sentence.

Brunetti smiled and opened the file that lay on his lap.

'Who pays them?' she asked.

'GCM Holdings,' he answered.

'Never heard of it.'

'Me neither,' Brunetti said. He pulled out his phone.

'Who are they?'

Brunetti pressed in one of the autodial numbers; both of them heard it ringing.

'Who are they?' Griffoni repeated; perhaps he had not heard her.

He turned aside from the phone and said, 'We'll know when we get back.'

The phone clicked, and a woman's voice said, 'Ah, Commissario, how can I help you?'

26

And so it was. They went directly to Signorina Elettra's office from the boat and found her – it must be said – preening. A number of papers lay on her desk.

'Casati's employer?' Brunetti asked when they entered, nodding in the direction of the papers.

'*Sì, Signore*, in a way,' she said with an easy smile. 'In its current incarnation, it's a construction company, owned by Gianclaudio Maschietto.' She nodded towards the screen. 'There's more.'

Brunetti thought he had read the name of the owner, a successful entrepreneur in the north-east. 'I know his name, but that's all.' A whiff of memory came, and he added, 'Something about a church?' He glanced aside at Griffoni. 'You, Claudia? Anything?'

She tilted her head and stared at the wall. 'No. Not even the name.'

Signorina Elettra nodded to confirm his memory. 'I've

made you each a copy of what I found. If you'd like to read it, I'll make some calls.'

'To friends?' Brunetti asked.

'To friends,' she assented.

'Come on, Claudia,' Brunetti said and picked up the papers. Seeing how many there were, he suggested they go to his office to read them and leave Signorina Elettra to get on with her work.

The windows of his office had been closed for some time, and it took Brunetti a moment to decide whether it would be better to leave them closed or to let the air into the room. The windows faced east; he pulled them open and was enveloped in a Saharan wave of desiccated air.

Well, it was done, and at least the air had a whiff of the sea. He passed one set of papers to Griffoni and went behind his desk, removed his jacket, and sat.

It felt to him a bit like being back at university, two classmates sitting in a small space, reading together. It was all standard fare: the company named Romina Rimozione was established more than forty years before, only nine employees at the beginning, now more than a hundred, with offices in Padova, Treviso, and Marghera. The first business was transport: quick delivery anywhere in Europe. The company had expanded into building: houses and schools, then office buildings and even a part of the airport. One early success was a contract to transport materials from the Marghera industrial area, soon followed by another to remove waste metal from a factory complex in the same area. Construction of a shopping centre outside Pordenone, sub-contract for the laying of track for the new tram between Mestre and Venice. Somewhere in the middle of the expansion, Romina disappeared, as did the idea of removals, and the name of the company was changed to 'GCM Holdings'.

He checked the articles and saw that Signorina Elettra had arranged them in chronological order, as though wanting them to feel participant in the continuing success of the company.

There was only one article of any length about the owner and guiding spirit of the company. Gianclaudio Maschietto, 83, was born in Piove di Sacco and currently divided his time between his birthplace and Venice. The article had photos of the church he had built and donated to his birthplace and quoted him as saying, 'It is my duty to God and my fellow citizens that I do this.' Presumably, he meant building the church, which Brunetti thought grotesque, a cement box with a sharply slanted tile roof and stained-glass windows that looked like scenes from religious comic books.

There had been a spurt of articles six years before, when Maschietto had withdrawn from the daily running of the company, passing control to his son, Francesco, who became CEO, his father retaining only a non-voting position on the board.

Finished reading the articles, Brunetti looked across at Griffoni, who was studying the photos of the stained-glass windows. She looked at him and sighed. 'It looks frighteningly like the new church in the village my mother comes from.'

Griffoni tapped the sheets of paper on her knees, forcing them back into order. 'To build the new church in my village, they tore down a small chapel from the sixteenth century.' When she saw his startled look, she said, 'That was fifty years ago.'

Brunetti wondered if this were meant to make it less awful. It didn't.

'What do you think?' he asked.

'I'd like to know why his company is paying for Bianchi.'

Brunetti turned a few pages and found what he was looking for. 'It says here that the original company was working in Marghera from the early eighties.'

'Umm,' she said. 'I read that.' She flipped a few pages, then lowered the papers. 'Do you think the accident would have been reported in the press? Two men were badly injured.'

'If the damage was big enough or people were killed, it would be,' Brunetti observed.

Griffoni thought about this for a moment, pulled her lips together and nodded a few times. 'Of course, we believed what he told us, didn't we? Because he's handicapped. There could have been more people involved.'

Brunetti flirted with the idea of adding, 'And because he's good to his dog,' but good sense prevailed. 'Shall we go and see what else she's found?' he asked, instead.

Together they went down to Signorina Elettra's office, where they found her still at her computer. As they entered, Brunetti saw a new pile of papers lying in the tray of the printer and asked, 'Are those for us?'

'Yes,' Signorina Elettra said without bothering to look up from the screen. 'They're about the fire.'

Brunetti went and picked up the papers, and again there were two copies of each page. He went to the windowsill and sorted them into two piles, handed one to Griffoni. She leaned back beside him and started with the top page, instantly intent.

Brunetti remained where he was and started to read his copy.

The *Gazzettino* carried a story about a fire in a warehouse at a complex of offices and factories in Marghera in which at least two workers were killed, three injured, and two others reported as missing. The fire – for which no cause was given - had started in the warehouse in the late afternoon. Four brigades of firefighters had responded to the call and fought the fire until it was extinguished in the early morning.

The following day, *La Nuova di Venezia* confirmed the number of injured and killed but reported that the two missing workers had been on assignment in another part of the industrial complex and had not been involved in the fire. The captain of the firefighters was quoted as saying that the likely cause of the fire was a short circuit in the electrical system.

There was the usual comment on the large numbers of 'white deaths', on-the-job deaths of workers, and the standard interviews with the friends and family members of the two dead men, whom they remembered as serious, careful workers whose loss would be mourned by their colleagues and loved ones. The injured workers, Zeno Bianchi, Davide Casati, and Leonardo Pozzi, had been transported to hospitals in Padova and Venice and were all reported in *'condizione riservata'*.

By the third day, the story had moved farther back in the papers, and on the fourth there was a photo of the then-mayor visiting the site, surrounded by firefighters and various unnamed officials, all of them wearing coveralls, boots, and helmets, the mayor turned in half-profile, the better to be recognizable in the photo. After that, nothing, although Brunetti could still hear the thuh, thuh, thuh of the printer.

Without asking, he went and collected the pages, separated them, and handed one copy to Griffoni.

These dealt, though not until a year had passed, with Gianclaudio Maschietto, who had given an interview to *Famiglia Cristiana*, in which he declared that the events at his warehouse in Marghera, still fresh in his mind, as well as the recent death of his wife, had so burned into his soul – perhaps not the most opportune choice of word, Brunetti reflected – that his thoughts had turned to God, in whose name he would devote some of his wealth to aid the spiritual and physical welfare of his fellow citizens. Thus the construction of the church and the endowment of three beds in perpetuity at a *casa di cura*, to be given to workers who suffered crippling injuries in on-the-job accidents.

Years passed before Maschietto appeared again, this time, only six months ago, named among the forty people – almost all men – put forward as possible candidates for the state honour of *Cavaliere del lavoro*, to be awarded later in the year to twenty-five of them.

The printer was silent, the tray empty, and they had learned very little that would aid them in understanding the circumstances of Davide Casati's death.

'Three beds?' Griffoni asked, reading his mind.

'We didn't know to ask, did we?' Brunetti answered.

'A short circuit?'

'It's what the firemen said,' Brunetti answered and turned to Signorina Elettra, who was taking silent part in this conversation. He lifted his chin in inquiry.

'There was nothing else in the papers,' she said, 'so it's likely that was the cause; the insurance investigators don't seem to have found anything else,' she went on, then asked, 'What happened at Villa Flora?'

Brunetti briefly explained their conversation with Bianchi, and then the three of them passed some time in silent consideration of this. Brunetti glanced through the papers again, and Griffoni pulled out one page and read it through. Signorina Elettra kept her attention on the screen, but her eyes did not move along the lines of text.

Finally Brunetti said, 'Claudia, would you call Signora Segalin and tell her we discovered when we got back to the office that we were also meant to inspect the condition of the residents who occupy the other two beds endowed by GCM Holdings?'

'What if Bianchi's told her who we are?' Claudia asked, setting the papers on the windowsill behind her.

'I doubt that he would,' Brunetti answered.

'One moment,' Signorina Elettra said, tapped in a few letters, and then read out the phone number of Villa Flora. She picked up her desk phone, dialled, and held the receiver out to Griffoni. Griffoni took the phone and leaned one hip against Signorina Elettra's desk.

'Good afternoon, this is Dottoressa Griffoni. I visited earlier with my colleague, Dottor Brunetti. Could I speak to Signora Segalin, please? Yes, thank you.'

She looked up at them and made an arc in the air with her free hand to show that the call was being transferred.

'Ah, good afternoon, Signora,' she said, her smile slipping down the line. 'So good of you to speak to me again . . . No, nothing really important, but I have to tell you that we've all been victims of bureaucratic incompetence . . . No,' she said with a small, complicit laugh, 'I didn't think you'd be a stranger to it, Signora. Which of us is?

'It's about the other beds in the GCM endowment. Yes, precisely. Could you tell me if the other beds are occupied and, if so, by whom?'

A long silence stretched out until Griffoni said, 'Yes, it's to complete our files . . . Ah, I didn't know that, Signora. When was it cancelled? Ah, of course, of course. But the second one remained?'

Griffoni reached over, pulled a piece of paper towards her and took the pencil Signorina Elettra held out to her.

'Leonardo Pozzi? Yes, thank you. And how long has he been there? . . . Oh, really? Ah, the poor man. Does anyone come to . . . ? Yes, I can understand why the staff would . . . Of course. Of course.'

Griffoni stared at the floor while speaking, intent on saying the right thing and keeping the correct tone. Signora Segalin went on for a long time, and Brunetti imagined her eyes flashing out useless signals to cue her listener to the proper emotional response. Griffoni did not disappoint, umming and ahhing and saying 'yes' or 'no', both with the special emphasis one uses with a person who wants affirmation, not only of the fact reported but of the emotional weight of that fact.

'Would it be possible for us to come and speak to him, do you think?' Griffoni looked across at Brunetti and held up a hand, then shook it in the air a few times, as one does when in possession of important information.

'Yes, that's very kind of you. When would be the best time, do you think? You certainly understand these things far better than we do.' The flattery was blatant, but Brunetti could imagine the flashes of delight from Signora Segalin's eyes.

'Fine, then we'll be there tomorrow morning at eleven. And thank you so much for your efficiency and help.' Griffoni made a few positive, warm noises and hung up.

She handed the pencil back to Signorina Elettra and pushed away from the desk. She looked over at Brunetti and said, 'The second bed is still occupied by Leonardo Pozzi. He's been there a shorter time than Signor Bianchi, but that's because he was in the hospital longer and was moved to Villa Flora four months later.'

She turned slightly to her right and looked at Signorina Elettra before continuing. 'Pozzi was injured far more seriously than either of the others,' she began and lowered her head while she said, 'He lost both legs.' Before they could inquire, she said, 'He was hit by pieces of one of the barrels that exploded and didn't bleed to death only because . . . because the wounds were seared closed.' Here she glanced at both of them, and looked down at the floor again. 'That was the phrase Signora Segalin used. By whatever was in the barrel.' She let them think about that for a moment and continued.

'Signora Segalin said that he has become more isolated as the years pass, and now he seldom speaks to anyone.' She put her hands together and rubbed at her left wrist, as though she had broken it once and it ached at times.

Brunetti asked, 'And the third bed?'

'The money for it was cancelled when the third man injured in the accident didn't accept the invitation to Villa Flora and chose to remain in a state facility, instead.'

'Casati?' Brunetti asked.

'She didn't give a name, and I didn't want to interrupt her to ask.' She paused a moment and then added, 'From what you've told me about him, it seems likely.'

'If they're paying for two beds,' Griffoni said, 'then they've spent more than four million Euros to keep them there all this time.'

Brunetti heard Griffoni say something under her breath and turned to ask her, 'What?'

'Seared,' she said, told him she'd see them in the morning, and left without saying anything else.

27

The same driver took them back to Villa Flora the next morning, both of them disguising their eagerness to meet Leonardo Pozzi. They spoke of the terrible heat and the comfort of having a car with air conditioning; they spoke of the desiccated crops on either side of the road; they spoke of anything other than the second man at Villa Flora.

Signora Segalin opened the door to them again, today wearing what appeared to be the same suit in dark grey. The flash of her smile was subdued, perhaps in proportion to Signor Pozzi's greater disability. 'I've told him you're coming to visit,' she said as soon as they'd shaken hands.

'Was he interested?' Griffoni asked. They had decided that she, having been the one to speak to Signora Segalin the previous evening, should speak for them both.

'It's sometimes difficult to know what he thinks,' Signora Segalin said and flashed a small smile. 'Because he speaks so little. And now that he and Signor Bianchi don't seem to talk to one another any more, we can't ask him to help us communicate with Signor Pozzi.' She said this as one would speak of a spat between children.

Griffoni let out a little 'oh' of surprise. 'I didn't know they knew one another. Certainly Signor Bianchi didn't mention him yesterday.'

'I suppose he wouldn't. Not now,' Signora Segalin said. Like many people who worked with patients, she was glad to show how much she knew about their private lives, sure proof of her close involvement with them. 'They've been good friends for years. They often ate together. But recently they've stopped speaking to one another or going to visit.'

'Oh, I'm so sorry to hear that,' Griffoni said, impressing even Brunetti with the sound of her sincerity. 'I hope it doesn't last.'

Signora Segalin smiled at this proof of the other woman's goodwill. 'Well, these things happen sometimes between patients, but they usually calm down after a while. I'm sure that will happen with them.' She couldn't have sounded more certain. 'All they have is one another, in the end.' She turned away and started down the corridor on the other side of the building from where they had been the previous day. They walked to the very end; Signora Segalin stopped in front of an open door and tapped a few times on the jamb, then entered and waved them in after her.

Aside from the heat, which enveloped them as soon as they entered the room from the air-conditioned corridor, they could have been visiting a celebrity in a hotel suite: there was a large bouquet of the by-now-familiar roses in a crystal vase, what looked like an Isfahan carpet on the parquet floor, and three prints of Longhi harlequins on the walls. Through a door, Brunetti glimpsed a carpeted bedroom and a brocade-covered bed. The same garden that spread out beyond the other wing of the building bloomed behind the windows in this room. It was hard to concentrate on details, however, so overwhelmed were they by the heat and humidity.

Upright on a grey velvet sofa sat a tall man of extraordinary thinness, his lap covered with a light blue cashmere blanket. His hair was dark brown with no sign of grey and cut close to his head. His eyes were an even darker brown and displayed absolutely no interest in them, nor in Signora Segalin. Two deep lines curved outward from either side of his nose and arched to below his mouth, but aside from them his face was almost entirely unlined. He appeared to be about ten years younger than Casati and Bianchi.

He wore striped pyjamas that had not been slept in under a dark blue dressing gown, with a paisley scarf tied at the open neck of his pyjama jacket. The sight of the woollen dressing gown made Brunetti reach up and loosen his tie. Pozzi's hands lay folded in his lap. As they approached, Pozzi's face remained calm, uninterested, his attention entirely absent.

Brunetti and Griffoni stopped a few metres from him, reacting automatically to the force field of indifference he projected. Signora Segalin either didn't notice or didn't care – perhaps she just wanted to introduce them quickly and escape the heat in the room – and continued until she stood near to where his feet would have been, had anything but the empty legs of the pyjamas been visible at the front of the sofa.

'Signor Pozzi,' Signora Segalin began, speaking with exaggerated clarity, 'these are the people from social services who would like to talk to you.' She stepped aside and motioned them forward, but neither of them moved.

Pozzi turned his head towards them; Brunetti noticed

that his shoulders moved when his head did, as though his neck were not able to turn on its own. It gave him the look of a robot, some of whose parts had been scrapped.

Signora Segalin again motioned them forward, this time impatiently.

'Perhaps Signor Pozzi feels more comfortable if we stay here,' Griffoni suggested.

'Nonsense,' Signora Segalin said and busied herself moving chairs around until two of them stood facing Signor Pozzi, whose eyes had moved to Griffoni's face. In her haste, Signora Segalin yanked one of the chairs into the edge of the carpet and stopped only when she could move the chair no farther. Saying nothing, Griffoni moved towards the chair and lifted it to allow the edge of the carpet to fall smooth again, then she smiled at Signor Pozzi and sat.

Brunetti nodded his greeting, pulled the second chair slightly farther away from Pozzi, and sat, careful to sit far back in the deep seat.

Signora Segalin glanced at her watch and asked Brunetti, 'Would you like me to stay and help?' as though she were a reluctant translator unable to disguise her eagerness to finish and leave.

'That's very kind of you, Signora,' Griffoni said in her most polite voice. 'But we've already taken up too much of your time.' She stood and moved around behind her chair to enforce her words by taking Signora Segalin's hand in both of hers to give it a squeeze that showed her thanks.

'Well, then,' Signora Segalin said, 'I'll leave you alone to talk.' Then, to Pozzi, in what she tried to make sound like a friendly voice, 'I hope you have a pleasant visit.'

The door closed, and the three of them sat, at least two of them beaten down by the heat. Brunetti and Griffoni let a few minutes pass by before she said, 'Signor Pozzi, we've come to talk to you about the events that led to your coming here to Villa Flora. You've been here a long time, haven't you?'

Pozzi nodded, bending his entire torso forward to do it.

Griffoni smiled her thanks for his answer and said, 'You were working for GMC Holdings at the time, weren't you?'

Pozzi considered her question for a long time and finally said, 'CM.'

Brunetti restrained the impulse to look at Griffoni.

She smiled and said, 'Excuse me?'

'CM,' Pozzi repeated. 'GCM.' His lips barely moved when he pronounced the letters and drew softly closed with the last.

'Of course,' Griffoni said, raising a hand to her forehead, as if to reprove her offending memory. 'GCM.'

Pozzi nodded, again moving his body.

'Were you working for GCM Holdings then? And thank you for the correction, Signor Pozzi.'

Brunetti watched the other man's face, keeping a neutral expression on his own, even allowing his attention to appear to drift away. He looked around the room and became fully aware of the bookshelf behind Pozzi's left shoulder.

He ran his eyes along the shelves, wondering what sort of books a crippled factory worker would find interesting, though he did not phrase it that way, not even to himself. The first thing he noticed was the height and thickness of most of the books, and then he adjusted his eyes to the distance and started to read the perpendicular titles: Goya, Tiziano, Velázquez, Holbein, Van Dyck, Moroni.

He moved his eyes back to Pozzi and saw that the man had been watching him as he discovered the titles of the books. Their eyes met, and Brunetti gave a relaxed smile and small nod of approval.

Griffoni was drawing breath, no doubt to repeat her question, when Brunetti cut her off by saying, 'I didn't know the Hughes book had been translated into Italian.'

Pozzi answered in an entirely conversational voice. 'It hasn't been, as far as I know. I read the English text.' When Brunetti said nothing, Pozzi added, 'I've always liked the way he writes, ever since *The Shock of the New*.'

'It's been a long time since I read it,' Brunetti said, 'but I still remember my surprise when he explained the change in the way people perceived landscape once they could move through it smoothly in a machine.'

'And fast, without the viewer being joggled along by a carriage or a horse,' Pozzi added. 'It's so obvious, isn't it? But, as you say, so surprising to realize.'

'It's nice to see the Moroni,' Brunetti added. 'I've always liked his work.'

'It must be wonderful to see the real paintings,' Pozzi said with the wide-eyed wonder of a lover of art and without a hair's breadth of self-pity. 'I wish . . .'

Brunetti thought a long time before he risked saying, 'I think there are two or three in Milano, but not in the same museum. And the Accademia Carrara in Bergamo is full of them. Can't you get them to take you there?'

'It's not so easy,' Pozzi said.

'Why?' Brunetti asked, his question implying something – laziness, perhaps – on the part of the staff or perhaps on Pozzi's part. 'They must have some sort of van here, so all they'd have to do is put you in a wheelchair and take you there.' He smiled as at a sudden revelation. 'With the handicapped sticker, they can park just about anywhere, so they don't have to worry about that. And you'd probably be right in front of the building. Nothing's easier.'

It came to Brunetti that for this man nothing was easy, so his remark must have seemed a taunt or a provocation. 'I mean nothing's easier than to arrange it, Signore; not to do it. Only you know how difficult that is.'

Pozzi raised his eyebrows, as though in appreciation of Brunetti's frankness, and returned his attention to Griffoni. 'You asked me if I was working for GCM Holdings, Signorina. May I ask you the reason for your curiosity?' How had Pozzi learned to speak like that? Brunetti wondered. A factory worker certainly had not learned it from the people with whom he had worked, and Signorina Segalin said he spoke very little here. Brunetti glanced around and saw no television, nor was there sign of a radio; not that either provided much in the way of an example of how to speak. Books, then?

'Because we are not from the social services, Signor Pozzi,' Griffoni said, speaking in her normal voice and not that of the fresh-faced woman from the social services she had been impersonating until now. 'Signora Segalin has confused things. We're from the police.'

Pozzi watched Griffoni for a long time, his now indisputably intelligent face changing, as though he were considering the possibility of returning to the listless creature he had been when they came in. Brunetti saw the man's attention appear to go in and out of focus, his expression dull-witted and then astute, only to lapse again into complete apathy. Finally Pozzi asked, 'Are you here about the fire?' in a voice so neutral it could have been that of a machine.

Surprised, Griffoni asked, 'Did Signor Bianchi tell you?'

Surprised in his turn, Pozzi asked, 'You spoke to him?'

'Yes. Yesterday.'

'What did he tell you?'

Griffoni turned and gave Brunetti an inquisitive look: it was his investigation, after all.

The man liked Moroni, Brunetti reflected. He nodded to Griffoni.

'He told us what happened in the fire,' she said.

'Ah,' Pozzi said, prolonging his response until it was a sustained, low noise. 'That he tried to stop Casati from lighting a cigarette?'

'Yes,' Griffoni answered.

'And Casati carried him from the building?' Pozzi asked, as though he were now the person conducting the investigation.

'Yes.'

'Well, at least that's true,' Pozzi said.

'What isn't?' Griffoni asked.

Pozzi gave a weak smile. 'I probably spoke too soon. It's more likely that he asked Casati for a light: they both smoked in places where it was prohibited. I caught them a number of times.'

'And reported it?' Griffoni broke in to ask.

'Yes. Always.'

'Did it stop them?' she asked.

'I doubt it,' Pozzi said with the air of someone explaining a simple human truth to an even more simple-minded person. 'But I wasn't with them when the fire started, and one should never jump to conclusions, should one?'

'If they didn't start it, what could have caused the fire?' Brunetti asked.

Pozzi appeared to think about this before he said, 'Carelessness, neglect, negligence, contempt for safety standards and for the workers.' He saw their surprise. 'But above all, a desire to spend less money: always and ever. That was their goal.'

'Of the company?' Griffoni asked.

'Yes.'

'Yet you worked for them?'

'Yes,' Pozzi said, looking down at the blanket and pulling it closer to his chest, as though eager for the warmth it provided. The gesture made Brunetti suddenly conscious of the sweat soaking into the back of his jacket and under his arms.

'What were you doing for them?' Brunetti asked.

'We had a contract to dispose of some of the materials used in the petrochemical plants,' Pozzi began. 'Once the materials were collected and put into barrels, they were shipped to the various plants that would treat them. I was the logistical engineer in charge of the project.'

'Contaminating materials?' Brunetti asked.

Pozzi looked at the back of his right hand and carefully spread out the fingers, as though he'd been asked to prove that they were all there and was proud to be able to show that they were. Looking back at Brunetti, he added, 'Whatever was on the list of what had to be removed.'

'Such as?'

'Molybdenum, chrome, dioxin, arsenic, mercury,' he said, banging down on each word as though his voice were a hammer. 'Many more, I'm sure; those are the ones that come to mind after all these years. And, of course, a great deal of highly flammable liquids.'

Brunetti, struck by the ease with which he pronounced the last two words, asked, 'You don't think about it any more?'

Pozzi tilted his head to one side as he considered this, then said, 'No, I suppose I don't; not any more. I try to think about paintings and lines and colours and how objects are placed to create perspective and how difficult it is to paint eyes.'

'And where did these materials go?' Brunetti asked, not interested in the problems of perspective.

'They were supposed to go to Germany and Sweden, and Austria, all countries which had, and have, far better facilities for processing them than we do.'

'"Supposed to go"?' Griffoni asked, joining the conversation again.

Pozzi smiled for the first time, and Brunetti saw that he must have been a handsome man, before the accident that had reduced him so. 'Very good, Signorina,' he said, his delight audible. Brunetti suddenly found himself annoyed at Pozzi's condescension, as though he believed his knowledge combined with his handicap conveyed some special merit and thus put him in charge here.

Griffoni replied coolly, 'You said it in such a way that I was compelled to ask, don't you think, Signore?'

Pozzi's smile evaporated and he said, 'But so few people pay serious attention to what is said to them, Signorina, that you deserve the compliment.' Brunetti wondered if Pozzi had so little interaction with people that he believed this.

'And did they go to those countries?' Brunetti asked.

Pozzi turned the upper part of his body towards Brunetti and answered, 'That was not part of our mandate, Signore. We delivered the barrels to the trucks or, in some cases, to the boats; the people to whom we delivered them signed off on our invoices and took possession of the shipment.' In case they did not understand, he went on, 'We had no involvement beyond that. And no interest.'

Saying nothing, Brunetti waited for Griffoni to take charge again. She did by asking, 'Do you remember the names of any of these companies?'

'No; not after all these years.'

'Did you ever learn where any of the shipments were going?'

'As I told you, I don't remember the invoices.'

'That's not what I'm asking, Signor Pozzi,' she said with the first hint of impatience. 'I'm asking if you ever learned where they were going.'

'I didn't ask,' Pozzi replied.

She leaned forward and spoke with exaggerated emphasis. 'Again, you seem to be misinterpreting my question. Did you ever learn where they went?'

'No.'

'Did you ever hear speculation about where they might be going?'

'Speculation?'

'Among the people with whom you worked.'

His answering smile was soft and pleased with itself; Brunetti didn't like the sight of it.

'There's always speculation, isn't there?' Pozzi asked. How many witnesses had Brunetti listened to who spoke in the same way? Thinking themselves so much cleverer than the person who questioned them, they would answer with rhetorical questions, try to split hairs that would have been invisible to a Jesuit.

Brunetti saw it now: Pozzi was a cat, who saw them as two small mice. Swat, swat, keep the claws in at the beginning, perhaps all the time. But swat and have what fun you could with them. 'Did you believe any of the stories you heard?' Griffoni asked.

'Shall we say I found some of them interesting?' Pozzi answered.

Griffoni said nothing. Brunetti studied her profile and saw her tongue moisten her lips before she asked, 'Which ones were they?'

'I heard that some of it went to Nigeria, that some went to Campania.'

'I've heard about those,' she said with a lack of interest.

As if to goad her into being interested, Pozzi said, 'And some of them were like the little piggy in the English nursery rhyme. "This little piggy stayed home",' he said, his pronunciation showing that his knowledge of English was confined to reading.

'I'm afraid I don't understand,' she said. 'Not your English,' she quickly added, which Brunetti saw as a wise sop to her listener's vanity, 'but the meaning.'

'Some of it stayed home, Signorina,' he said with an enigmatic smile, the sort an attractive woman used when her answer could have been a yes as readily as a no.

Pozzi had said that some of the barrels had been delivered to boats. Brunetti suddenly pictured the many landing stages and docks with which the petrochemical area of Marghera was studded, all with easy access to the vastness of the *laguna*. And then he remembered diving into the water of the *laguna* and swimming back and forth to cool himself while waiting for Casati to return from collecting his last sample. He had dived down like a cormorant and swum underwater for as long as he could, holding his breath until compelled to plunge through the surface and draw in deep gulps of the life-saving air.

And then Casati had arrived, swimming with one arm raised, holding the vial safe from the water so that the soil inside could be sent for examination to see if it contained what was killing his bees.

'*Oddio*,' Brunetti whispered under his breath. 'They dumped it in the *laguna*.'

28

Years later, Brunetti would remember the smile that appeared on Pozzi's face as he savoured Brunetti's last words. It began with his lips, which closed together, pressure from the centre forcing the corners up very slowly. His expression softened; tension disappeared from his face for a fleeting moment. His hints and ambiguous answers had finally registered with the police officials, and at least one of them now understood what had happened all those years before.

Brunetti turned to look at Griffoni, and he saw her face when she understood his words: there was no smile. Brunetti saw that Pozzi was also watching Griffoni. Her effect on him was evident: he squeezed his eyes together minimally to bring her face into sharper focus, the better to enjoy her expression, the result of her growing awareness of what he knew. The muscles of Pozzi's lower face relaxed again, and the lines from his nose to his mouth disappeared. Years fled from him, and the young man he might well have been, before the flesh of his legs had been cauterized, made a brief appearance in the room. And then that man dissolved, still able to run from the room, leaving behind this other person. His shell? His lesser self? His remains.

Something horrid had slipped into the room with Pozzi's words, carried ever closer by years of rumour and suggestion and half-understood remarks. Brunetti had been listening to stories for years: when the trees in the park of San Giuliano, near Marghera, died within a year of being planted, it was said that the barrels of toxic waste on which the park was built had begun to leak. He'd heard endless jokes about the clams from the *laguna* and how much easier it was to find them at night because they glowed in the dark. Fact existed as well: he had read the statistical tables of the tumours that had laid waste a generation of workers in the factories from which GCM Holdings and companies like them had been paid to remove toxic materials.

Yet here was Pozzi talking about nursery rhymes, as though he found humour, not horror, in what was still befalling others, the pollution of the *laguna* no more than a piece to be used in a game only he knew how to enjoy. It came to Brunetti that Pozzi wanted them to be surprised but was incapable of understanding why they might be shocked.

'Ah,' Brunetti said, 'so all we've been hearing for years is true?'

Pozzi was transformed into the teacher proud of his student. 'All of it, I don't know, Signore. But some of it, yes.'

'If you've known about it for all of this time, why haven't you ever said anything?' Brunetti asked, as though he were piqued by curiosity, not by indignation; no, never that.

Griffoni had herself become a clam, stuck to something hard under metres of murky water and thus invisible, barely breathing. Brunetti kept his eyes on Pozzi, as though they were alone in the room.

'Because, as you know from the Bible, it is far better to invest a talent than to bury it,' Pozzi said, then smiled in anticipation of Brunetti's response.

Brunetti forced himself to produce a grin and then cite the same passage in a discreet compliment to Pozzi. 'What is it that you've done, you good and faithful servant?'

'I did as the first servant did: I invested the talent wisely.'

'And how did you do that?' Brunetti asked, telling himself to behave as though he were being told another story, another nursery rhyme.

Pozzi looked off into a corner of the ceiling, and Brunetti could all but see him putting his words in order, shifting them around so as to put the hero in the right place at the right time, where he was sure to do the one right thing. Brunetti noticed that Pozzi actually looked bigger than he had when they entered the room.

'I invested it in my future,' Pozzi finally said with a very small smile.

Brunetti allowed his eyes to travel appreciatively around the entire room, his gaze lingering longer than necessary on the bookcase, consciously avoiding the place where Griffoni sat, before he returned it to Pozzi. He thought of complimenting him on the room, but, much as he tried, he could not bring himself to speak those words. Instead, he indicated the room with a wave, and nodded.

Taking Brunetti's gaze as a compliment, Pozzi continued. 'It took me some time to realize that I had something to sell and had a buyer.'

'You make it sound easy,' Brunetti said, relieved to find the words sounding normal.

'I was in the hospital for months, you know?' Pozzi asked, and Brunetti responded with a shake of his head meant to suggest ignorance of and sympathy for this fact.

'Then they sent me to a rehab facility. State run. They gave me a bed and one hour of rehabilitation a week.' He looked at Brunetti, raised a hand to shoulder height, and ran it down the front of his torso and out into the air at the height where his knees might still have been. 'They would have let me lie there until I died.' Brunetti was familiar with such places.

'After I'd been there for a month,' Pozzi continued, 'some of the men I had worked with came to visit, and they told me about the two who died and about Casati and Bianchi. They said Bianchi had been in a private clinic and had gone to a private nursing home when the clinic released him.' He let that sink in and then added, 'And I was lying in a room with three other men, with one hour of rehabilitation a week.'

Neither Griffoni nor Brunetti said a word; their silence led him on.

'So I called GCM and told them I'd like to speak to one of their lawyers, and when they asked what it was about, I mentioned the fire.' He paused to observe Brunetti's reaction: Brunetti did his part and showed every sign of interest.

Apparently pleased with what he saw on his listener's face, Pozzi continued. 'When they transferred the call, I told the person who I was and where I was, and why. I told him I'd had a long time in the hospital to think about what had been going on before the fire and wanted to discuss it with them before contacting the authorities.' Pozzi could not suppress a smile, the same sly smile that Brunetti didn't like.

'Their lawyers came the next day, two of them. That they were so eager was enough to tell me I'd already won, so I said I knew about how Bianchi was being treated, and I wanted everything he had, but with rehab every day and enough money every month to be able to live as I pleased.' Pozzi looked at Griffoni, as though he wanted to be sure she was following his story, and she nodded, though she did not smile.

It was enough, however, to persuade Pozzi to continue. 'I told them I was willing to make the same agreement with them that Bianchi had.' Pozzi threw his head back in a motion of pure glee and, eyes on the ceiling, added, 'I didn't know what Bianchi had given them, but I knew what he got.'

'You knew where the barrels had been sent?' Brunetti asked, wanting to be sure.

'I was the logistical engineer,' Pozzi said by way of answer. 'Remember?' He forgot to smile when he asked this, then continued. 'I told them I'd made copies of company invoices and left them in a safe place.' When Pozzi turned to check the expression on Griffoni's face, he smiled and said, 'It was my insurance policy, Signora.'

'I see,' she answered and relapsed into silence.

'And?' asked Brunetti, though the fact that Pozzi was a patient in Villa Flora made it obvious what the response had been.

Pozzi turned the same smile to Brunetti. 'They gave it to me: this place, rehabilitation, and they fitted me with artificial legs.'

When he saw Brunetti's involuntary expression of surprise, Pozzi said, 'Yes, I've got them. Like that South African guy who killed his girlfriend.' He paused, and in the absence of Brunetti's question, volunteered: 'They're in the other room. I ask them to put them there during the day because it's easier not to use them all the time.'

Brunetti nodded and then asked, 'Bianchi. Do you see him?'

Before answering, Pozzi glanced toward the door, as if fearing his words might slip away down the corridors and work their way into Bianchi's room. 'I never liked him when we worked together, so I don't see any reason why I'd like him now.' Then, as though to erase all doubt, he added, 'Besides, he can't read, so what would we talk about?'

'Of course, of course,' Brunetti muttered.

A new look, self-satisfied and smug, passed across Pozzi's face. 'The lawyer probably thought he was dealing with some crippled idiot. He asked me to sign a form saying that the company had maintained the highest professional standards of security in the areas assigned to them for clean-up.' Then anger replaced self-satisfaction. 'What did he think I was?'

'He underestimated you, I can see,' Brunetti said, speaking the truth.

Pozzi preened at the compliment. 'He did, indeed.'

'What did you have to give . . . ?' Brunetti began but let his voice trail off, wondering how far Pozzi would let himself go before he remembered that he was talking to a policeman.

Pozzi's expression changed, and he said, 'I gave them nothing, Signore. I told them I understood their pre-occupation, and I had no idea of making trouble for anyone, so long as they sent me here.' Pozzi looked up and waved around the room. Then he smiled. 'They're businessmen; they understood the conditions: so long as I was here, I'd say nothing. It would not be in my best interests.'

'Of course,' Griffoni said and nodded in approval.

Brunetti decided it would be wise to lead Pozzi away from the topic of his dealings with GCM, and so said, 'You mentioned Signor Casati.'

Pozzi cut him short. 'He was a fool,' he answered with a thin, mean-spirited smile. 'The men who came to see me told me Davide spent three months in a public hospital. Can you believe?' he asked with the astonishment a dowager would express at the idea of helping with the dishes.

Brunetti limited himself to raising his eyebrows and was happy to see Griffoni shake her head at the very thought.

Pozzi pulled the blanket up higher and said, smiling, 'May I offer you something? A coffee?'

Brunetti saw that this was an opportunity for Pozzi to impress them by giving an order and having it obeyed, so he answered in his most polite manner, 'That's very kind of you, Signor Pozzi, but we had coffee on the way here, and we have to be back in the city for lunch.'

Griffoni leaned forward and smiled. 'Perhaps another time?' The words were filled with a warmth that suggested she'd gladly accept a later invitation.

She sat back in the chair, smiling, and crossed her legs. As she did, Brunetti saw a look of raw longing pass across Pozzi's face, a look that brought back to life that younger, different man, the one with all of life ahead of him, and not the small, useless shell of a man who sat clutching at his blanket.

Griffoni might have seen the expression as well, for she said, her voice filled with curiosity that sounded real and concerned, 'Could you tell us about the accident?'

Another savage smile swept across Pozzi's face, driving the younger man back to where he had been sent the last time. Then he laughed, a rusty sound, as though he were imitating a noise he had heard long ago and thought he remembered well enough to imitate. This went on for a long time until Pozzi had to lean his head against the back of the sofa. His hand wiped at his eyes, and he pulled in deep breaths until his normal breathing returned.

'I don't know what happened,' he said and stopped to take a few more breaths. 'That's what's so funny: I have no idea.'

'But you were there,' she said.

'I was there, yes, in my office at the back of the warehouse. I heard a noise, and at first I thought it came from one of the small tankers we were using to transport liquids. Sometimes they made a lot of noise when they banged into the loading dock. But when I heard it again, I realized it came from the other side of the building, not the side that ran along the canal.' He tilted his head to his right to indicate a place behind him.

'I walked,' he began but stopped for some time after that verb, then continued, 'over to the door, which led into the warehouse, and when I opened it, I saw that the central part of the warehouse was on fire and the noise was the explosion of barrels.' He looked from Griffoni to Brunetti and back again, but neither of them spoke.

'I couldn't move. I couldn't think. All I saw was a strip of fire between me and the door. That was the only way out. Then I saw some men standing on my side of the fire and I started to run towards them. I don't know why I did that; maybe I thought we'd be safer – somehow – if we were all together. When I got to them I saw that it was Casati and a man I couldn't recognize, who was screaming and clawing at sticky stuff that was all over his face. He stood still and screamed until finally Casati picked him up and started running for the door, running through the fire, which I could see was only a narrow strip. I ran past them because I wasn't carrying anyone, and I jumped over the flames.' Pozzi paused, repeated the single word, 'jumped', and stopped. Then, as if he'd just come back from somewhere, he went on. 'I saw the light outside and realized I was safe, but then something hit me from behind and knocked me over. That's all I remember.'

Brunetti saw that, although Pozzi was shivering, his face was covered with sweat. Hurriedly Pozzi wiped his right hand across his eyes and left it there for a time, then wiped each eye separately; when he pulled it away, his face was dry.

Griffoni looked at Pozzi with an appreciative smile. 'Well,' she said, 'you must be quite a negotiator.' When Pozzi did not respond, she added, 'GCM must have seen the report from the firemen, that it was a short circuit.'

'Of course,' Pozzi said.

She smiled again.

'So they knew the insurance company would have to pay?' she asked.

'Yes.'

'Pay GCM, that is,' Brunetti clarified. 'As a company.'

Brunetti did not have to make the obvious point that GCM could then make its own decisions about compensation and the care of the injured workers. Nor did he have to remark on the legendary delays of both insurance companies and employers in matters of compensation.

Griffoni gave the room another once-over, nodding in approval at everything she saw. 'Is all of this what you got from them?' she asked, much in the manner of a teenager asking a rock star for an autograph.

Pozzi nodded but said nothing, glancing first at Griffoni and then at Brunetti. He gave Brunetti the impression that he was beginning to regret having been so forthcoming. Brunetti thought then of his mother and of the basic principles she had taught him when he was a child. Don't lie, say please and thank you, be polite to old people and help them if you can, never tease a cripple, eat everything on your plate and do not ask for more, never borrow money, keep your promises.

'Where would you go if GCM stopped paying for you here, Signor Pozzi?' Brunetti asked idly, speculatively.

'What?' Pozzi asked, startled.

'If, for any reason, GCM cancelled their contract here, as they did with the third bed? If they cancelled the first and the second, as well? Where would you and Signor Bianchi go?'

'But why would they do that?' Pozzi asked. His face was drained white, making the lines near his mouth suddenly deeper.

'It was just a thought, Signor Pozzi,' Brunetti said. He put his hand to his chin and did his best to appear to be mulling over Pozzi's question. 'You know an investigation into the clean-up of Marghera's been going on for years,' Brunetti continued, then waited until Pozzi nodded. He failed to remark that it had been going on so long that most people had forgotten about it. 'If your former employer learned that new evidence had been produced about their part in the clean-up, do you think they might, er, review your position here?'

'Millions,' Griffoni said, freed by Brunetti's question to launch her own attack. She'd interrupted as though she'd just seen that amount flying past and called out its name to catch its attention. 'I'm sure they'd like to stop paying all that money.' She smiled amiably.

Pozzi's mouth gaped in surprise. He joined his hands

together and then separated them and pressed them flat on his thighs. Brunetti averted his eyes and his curiosity from those thighs.

Never tease a cripple. 'If they thought the information came from you or Signor Bianchi, then I suppose you'd have to content yourself with whatever facility your state pension would permit you,' Brunetti mused aloud.

Griffoni smiled and added, 'I'm sure they'd let you take the prosthetic legs with you, Signore.'

As though she'd struck him a blow in the chest, Pozzi gasped and bent forward, one hand clutched to his heart.

'And since you'd both be coming from the same place, and you'd been colleagues at work, years ago, they'd probably try to put you and Signor Bianchi in the same room,' Brunetti added. This was the way mobs worked, he realized: one person started it, and then the others joined in, always an escalation, always harder blows, a few kicks once they were down, surround them, and then go in for the kill.

Pozzi's hand was still on his heart but his breathing had slowed. 'What do you want?'

Griffoni glanced at Brunetti, an expression of innocent surprise on her face. She said nothing; now, Brunetti saw, they were slowly walking around their prey, looking to find the weak point where they could begin.

'You said, "This little piggy stayed home", Signor Pozzi. Do you think you could tell me exactly where it stayed?' Brunetti asked in a friendly voice, quite as though he were asking where he might find the barber who had given this man such a good haircut.

'I don't remember saying that,' Pozzi said.

'How strange,' Griffoni said. 'I remember hearing you say it.'

Brunetti looked at her. 'So do I.' He waved a hand towards what he knew to be the empty pocket of her skirt and asked, 'Was the tape recorder on?'

She glanced at her watch and pushed at the dial on the right. 'Yes, Commissario. It was.'

Brunetti smiled across at Pozzi and said, 'What a relief we have the recording, Signore, should there be any question about our conversation.' He gave what he hoped was a reassuring smile and said, 'Now, as I was saying, just where was it the little piggy stayed?'

Pozzi turned his head and looked towards his bedroom, and Brunetti realized he was probably looking for his legs and regretting that they were in the other room. Pushing aside shame, Brunetti said, 'We'd also like to know what happened between you and Signor Bianchi.'

Like a goaded animal, Pozzi squealed even before the stick hit him. 'How do you know about that?' he demanded, not even bothering to deny it.

Brunetti shrugged; Griffoni sat quietly and said nothing.

Pozzi looked at the door that he would have been able to reach had he been wearing his legs. His hand moved to the right pocket of his dressing gown, but he merely patted the *telefonino* that must be there; he did not pull it out. Perhaps he feared that these people would take it from him?

When it became evident that neither of them was going to answer him, Pozzi said, sounding like a grumpy child, 'He told me about his conversation with Casati. Casati had told Bianchi he was going to call the police.'

'Why would Casati do a thing like that, Signor Pozzi?' Brunetti asked.

Pozzi considered the question, looked past Brunetti and out the window at the roses. When Brunetti saw the tightness around his eyes disappear, he knew he was going to lie: after so long a pause, only the truth would be stressful, a lie a relief.

'Bianchi told me he didn't say,' Pozzi answered.

'Why would Casati do a thing like that?' Brunetti repeated softly, as though Pozzi had not answered.

Pozzi was taken aback by the question, as though he had never thought about what another person might desire. He made no attempt to hide the irritation in his voice. 'How would I know what went on in his head?'

'I thought you knew him, that you'd been friends.'

Pozzi snorted at the idea. 'We worked together, years ago. That's not friendship.'

'What is?' Griffoni interrupted to ask.

When Brunetti glanced at her, he could tell that the question was a real one, and for some reason it was important to her. He decided to see if Pozzi would answer her.

Pozzi returned to his study of the roses, and Brunetti began to feel overcome by the heat of the room and the sight of this man covered and draped in wool. He found himself thinking about the cause: did the loss of his legs slow down his circulation and thus make him more vulnerable to the cold? What did he do in the winter?

'I don't know,' Pozzi finally said. 'Bianchi was his friend. Why don't you go and ask him?'

'Maybe we'd better,' Brunetti said, and got to his feet.

29

Neither of them wanted to deal with Signora Segalin, so by common consent they let themselves into the rose garden and started across the grass towards the gazebo, where a man sat in a wicker chair, back turned to them, his attention and voice directed at someone they could not see. When they recognized Signor Bianchi's voice, they found themselves in the embarrassing position of seeming to sneak up on him.

Before they could announce themselves, however, Bianchi said, in an artificially loud voice, 'I think our guests have come back, Bardo. Why don't you go and say hello to them?' The head of the dog appeared under the back of Bianchi's chair, and when the rest of his body arrived, he trotted down the stairs to greet them. Either he had recognized their smell, or Bianchi's voice had established the tone, for he came to them quite cheerfully and sat.

Griffoni stooped down and rubbed his head and neck.

The dog's tail stirred the gravel. He got up, moved to Brunetti and sat down again. Brunetti bent and patted his head a few times, saying, 'It's good to see you again, Bardo,' then pressed a knuckle to his lips, hearing himself using that verb.

'You've come back to ask more questions?' Bianchi asked, speaking loudly enough for them to hear him clearly.

'Yes, we have,' Brunetti answered. 'We've just been speaking to your colleague, Signor Pozzi.'

Bianchi turned in his chair to face them. 'I imagine he wasn't much help to you.' He called to the dog, who ran up the steps and jumped into his lap. 'He's a very evasive man,' Bianchi said. Then, sounding almost hospitable, he added, 'Bardo seems to like you both, so why don't you come up here and sit with me? That woman's left the chairs where they were yesterday.'

While they were coming up the steps, Bianchi said, taking a childlike pride in it, 'No one manages to sneak up on me,' not explaining whether it was his hearing or Bardo's that had detected and identified them.

'But he didn't bark,' Brunetti, who had taken the seat facing Bianchi, said.

'That means he trusts you.'

The fingers of Bianchi's full hand dug in under Bardo's neck, and Brunetti thought he heard the dog sigh in contentment. As he watched, Bardo's eyes went out of focus with joy.

'Signor Bianchi,' he began, 'we'd like to ask you some more questions about your old friend, Davide Casati.' Bianchi remained silent, so Brunetti added, 'I knew him, but only briefly. We rowed together in the *laguna* and spent days talking to one another. Not about anything in particular, just talk.'

Bianchi nodded, his hand still busy under Bardo's neck. 'It's good to talk like that, to another man,' he agreed.

'Did you and he row together?' Brunetti asked, responding to something in Bianchi's voice.

'No, I never had a feeling for the water, the way Davide did. Anyway, we were much younger then. Different people.'

'When you worked together?'

'Even before. We knew one another for a long time.'

'Were you close friends?' Brunetti asked, acutely aware of Bianchi's use of the simple past tense.

'Brothers are no closer.'

'But you argued with him?' Brunetti asked.

Bianchi lowered his head, a habit, perhaps, from sighted times. 'We disagreed.'

'About?'

'He asked me for my advice, and when I gave it to him, he refused to listen to me.'

'What did he ask you?'

Bianchi's non-gaze remained lowered; he gave no indication of having heard what Brunetti said. He continued to scratch Bardo's neck; then his hand stopped and lay quiet on the dog's head. 'I don't know what colour Bardo is,' he surprised them both by saying. 'And even if someone told me he was brown and white, it wouldn't mean anything to me because I've forgotten what colours look like. I can't see them in my mind any more.'

Brunetti noticed that Bianchi drew in his lips after he said that, showing dismay and perhaps resignation. Then he said, 'He told me he was going to cause trouble.'

'About what?' Brunetti asked.

'I don't think it matters now. I've seen too much trouble in my life. I don't want to see any more.'

The word pounded at Brunetti: was he the only one to hear it? 'Was it going to be his trouble, or yours?'

Bianchi said nothing.

'Which?' Brunetti insisted.

'If it was his trouble, it was my trouble, as well.'

'Is that why you disagreed? Because you didn't want trouble for yourself?'

Bianchi's face lifted towards him so quickly that Brunetti couldn't stop himself from pulling back from the man's anger. Bardo responded to the motion by jumping down from Bianchi's lap and going over to Griffoni. He put one paw on her knee, and she bent down to pick him up. He sat upright, alert, eyes turned towards his master.

Speaking slowly and pronouncing his words very clearly, Bianchi said, 'I didn't want *him* to have trouble. I told you: I've had a lot of trouble; I didn't want him to have it, too.'

'You've already had the same kind of trouble, you two,' Brunetti insisted. 'Remember, I told you I went swimming with him, so I saw the results of the trouble he'd had.' Brunetti felt suffocated by the word and by the constant emphasis on seeing, seeing, seeing.

'I tried to make him understand that he'd never live in peace if he didn't listen to me,' Bianchi said, voice lowered and slowed under the weight of sadness.

'And now he's dead,' Brunetti declared.

Bianchi said nothing and patted at the spot on his lap where Bardo had been, as though in want of the comfort of the dog's presence. Finally he said, 'Yes. Now he's dead.'

'Because he didn't listen to you?' Brunetti asked.

Bianchi's shrug pushed up the shoulders of his woollen jacket, a different one today, but no less heavy. He sighed deeply. Bardo responded by jumping down from Griffoni's lap and returning to Bianchi's, this time curling up and batting his tail against his master's chest. The blind man put his good hand on the dog's back, and his tail grew quiet.

Bianchi moved his head from side to side a few times and finally said, 'No, not because of that but because he couldn't listen to anyone.' After a moment's thought, he added, 'Or wouldn't.' He gave a half-smile and asked, 'It's strange, isn't it, the way we always say "can't" when what we really mean is "won't" but aren't honest enough to say it?'

Griffoni raised a hand and gave a small wave that caught Brunetti's attention. Bardo watched the gesture, but Bianchi could not. She gave a grimace of disbelief, then raised her right forefinger and waved it back and forth to signal uncertainty. Brunetti, too, had heard the change in tone when Bianchi passed from sombre reflection to rhetorical deflection.

'What did you tell him that he wouldn't listen to?' Brunetti asked.

Bianchi shook his head, as though to express his disbelief that this man could continue to think any of this important. For a moment, Brunetti feared Bianchi would make some enigmatic remark to the dog by way of answer: if he did that, Brunetti might be driven to tease another cripple. His thoughts slid away and he considered why teasing cripples was so much worse than hurting them. They were cripples because their bodies had been damaged in some way, not their dignity. Teasing attacked any pride that had managed to survive. How was it that his mother had understood this?

'. . . for his wife's death,' Brunetti heard Bianchi say when he returned his attention to the other man.

Brunetti did the best he could to disguise having wandered off. 'I'm afraid I don't understand,' he said.

The tilt of Bianchi's head showed his puzzlement. 'I think what I said was clear enough, Commissario. He blamed himself for his wife's death, however absurd that might be.'

'Why did he blame himself?' Griffoni interrupted to ask.

Bianchi shrugged. 'He told me that he hadn't protected her. He said he should have known about the danger.'

No one spoke for some time until Griffoni broke the silence to ask, 'How did your conversation end?'

Bianchi cleared his throat and then, still facing Brunetti, he answered Griffoni's question. 'We argued. It was the first time in all those years. I tried to stop him, but he wouldn't listen to me.'

'Because you disagreed with him?' she asked.

Bianchi took a deep breath, expelled it and said, 'No, not that. Because I couldn't explain.'

'Why was that?' she asked softly.

'Because I lied to him about this place from the time I came here.' After he said that, Bianchi lowered his head and put his good hand over his eyes, as though he wanted to hide from these sighted people.

'Why?' she asked.

'I didn't want him to come to visit. If he did, he'd see what it was like and know what I did,' Bianchi said.

Brunetti noticed that the other man's face was covered with sweat and that his dark glasses had started to slip down his nose. Because Bianchi's good hand was still on the dog's head, he used the thumb of the other to shove them back into place, a gesture Brunetti observed with something akin to disgust.

'And if he had found out?' Brunetti asked, fully aware of what the other man was talking about. 'Why would that change things?'

Bianchi snapped out an answer without thinking. 'Because he'd understand who was paying for it all. That they offered, and I took it. Like Pozzi.' He said the other man's name with despair, the way a Christian would speak of Judas.

'And he didn't,' Brunetti said out loud.

Bianchi shook his head. Griffoni and Bardo remained motionless and silent, the dog because he was asleep and the woman because she did not want to make any sound that would draw Bianchi's attention away from Brunetti.

'Why wouldn't he let them pay him?' Brunetti demanded.

With a dry laugh that held no humour, Bianchi said, 'Because he was a better man than either of us.' He shifted his body to one side, removed his hand from the dog, and reached into the pocket of his trousers. He pulled out a white handkerchief and shook it open. He moved it to the other hand, which took it between thumb and last finger. Then he reached up with his undamaged hand and placed his thumb and first two fingers on the rim of his glasses.

Griffoni and Brunetti lowered their gaze; they kept their eyes on the ground for some time, until Bianchi said, 'We all had suspicions – everyone who worked there did – about what they were doing, where the trucks were going and what was in them.' They looked at him again and saw that his face was dry, the dark glasses back in place, no sign of the handkerchief.

'But that was years ago, and who knew then or cared about those things?' Bianchi said, now back to his old friend, the rhetorical question. 'So long as it disappeared, what business of ours was it where it went? Besides, we were workers, tough men with wives and families to take care of, so we had no time for . . .' He stopped and began to run his hand down Bardo's sleeping body, careful to pick it up before reaching the tail and to return it accurately to the back of the dog's head.

Brunetti found it strangely peaceful to watch Bianchi do this and so said nothing for some time. Finally, when Bardo stirred in his sleep and flopped over to his other side, Bianchi removed his hand and said, 'No time to think of anything or anyone beyond our own small circles, and no time to think of the future and what we were doing to it.'

'What happened?' Brunetti asked.

'The accident, of course,' Bianchi said, sounding disappointed at Brunetti's obtuseness.

'No, I mean what happened to Casati? To change him so.'

'Ah,' Bianchi said, 'of course.' And then he didn't speak for a long time.

'I think it must have been the pain and the slowness of time passing,' he finally answered. 'When you're in pain, you need to think of something so that at least part of you can be free of the pain, so that your mind can go somewhere where there's no pain.' As if to stop them from questioning this, he continued, 'I'm talking about pain that goes on for weeks and that you think is never, not in your whole life, ever going to end.'

Again, Bianchi sighed. 'That's what changed him. He was in the hospital for months because his wounds didn't heal the way they should – that's what happens with big burns like the ones he had – and he kept getting new infections.' He paused, as if to give them time to speak, but neither did.

'That's when he changed, during those months. Franca moved into his room and refused to leave when the nurses told her to. She sent Federica to stay with her brother, and she went to the hospital with a suitcase and stayed until he was well enough to go home.' Bianchi stopped suddenly and sat silent, as if playing back the memory of what he had heard. Then, more insistent than he had been, he said, 'That's why it was so terrible for him when . . .'

'When did he tell you all this?' Brunetti asked.

'Oh, he never did. That is, not directly, in one telling. It sort of slipped into what he said when we talked over the years.'

'That's a long time,' Brunetti said. 'Did you ever meet him again?'

'No. Talking was enough,' Bianchi said, sounding as though he didn't really believe it. 'Davide'd gone to live on Sant'Erasmo. He had his pension. At first he didn't want to take it, but his wife told him he deserved it.'

'He believed her?' Brunetti asked.

'He earned it,' Bianchi shot back.

After letting some time pass, Brunetti asked, 'Is that all he got from them?' He glanced around the gazebo and out into the rose garden but said nothing.

When the expression on Bianchi's face showed Brunetti that he was not going to get an answer to that question, he asked, 'What about Pozzi?'

Bianchi's mouth tightened at the mere mention of Pozzi. Brunetti watched his face as the blind man considered the question and was struck by how much the eyes revealed: hide them and there were no easy clues. 'He earned it, too,' Bianchi finally said.

'To stay here?' Brunetti asked.

'Yes.'

'And you? How did you earn it?' Brunetti responded without hesitation.

Bianchi's body stiffened at the abruptness and aggression

of Brunetti's question. Again, Brunetti studied the eyeless, unresponsive face. The answer was long delayed, and when it came, Bianchi rationed out his reasons in a soft, level voice. 'With pain,' he said acidly. 'And then with laziness. Fear. Shame.' Brunetti thought he had finished and was about to speak, when Bianchi added, 'Greed.'

Brunetti and Griffoni exchanged a glance, but neither chose to speak.

Bianchi made a noise, half grunt, half laugh. 'We're a bit like animals, Pozzi and I. We were born in the forest and lived there for a long time, but then we were captured and turned into house pets, and now we're too well trained and housebroken to be able to go back to the forest. So we stay here, where we're fed and cared for and safe.' He nodded a few times, as though he'd been listening to a comparison he'd never thought about before and found it accurate.

He put his good hand on the dog's head. 'Even Bardo's braver than we are: he still barks and growls and bites.' He smiled at them and added, 'They told me that, last week, he caught a baby rabbit and tore it to pieces.' He smiled again, at the thought, proud of his dog. 'While Pozzi and I sit here and wait for lunch to be served.'

'While Casati went back to the forest?' Brunetti asked.

Again, Bianchi made the grunting noise. 'Yes, I suppose you could say that.'

'At what price?' Brunetti asked.

Bianchi's head moved a bit to the left so that his face was pointing in the general direction of Brunetti. 'Do I have to answer that, Signor . . . I'm sorry, I've forgotten your name. And your rank.'

'Brunetti. Commissario. And no, you don't have to answer any of our questions.' He knew there was no wisdom in saying anything more, but said it anyway. 'At least legally, you don't have to say anything.'

'Ah, the policeman as philosopher?'

Instead of answering, Brunetti thought about these two men: Pozzi reading about painting and the history of art, and Bianchi rich in metaphors and conscious of the seriousness of their conversation.

'It's hard to believe that either of you worked in a factory,' Brunetti said.

'You mean Pozzi and his paintings?'

'Yes.'

'And me with my speculation?'

'Also.'

'We've had more than two decades to ... develop new interests,' he concluded ironically.

'Not everyone would have spent the time that way.'

'Not everyone is crippled.'

Brunetti thought it better to let some time pass before he said, 'What did Casati have to do?'

'We had to be certain that he wouldn't say anything.'

'"We"?' Brunetti inquired harshly, tired of Bianchi's posturing.

Bianchi lowered his head so that his voice was directed at Bardo. 'Now's when I have to tell the truth, Bardo. And luckily you won't understand it, because you wouldn't love me any more if you knew.' He placed his palms over the dog's ears and went on. 'I told them. Years ago, when I first came here and he'd gone to live on Sant'Erasmo, I asked him what he was going to do, and he told me he had no desire to cause trouble. He said that what had happened to us was punishment for what we'd done, and that was the end of it for him.' He paused, then added, voice moving from irony to pain, 'He'd never lie to me.'

'Did you tell them what he'd said?' Brunetti asked, not certain but willing to risk the question.

'I told them what he'd told me, that he'd never talk about what we did.'

'How?'

'What do you mean, how?'

'How did you contact them?'

'I'd call Signor Maschietto every few months, or he'd call me, and when he retired, I started to speak to his son.'

'To pass on everything Casati told you?'

The sharpness of the question surprised, but appeared not to offend, Bianchi. He paused for a while in silent thought and finally said, 'If it regarded the company, yes.'

'What was the last thing you told them?' Brunetti asked.

'That he'd found . . .' Bianchi began, and then cleared his throat a few times before starting again. 'That he'd found what was killing his bees. He had lab reports, and he understood what it was doing to the soil and the water.' Bianchi stopped and turned his face aside, a gesture that no longer had a purpose. 'He said that was the end of it for him. That he couldn't stand it any more.'

'What did that mean?'

'That's what I asked him,' Bianchi answered defensively. 'First he said he wanted to call you.'

'Me?' Brunetti asked.

'The police,' Bianchi explained. 'But then he said he wasn't sure any longer.'

'What did you do, Signor Bianchi?'

Bianchi took his hands from the sleeping dog and gripped the arms of his chair. 'I called Maschietto and told him.'

30

Well, Bianchi hadn't wasted any time, had he? Brunetti asked himself. No sooner had a confidence been entrusted to him than Bianchi was on the phone to exchange it for . . . for what? Some grilled chicken breast for Bardo?

Fighting down his disgust, Brunetti asked, 'You called the son and told him what you just told me?'

Bianchi sat silent and then suddenly made a short moaning sound. 'I didn't tell him that Davide had talked about calling the police. Believe me,' he cried. With no warning, he pulled off his glasses and pressed the elbow of his sleeve against his eyes, held it there a moment and then pulled it away. Equally without warning, Brunetti and Griffoni saw what the exploding waste had done to his face and eyes all those years ago, and the sight turned away Brunetti's wrath.

Brunetti sat quietly for a long time, trying to think of something to say or ask and fighting the temptation to refer to thirty pieces of silver.

In ordinary circumstances, Brunetti would have assaulted Bianchi with sarcasm, but the flashing sight of Bianchi's face had made that impossible.

'I warned Davide,' Bianchi said in a firm voice. 'I told him not even to think about telling anyone.' He raised a hand and waved it in the general direction of Brunetti and Griffoni. 'Especially the police.'

'Who else would he tell?'

Bianchi tossed up his hands in exasperation. 'For all I knew, he'd go and tell his wife.' The words were no sooner said than Bianchi stopped, stunned, hands still raised. He slowly lowered them to the arms of his chair, careful not to disturb the sleeping dog.

Brunetti glanced at Griffoni but said nothing. She raised her eyebrows faintly, unable to overcome the habit of making no evident response to whatever a witness said. Brunetti patted the air with his right hand, enjoining her to patience.

Moments passed and all of them were silent until Bianchi finally said, 'That's what he'd do, go and talk things over with her. It's crazy, but he did it all the time.' He nodded in affirmation and then went on, his voice slowing, as though his words were feet, growing heavier as each step took him up a long staircase. Exhausted, he reached the top. 'And she'd tell him what to do.'

He turned his face towards where they were sitting; his mouth remained open, as if only this way could he find enough air to breathe.

When the sound of his heavy breathing became unbearable, Griffoni asked with perfect timing and oh, so casually, 'Did you know her?'

Bianchi pulled his lips into his mouth and took a few deep breaths through his nose. 'I met her a few times over the years.'

'What was she like?' Griffoni asked.

Bianchi thought about this, then answered, 'All I remember is that she was small and I thought at the time that she was very pretty. I have another memory of very big, dark eyes. But it's only a verbal memory.' A long time passed before he said, 'Davide loved her. From the first time he saw her, he was lost for her. And it stayed like that all the time they were married. I think he forgot there were other women in the world.'

As he spoke, Bianchi's voice had grown incantational, the voice of a person telling a fairy tale. Casati was the prince, his wife the princess. But where was the dragon?

'When she died,' Bianchi began, not bothering to name the kind of dragon that had killed her, '– and she was sick a long time – he was lost. At the beginning he said it didn't make any sense to be alive except to help his daughter and her family because they needed him. He said the same thing about the bees, that they were a reason to live for because they needed him, too.' Bianchi lowered his head as he spoke. 'That's crazy isn't it?'

He nodded a few times to enforce the strangeness of this. Then he repeated, 'Bees.'

It came to Brunetti to ask Bianchi why bees were different from Bardo, but he said nothing, true to his mother's injunction and certain that it was not his business to ask people to see things as he did.

There seemed little more they could do or learn here. He got to his feet; Griffoni did the same. Unable to shake the habit of sighted life, Bianchi raised his head to face them.

'I didn't have a choice,' he said in a voice he struggled to keep calm.

Brunetti wanted to tell him that, although he had not

had an easy choice, he *had* had a choice, but he said nothing, unable to free himself of his pity for this man.

'We have to go now, Signore,' he said.

Bianchi stood up so quickly that Bardo was forced to make a heavy landing in front of him. With great scraping of nails on the wooden floor, the dog scuttled aside and took refuge under Brunetti's chair, planted himself there and looked up at his master.

Bianchi put out his good hand, but he had turned away from them instead of towards them when he stood, so they both chose the option of not seeing it.

They left as stealthily as they had come: no one questioning their presence nor their departure.

Outside, they walked silently to the waiting car and got into the back seat. The driver, saying nothing, started towards Venice.

When the villa was behind them, Griffoni turned to Brunetti and asked, 'What happened?'

He shrugged and looked out the window as the car made its way down the highway leading back to the city. When had things become so ugly? Brunetti wondered. When had all these horrible buildings and factories and parking lots, these endless discount stores and shopping malls, sprung up like monsters spawned from dragon's teeth?

He waited a long time to answer Griffoni's question, and when he did, he said, 'I don't know. Maybe his wife told him what to do. It looked like an accident.'

'But before the fire? How could he just take that stuff out and dump it?'

The answer seemed simple enough to Brunetti. 'Because he wasn't living there and he was younger. His wife was healthy and he didn't have any bees, so it didn't matter to him.'

'You said he was a good man.'

'He became a good man,' Brunetti corrected her.

'People don't change,' she answered, voicing the wisdom Neapolitans had learned over centuries.

'If they suffer enough, they do,' Brunetti said, then quickly amended it to 'or can.'

Brunetti's attention drifted from Griffoni and back to Casati, that solitary and often silent man. He had been a married man and a father when he worked on the clean-up and all that entailed. He had surely known what was being shipped south and what was being taken out to be dumped willy-nilly into the *laguna*, and he might even have helped move more toxic waste to what was now a park with a view across to the beautiful profile of the city. And it hadn't bothered him one whit.

People seldom consider the consequences of their behaviour, Brunetti knew. Desire justified all. He had no idea of what Casati could have desired all those years ago, before he became the man he was when he died. Nor did he know what he had desired just before he died.

31

When the car entered the state highway, Griffoni turned to him and said, 'Well?'

'Did he fall or did he jump?' Brunetti asked rhetorically, distressed by his uncertainty.

Griffoni's face showed her surprise, even something stronger. 'Is that a joke?'

This was the first time she'd responded to his words and not his tone, and her failure disappointed Brunetti. 'Hardly,' he answered, sober now at the thought that both possibilities led equally to death. In the face of that, speculation seemed pointless.

Brunetti had been considering possibilities for days, altering them to conform to each new piece of information. 'He must have gone to talk to his wife.'

'To tell her what?'

'I'm sure he'd already confessed that what he'd done had

helped to kill her, and now he went to tell her he was killing his bees.'

'Don't you think that's a bit melodramatic, Guido?' she asked, making no attempt to disguise her exasperation. 'Men don't kill themselves because their bees die.'

Brunetti had recently read a book that said a goshawk could see the veins in the wings of a butterfly: who knew what could be seen? Or felt. Possibility was limitless, each of us a separate universe of choice and capacity.

'Most people don't, I know,' he agreed, to content her.

A car was suddenly in front of them, though neither of them knew how it had got there. Their driver swore aloud and braked sharply, avoiding contact and managing to fight his way out of a skid that pulled them to the right. The other car slipped into the left lane and sped past two more cars and then two more, and then was blocked from their sight by the cars in front of them.

'There was a child in the seat beside him,' the driver said in a shaken voice, then added, 'Excuse me for cursing, Signori.'

'It's nothing,' Griffoni answered for them both, as if a woman would be more offended by profanity than a man and thus in charge of accepting the apology. She turned to Brunetti and said, 'I'm becoming a Venetian. My heart's still pounding.' At his puzzled glance, she explained, 'That's how people in Naples drive all the time, but now it terrifies me.' She smiled, then laughed, then shook her head to express her wonder.

'I've changed,' she said, and he sensed it was not a joke.

Their fear had somehow united them, and at last Griffoni asked, 'You knew him. What do you think?'

Brunetti waved a hand back towards where they had been. 'You heard what Bianchi said: he didn't see any sense in living after she died. Except for his daughter and his bees. And now,' he went on, 'his daughter is married, has a family, and no longer needs his protection, and his bees are dying. Because of what he did.'

'Why are you sure of that?' she asked.

'Signora Minati interpreted the lab results for him, so he knew – maybe for the first time – the names of what they'd put in the water and dumped in the *laguna*.' Brunetti saw that he had her attention, so he went on, telling her what he'd thought about in the last days. 'His wife died of a rare form of cancer. When we were near some of his beehives,' he said, choosing not to tell her he had been swimming near them, 'I saw a sheet of metal under the water. It could have been the lid of a barrel.'

Griffoni was silent for a long time and then said, 'You spent time with him. Did he seem like someone who would do that?'

'What?'

'Poison the *laguna*,' she said, mincing no words.

'The man I knew wouldn't do that,' Brunetti said, defending a friend.

'And the one you didn't know?'

Brunetti had only heard about him, a normal working man, who wanted to keep his job. The words broke from him, unconsidered, unwanted. 'Probably. I told you that.'

Griffoni looked out of the window on her side of the car. Fresh growth lurked everywhere, as if in hiding from the buildings that had stolen its place. Nettles slipped through cracks in cement, vines crawled up electric poles and along the wires; the earth had been ploughed and bulldozed, but it had covered itself with green shoots after the first rain. Raw nature quickly encircled, then covered, abandoned tyres and paint cans, piles of dumped building materials, milk crates, bicycle carcasses. Like people, it suffered, changed, and found survival.

Brunetti remembered the sight of Casati's dead hand, the frond-like undulation of his fingers and his hair. At least he had been discovered by a friend and not some unknown diver who would not care what Casati had done and why he had had to do it.

They said little after that. At Piazzale Roma, Foa was waiting with a boat, but he must have sensed their mood, for he did no more than greet them and open one side of the swinging doors to the cabin at the back.

As they travelled up the Grand Canal, Brunetti was assaulted by beauty and looked around him, as he sometimes did, with eyes he tried to make new, as though he were seeing this for the first time. He sneaked a glance at Griffoni, who was sitting on the left side of the back seat, facing that side of the canal, the one she preferred.

They passed the train station, then under the bridge, Brunetti moving his head easily from side to side. Parched garden on the right, its roses visibly in pain from lack of water; the Casinò that had lured so many people to their ruin, the *palazzo* where his last professor of Greek had lived; another bridge, the restoration said finally to be finished.

Again he glanced at Griffoni, but she seemed no longer to be there. He thought for a moment that he could push her sideways and she'd fall over without knowing it.

Another bridge, then open water on one side. On the other was the Basilica and the Palazzo, and Brunetti had the sudden realization that, though none of this belonged to him, he belonged to all of it.

By the time they got to the Questura, Brunetti had left those thoughts behind and was planning to call Signora

Minati to ask for the name of the chemical that had been found in Casati's earth to see if it was the one repeatedly named in the articles about the clean-up of Marghera. His reluctance to upset Federica again made him want to speak to Massimo about Casati's state of mind in the weeks or days before his death, to learn – even to invent if necessary – something he had said that spoke of hope or plans for the future. Massimo, he believed, was a man who would gladly lie to save his wife's peace of mind. It came to him then that there was little purpose, and some risk, in asking these painful questions. If Casati's death continued to be considered an accident, Federica would be spared the inevitable guilt of suspecting she had failed to save him from despair and somehow prevent his death.

Inside the door, the officer at the desk got to his feet as they came in and addressed Brunetti. 'There's a man here to see you, Commissario.'

Brunetti raised his chin in silent interrogation.

The man looked at his feet then up again, as though he had a mistake to confess. 'I know him, sir, so I put him in that small room next to the pilots' office.' He waited for Brunetti to inquire about the man, and when he did not, the officer said, 'He said he has to talk to you.'

'Has he been here long?' Brunetti asked.

'About half an hour.'

'I'm going up to my office. Could you send someone up with him in about five minutes?'

'Yes, sir,' the officer said and returned to the cubbyhole by the door and to his desk.

Brunetti and Griffoni started up the steps. He waited for her to ask him what he was going to do. He had no idea; he had no answer.

At the landing where she would turn off to her tiny office, she said, 'I think I'll go home.'

Brunetti smiled. 'I'll talk to this man and do the same.'

She moved off to the left; halfway down the corridor, without turning round, she raised an arm in the air and gave a wave.

Brunetti entered his office and went to look out the window. The roses on the wall across the canal clambered every which way and showed no sign of thirst. Brunetti wondered if the earth somehow filtered out the salt in the waters of the canal and allowed the roses to flourish.

Behind him, a man coughed, and when he turned, he saw Massimo, Federica's husband. He stood in the doorway, his shoulders seeming to touch both sides. 'Ah, Massimo,' Brunetti said with real pleasure. 'Come in, come in. Please sit down.' He had spoken in the familiar '*tu*' on the island, and he saw no reason to change it because they were in the Questura.

Massimo came quickly across the room to take Brunetti's hand, but to do so he had to switch the leather briefcase he was carrying from his right hand to his left. They shook hands and Massimo sat in one of the two chairs facing Brunetti.

'I'm glad you came,' Brunetti began without introduction, then caught himself short and asked, 'How's Federica?'

'I want,' he began in a voice cramped with nervousness. 'I want to bring this back to you. A police boat delivered it to the house yesterday. I didn't bother to look at the name on it, so I opened it and took a look at what was inside, but it's yours.'

He opened the briefcase, a thick old leather thing with a dark plastic handle. He pulled out a manila envelope and showed it to Brunetti, who saw his own name on the front, c/o the address of the villa.

Massimo looked away, cleared his throat, looked back. 'She's thought about how much he loved us,' he began. 'So she accepts that it must have been an accident.' His face and his voice tightened. 'She mustn't know.'

Brunetti had no idea what the other man meant, no idea of what might be hidden in the envelope. Some relic of her father? Some evidence that would prove he had taken his own life?

'What is it?' Brunetti asked.

His question startled Massimo. 'Didn't you send it? They said they were returning your photos to you.'

'The police sent it?' Brunetti asked.

'I don't know who sent it, but a police boat delivered it.'

Brunetti opened the envelope and pulled out a pile of photos. He set them on the table. On top was one of the upside-down *puparìn*, then one in which he recognized his sneaker-clad foot beside the boat, and he realized they were the photos he had taken and asked Signorina Elettra to send to Rizzardi.

Massimo cleared his throat again. Brunetti moved the photos aside one by one with the tip of his finger and saw Casati's left hand, the skin puffy and white, the ring and watch visible, the ring cutting into the white flesh. Brunetti slid the photo aside after looking at it. There followed the photos of Casati's swollen face from every angle. As he looked at them, Brunetti's mind clouded over with horror, as it had when he had taken them. He glanced quickly through them and looked up at Massimo. 'Yes, I took them,' he said. 'But I don't understand why they sent them back to me.'

Massimo tapped insistently at one of them. Brunetti saw the familiar iron grating that Casati had used as an anchor, the rope that had circled and trapped Casati's leg snaking towards and tied to it.

'Don't you see it?' Massimo demanded.

What in God's name had he come for? Brunetti wondered. Was he going to claim they'd sent back the wrong ring, the wrong watch, the outlines of both of which he could see at the bottom of the envelope?

'I don't understand, Massimo,' Brunetti said, striving for calm. 'I don't understand what you're saying.'

'But you row, don't you? You've been on boats.'

Brunetti looked at the photo again and saw what he had seen the first time: the grating, the knot, the rope. He moved the photo a few centimetres closer. 'I'm sorry, Massimo. I still don't understand.'

Massimo poked at the photo again. 'Look at that.' He left his finger on it, obscuring whatever it was Brunetti was meant to see. When he removed his hand and put it in his lap, Brunetti saw that the other man had been pointing at the knot that tied the rope to the grating.

'That's not a boatman's knot,' Massimo said with complete certainty. 'No man who works on boats tied that. It's a landman's knot; it's nothing.'

Brunetti looked more closely. No, although the knot was double, it wasn't the double bowline he'd seen Casati tie. When he studied it, the knot looked like something one of his children would tie: two simple knots, one on top of the other, as if the person who tied it wanted to make sure it could not be easily untied. As it had not been.

'You think he didn't tie this?' Brunetti asked.

Massimo punched his finger on to the knot again. 'For God's sake, Guido, Davide *couldn't* tie this. It's a mess; no sailor could make it. It's stupid, useless.' In disgust, Massimo pushed the photo away from them; it slid over and stopped just at the edge of Brunetti's desk.

He looked across at Massimo. 'Where's the grating?'

'It was in the boat when they towed it back to us.'

'And the knot?' Brunetti asked.

'They'd untied the rope at both ends and coiled it in the bottom of the boat.'

Brunetti stared at the photo and imagined showing it to Patta or to a magistrate and trying to persuade them that this knot had been tied by someone other than the dead man, and that the small wound on the man's forehead had resulted from a blow, after which the rope had intentionally been coiled around his leg and . . .

Then Brunetti considered the response of judges to that hypothesis – he dared not call it evidence – and realized that there was no way this photo would ever make its way into a courtroom.

Nor would Bianchi ever be asked to risk his comfort by repeating his story, and who could question the largesse of the Maschietto family? Had they not given a church to their village?

The justice system had been looking into what had gone on in Marghera for decades, both before and after the so-called *'pianificazione'*. Sooner or later, they might have a look at GCM Holdings and its part in the clean-up. Or they might not.

Brunetti's speculations turned to Casati. Maybe he was somewhere, talking to his wife, taking care of his bees. Brunetti's mother would have liked this scenario; she was a woman who liked happy endings, even though she had seen few of them in her own life.

He looked across at Massimo. 'Did Federica see this photo?'

'No.'

Brunetti closed his eyes. Casati continued to speak with his wife, that small woman with large dark eyes. And his bees continued to explore the *barena* – why not make it a *barena* in which there was no poison, no death? – and bring back pollen and nectar and transform them by the magic of bees into honey, that sweetest of all things.

Brunetti opened his eyes and looked at Massimo. 'Good,' he said.

The Waters of Eternal Youth

The twenty-fifth instalment in the bestselling Brunetti series

Fifteen years ago the teenage granddaughter of the grand Contessa Lando-Continui was rescued at the last moment from drowning in the canals. But young Manuela's life was never the same again. Now aged thirty, she lives trapped in an eternal youth.

The Contessa, certain that this was no accident, implores Brunetti to find the culprit she believes ruined Manuela's life.

But once Brunetti starts to investigate, he finds a murky past and a dark story at its heart . . .

'There is no one better than Donna Leon at showing the ripple effects of a single traumatic event . . . Throughout this astonishingly consistent series Leon has recast the city in her own venerable image: full of surprises and hidden beauty.'
Evening Standard

'All the things that are wrong with the city appear in these books: corruption, decay and overcrowding are part of the scenery and Leon pulls no punches describing them. But she still loves Venice and Brunetti and so do her readers.'
Literary Review

'Effortlessly entertaining.'
Crime Time